One of Us Is Wrong

ONE OF US
IS WRONG

DONALD WESTLAKE
writing as Samuel Holt

ONE OF US IS WRONG

A Felony & Mayhem mystery

PRINTING HISTORY
First hardcover edition: 1986
First mass-market edition: 1987
Felony & Mayhem edition: 2006

ISBN: 1-93397-40-3

Manufactured in the United States of America

GOOD SAM

Times change. Cultures change. Markets change.

Everything changes. Sometimes a writer, having made some success, looks around and says, "Could I do it today? If I were just starting now, would I succeed or fail?" That question has led a number of writers to test for the answer by producing new work under what's called a protected penname, in which only the publisher and agent, in the commercial world, know who the writer really is. That was the reason for Stephen King's side trip as Richard Bachman, for instance, and it also led me, in the mid-eighties, to try the same thing. We found a publisher who agreed to keep the secret in return for a shorter-than-normal advance for a four-book contract, and Samuel Holt was born.

I knew that John D. MacDonald, when he started Travis McGee, wrote the first three books simultaneously, because it was his first attempt at a series character and he wanted to be sure the voice was consistent. I thought that was a fine idea, so I did the same thing, figuring out at least the beginnings of three stories, then working on all three, going back and forth among them. I liked that method, so when I finished those three I put together beginnings for three more.

Then the first book was published, and in the window of my local bookstore was a sign saying Samuel Holt was me. The publisher had told his sales staff the "secret," and encouraged them to pass the news on to the bookstores.

Samuel Holt was poisoned for me. The purpose of his existence had been removed. I tried to hit Undo, but it never really worked.

I still owed one more book on the contract, so I wrote it, but it was hard. I still liked the character and the story, but the goal was gone.

The fifth and sixth books, barely begun, were put away forever. In *You Have Five Seconds to Live*, Sam was going to meet a retired astronaut, so they would be two people both famous for something they didn't do any more. *Now I Am Six and Clever as Clever* had a concept I don't now remember.

Anyway, another twenty years has gone by and it has belatedly occurred to me that Samuel Holt has spent twenty years imprisoned for a crime he didn't commit. I like these books, and I like his voice. Also, since my identity was going to be kept secret, I was able to make use of my observations of some showbiz people from my sometime screenwriting career, material I'd never use under my own name.

Poor Sam. I've been denying him for so long. No more. Welcome to the light, Sam. These are your friends.

—Donald Westlake
May 2006

This is for Otto and Michael,
unindicted co-conspirators.

Fame is nothing but an empty name.

—Charles Churchill, *Ghosts*

The technique of murder must be presented in a way
that will not inspire Imitation.

—A Code to Govern the Making of Motion and Talking Pictures by
the Motion Picture Producers and Distributors of America, Inc.
March 31, 1930

The icon above says you're holding a copy of a book in the Felony & Mayhem "Hard Boiled" category. These books feature mean streets and meaner bad guys, with a cop or a PI usually carrying the story and landing a few punches besides. If you enjoy this book, you may well like other "Hard Boiled" titles from Felony & Mayhem Press, including:

Satan's Lambs, by Lynn Hightower
Season of the Monsoon, by Paul Mann
The Ganja Coast, by Paul Mann
Death of a Dissident, by Stuart Kaminsky
The Lime Pit, by Jonathan Valin
Yellowthread Street, by William Marshall

For more about these books, and other Felony & Mayhem titles, or to place an order, please visit our website at:

www.FelonyAndMayhem.com

or contact us at:

Felony and Mayhem Press
156 Waverly Place
New York, NY 10014

One of Us Is Wrong

"**W**HEN YOU INVEST IN A shopping center," Karen told me, "you don't *look at* the shopping center. It's not a shopping center, it's an investment, and what you look at is the people running the investment. Leopold Associates has an excellent history in this area. Did you read the backgrounder?"

"I'll go take a look at the place, just for fun," I said, because of course I had not read the backgrounder and didn't want to admit it. Karen Platt is my accountant, and she is absolutely serious; when she sends you a backgrounder, pages and pages of computer printout complete with charts and graphs and references to annual statements, she expects you to read it.

Well, I can't read backgrounders. On the show I could never read the plot summaries, the character descriptions. Just tell me what I say and what the other guy says, and I'll figure out the details for myself. That system worked pretty well on the show, so why shouldn't it work now, when the question was whether or not to invest two hundred forty-two thousand for three points in this shopping center in Woodland Hills? "I'll just wander by the place," I said. "Sit behind the wheel, kick the tires."

"Do what you want," she said, expressing deep disapproval. "But you should have read the backgrounder," she told me, and that was the end of the conversation.

Of course, Karen was right about my not needing to go look at the actual shopping center before either investing in it or not investing in it, and, in fact, that afternoon I didn't go over to the Valley at all, and might never have gone except that the following Monday my agent, Zack Novak, put me on hold.

I hate to be put on hold, and the reason is, *God* has put me on hold. I'm ready to go, ready to make use of myself, ready to show what I can do, and nothing ever happens. It's ironic, I suppose, because I started life as somebody with absolutely no drive or ambition, just another feckless kid drifting through the Mineola, Long Island, school system, with no goal out in front of me at all. Because I'm six-foot-six I got a basketball scholarship to a college upstate, but just fooled around and dropped out after the first year, sliding into the army instead. They sent me to Germany, mostly to be on the brigade basketball team, and assigned me to the Military Police to keep me handy to headquarters.

After the army I drifted, didn't want to go back to college, wasn't good enough for pro basketball, eventually got a job with my hometown police. A year and a half later, scenes for a movie were shot in Mineola, and a few of us cops were given short bits in it. An agent thought I showed promise and signed me. I went out to Los Angeles, enjoyed myself, and got a few acting jobs, but worked mostly as a uniformed security guard.

That first agent eventually dropped me, having changed my name from Holton Hickey to Sam Holt, so it was my second agent, Zack Novak, who put me up for the lead in a new TV series called *Packard* about a criminology professor who sometimes does private-eye-type work for his friends.

Packard was a big success; too big, maybe. It ran five years and was canceled only because we all ran out of steam; the audience was still there. A bunch of us got rich off that series, and as long as it stays in reruns, I'll stay rich. (I also wrote seven of the episodes, my only writing before this.)

You can't involve yourself in a TV series for five years without developing some strong work habits, and maybe even a taste for the work itself. By the time *Packard* went off the air three years ago, when I was thirty-one, I'd matured from an easygoing drifter to somebody who knew how to work and wanted to work. And the work wasn't there.

That's why I say God put me on hold. You'd think I could get a movie part somewhere, or a guest shot on a TV series, maybe even a play, but no. I'm too identified with Jack Packard, like that fellow years ago who was so identified as the driver in the Greyhound bus commercials ("...and leave the driving to us!") that he never worked again. Like him, I've been typecast as one specific character, and that character doesn't exist anymore. Other people—James Garner, for instance—got past that problem by taking other roles while still at work in their series, but I never did; I just drifted along for five years being Packard, and this is what I got: Sam Holt is Jack Packard, and Jack Packard is Sam Holt. I'm thirty-four, I have no money worries, and it's looking more and more as though, damn it to hell and back, I'm retired. "Come on, God," I say. "Gimme a break."

"I'll get back to you," God says, and puts me on hold.

Well, I'll take that treatment from God because I don't have much choice in the matter, but I won't take it from Zack Novak. Not from my *agent*. And *he* was the one who called *me*. "I know you've been wanting to work, Sam," he started with wonderful understatement.

"Yes, I've been wanting to—"

"Oop! Hold it! I'll be right back, Sam."

And he put me on hold.

I waited three minutes exactly by the digital clock on my desk, and then I'd had enough. "God can do this to me,

Zack," I told the silent phone, "but you can't." And I hung up.

After that, naturally, I didn't want to be home when he called back, so I remembered Karen and the shopping center in Woodland Hills and decided I would go look at the place after all.

And that's how I happened to be heading north on the San Diego Freeway seven minutes later in my red Volvo when the four swarthy men in the two Impalas tried to murder me.

2

THE FREEWAY AT THAT POINT is eight lanes wide, four in each direction, with a tall rail and fence divider. I was in the third lane, being passed on my left by a block-long moving van, when a golden Chevy Impala came up out of nowhere into my right flank, sideswiped me hard, bounced off, and accelerated away.

I slammed on the brakes, yelling, "Holy shit!" as I shimmied. I used to do some of the stunts on *Packard*; not enough to risk life and limb, but enough to know something about how it's done, so now I fought the wheel into a half turn right to keep away from that monster truck beside me, and I was still fighting for control when the other one took a shot at me.

Also a Chevy Impala, this one was a metallic green, and I had just enough time to see a grim-faced olive-skinned guy at the wheel, staring straight ahead, when he hit me. I was already rattled, the Volvo was bouncing around like a football, and there was no way this time I was going to stay in my own lane.

What saved me first was that I'd already hit the brakes, and the moving van was really moving, so most of him had already gone by when I invaded his territory. And what saved me second was that I actually did hit the van.

Slightly. Left corner of the front bumper ricocheted off the rear right edge of the moving van, which I don't think the driver of that big rig ever noticed, but what it did for me was keep me from flailing all the way over into the guardrail and fence by bouncing the Volvo backward into its own momentum.

Up to that point I hadn't really been thinking, just reacting, but I suppose with that first hit some thought such as "That clown's an idiot!" would have crossed my mind, and even with the second one I still would have been more inclined to call it coincidence—"Just my luck, two meatballs the same day!"—but when I finally had the Volvo under control and looked out at the world around me, and when I saw the golden Impala ease into my rearview minor just as the green one was sliding into position again on my right flank, I knew I was in trouble.

This was a Monday in February, a pleasant, sunny day after January's rains, about eleven in the morning. Traffic was moderate, and moving fast. And two Chevy Impalas, with a pair of swarthy men in each, had me boxed into the left lane of the San Diego Freeway, behind a fast-receding moving van, where they absolutely intended to give me a fatal accident, and no substitutions accepted.

One thing I've always had, and I'm glad of it, and that's good reaction time. The instant I realized what was happening, I leaned forward against the pressure of the shoulder strap of my seat belt, rested my brow on my crossed forearms on the steering wheel, and kicked down onto the brake pedal as hard as I knew how.

The Volvo didn't exactly stop on a dime, but it slowed abruptly, and a lot sooner than the guy behind me, who came climbing up my tailpipe, jolting me, giving me a rabbit punch in the back of the neck. But I'd known what was happening and the other driver hadn't, so when I accelerated again, the golden Impala got smaller and smaller in my rearview mirror, wobbling over to thump itself into the center divider.

I didn't have time to see what happened next back there, because I still had number two, Captain Green. He was staring at me open-mouthed, no longer pretending he didn't know I was there, while his passenger craned back over the seat, looking for their other team. I put on a spurt, Captain Green did, too, and then I slammed on the brakes again for just a second, accelerated, and steered over into him.

What he'd done, he'd braked when I'd braked, but he was still braking when I accelerated and rammed him, coming up from his left, hitting his left front wheel obliquely with my right front fender, driving hard, turning into him so that he went bouncing off into the lane to his right amid a blare of horns from the other traffic in the vicinity, while I spun back to the left, found my opening, and shot through it.

But not to freedom, not yet. Captain Green was still after me in a car that was bigger and heavier than mine, and on the open highway like this he would also be faster.

But Mulholland Drive was just ahead. I gave no hint to what I planned, staying in the third lane while he came roaring up in my mirror in lane two, and I only moved over to lane two myself at the last second to keep him from passing me.

That's what he thought. He feinted as though he'd go to lane one, then shot off at an angle into lane three, committing himself to the move, halfway into it when I peeled off, ran across the road at an almost dead right angle, and shot out the Mulholland Drive exit.

What he managed to do to follow me off that major road I have no idea, though I could hear it causing a whole lot of angry horn-blowing. Whatever it was—did he make a

U-turn on the San Diego Freeway?—just as I was heading up onto Mulholland, here the son of a bitch came again.

Well, that's why I'd wanted Mulholland. A ridge of hills runs east and west here, separating Los Angeles on the south from the San Fernando Valley on the north, and little-used Mulholland Drive is the mostly two-lane winding road that runs along the top of that ridge. My friend's size and weight and speed meant a lot less up here; what counted was my Volvo's maneuverability.

Parts of Mulholland are very dusty when it isn't raining. I ran through a stretch like that, chalky white clouds rising behind me as I sawed the wheel back and forth through the sharp and twisty curves, and when I came out the other side, my rearview minor was empty. Feeling very shaky, I slowed just a bit, and headed toward home.

3

WE DIDN'T DO A LOT of car chases on *Packard*— he was a criminologist, more cerebral, a kind of dry-cleaned Columbo—but we did do some. What the heck, it's television, you have to do some car crashes. I'd helped out with the stunt driving, and I'd sat back to watch the professionals do the rollovers and the arroyo leaps, and I'd thought I knew pretty much what it was all about. But now I understood that the difference between all of that and actually having four guys in two big, heavy Chevy Impalas try to pound you and your little Volvo into the concrete on the San Diego Freeway is the difference, as Mark Twain said, between the lightning and the lightning bug. My nerves were shot all the way home, my reaction time was terrible, and now that the emergency was over, my driving skills had gone all to hell; if a cop had seen me then, he'd have had reasonable cause to search the car for little packets of white powder.

There are two main entrances into Bel-Air from Sunset Boulevard, both featuring great white arches; no embarrassment or shyness about money around here. Coming out westward from Los Angeles through Beverly Hills, you come to the first and more grandiose entrance at Stone Canyon, but if it's me you're visiting, you continue on to what my friend Brett Burgess calls Bel-Air's servants' entrance; a somewhat more modest white arch at Bellagio, across the way from the west gate to UCLA. Turning north through this arch, you follow Bellagio as it twists and turns, becoming at different intervals Bellagio Way, Bellagio Place, Bellagio Road, and even Bellagio Terrace, before you turn off on San Miguel Way, which is labeled DEAD END and at the very conclusion of which I live. San Miguel is a continuous curve to the left from its beginning at Bellagio to its finish at my house, so you can't see one end from the other.

Normally, that's the route I take home, but when people are out and about with ideas of committing murder on me, I think twice about entering a street where I can't see who's parked in front of my house until after I've made the dead-end turn. Fortunately, I have a back way in.

Behind my house, my property extends southwest down a steep scrub-covered slope. Beyond my land are a few large houses facing the other way, onto Thurston Circle, from which, via Thurston Avenue, you can drive down to Sunset Boulevard just east of the San Diego Freeway. Between two of those large houses I have an easement, and a one-lane blacktop road that looks like a driveway for a house down there, but actually curves up onto my land; where it meets a fence, an electronically controlled gate, and a call box. I use that entrance only if I'm trying to avoid somebody, and at the moment I would say I was definitely trying to avoid somebody.

The same little box on my visor controls both front and back gates. Driving up from Thurston Circle, my own dear land ahead of me, I buzzed the gate open, drove through, and went on up as the gate automatically swung shut behind me. The blacktop stream continued up and around the left side of my house, where it joined the lake of blacktop in front of my garage, where Sugar Ray and Max, my two palomino-colored boxer dogs, came frolicking out of the shade to see if I wanted to play. "Not today, guys," I muttered as I stopped the Volvo and with some difficulty opened my door.

Max immediately presented her head for me to pat, which I did, while Sugar Ray stood happily and alertly in the background, waiting to be told to do something interesting. "Yeah, yeah," I said, and elbowed myself out of the car. I had to lean against it for a second until my dizziness waned, and then I walked around the Volvo, Sugar Ray and Max strolling with me, to assess the damage.

Jesus. And I walked away from that? The right side of the Volvo, formerly red, looked as though several people had been whamming away at it with sledgehammers, to the extent that sheet metal was scraping the sides of both tires— I could see white threads in the bottom of those new grooves—and that passenger door would never open again. The rear, where I'd encouraged the first Impala to cream himself, now looked like a caricature of the front end of Sugar Ray, and the front, where I'd nicked the moving van, was a crumpled Kleenex of red metal around a shattered headlight.

"I think the resale value on this thing," I told the dogs, "has just taken a nosedive." They grinned their agreement, and I left them and went into the house, where Robinson was fitting a frozen pie crust into a pie plate. "Quiche again?" I asked.

He didn't deign to answer, which was quite a spectacle. Robinson, when he's not deigning to answer, looks like Abraham Lincoln with a wasp in his nose. Speaking around the wasp, he said, "Mr. Novak has been telephoning and telephoning. I had to tell him I had no idea where you were."

"You should have put him on hold," I said, and went through into my bathroom, where I scrubbed my face in an effort to feel normal again. It didn't actually work, but at least I then felt coordinated enough to use a telephone, which I did, though not to call the ever-loving Zack. My first call was to Oscar Cooperman, my attorney, who took it in his car, which meant he kept fading in and out. "Where are you, Oscar?" I asked.

"God knows. Harbor Freeway? Somewhere."

"How soon can you get here?"

"Sam, I'm on my way to a closing."

"I'm about to phone the cops, Oscar," I said, "and tell them four guys in two automobiles deliberately tried to kill me just now on the San Diego Freeway. When the cops arrive—"

"Wait a minute, wait a minute, you're fading in and out."

"Tell your chauffeur to drive to Bel-Air!"

"Hold on. Hold on. You there?"

"Oscar, are you going to put me on hold?"

"This phone doesn't have hold," he said. He sounded wistful.

So I heard him giving revised instructions to his chauffeur, and when he came back to me, I told him the story twice, and when he'd assembled the parts he'd heard from each telling, he said, "Holy shit!"

"That's what I said. Precisely what I said."

"Who *are* these people?"

"I don't know. Not fans."

"You'd better call the authorities."

"Yes, Oscar, thank you for your legal advice, that's why I want you here for the interview. See you in a few minutes."

Call the authorities. That turned out to be easier said than done, since there seem to be several hundred police forces in the Greater Los Angeles area, each of which has its own narrow area of responsibility. Since my attack had come on the southern slope of the San Diego Freeway where it crossed into the Valley, the general consensus was that the Los Angeles Sheriff's office was what I wanted, and a female with a southwestern twang at that number assured me deputies would be right out to talk to me about my experience.

Then I called Zack, who said, "What happened to you?"

For just a second I wondered how he'd already heard about it, but then I realized he simply meant that he'd carefully filed me away under hold, and when he'd returned I was gone. "Don't ask," I said. "You were talking about work."

"There's a fellow," he said, "Danny Silvermine, he's got a pretty good track record, he's put together some nice packages in his time, never a major leaguer, you understand, but—"

"What does he want me to do?"

"Dinner theater." Zack, when prodded, was capable of cutting to the essence.

"Where?"

"A tour. Open in Miami, on to Houston, Chicago, possibly the Westbury Music Fair on Long Island, that's your old stomping ground, isn't it? Possibly finish here in L.A."

"Why, Zack? What's in it for me?"

"Work," he said. "Exposure. Keeps your name and face before the people. Good reviews, other people see it, say, 'Maybe Sam Holt is good for this part, that part.'"

"In other words, the money stinks."

"In spades. My commission won't keep me in Tums."

But, as Zack had said, it was work, exposure, the infinite possible. I sighed and said, "What's the play, Zack?"

"Well, that's the genius of it," he said. "Danny Silvermine's genius."

Oh, God; stunt casting. He wants me to do Uncle Vanya or Hotspur, or Willy Loman. I said, "All right, Zack, I'm braced. Lay it on me."

But I wasn't braced. *This* idea had never occurred to me. "Packard," he said.

I frowned, and the red light on the phone blinked. "Hold it," I said, and switched to in-house, and Robinson's voice said in my ear, "Two gentlemen are at the gate, claiming to be police officers."

"That's fine, yes, let them in." I switched over to Zack and said, "*What?*"

"I wish you wouldn't put me on hold, Sam."

"Somebody wants me to do a *play* about *Packard?*"

"Dinner theater," he said. "Danny Silvermine, it's his notion, we—"

"This is work? This is exposure? Zack, this is the last nail in my coffin! Packard is the reason I can't get any other part; if I go on the goddamn road with—"

"A new field, Sam. The theater. You show you're a real actor."

"Playing Packard; there's a stretch. Who's writing this masterpiece?"

"Well, uh...you did."

I didn't get that one the first time it went by. "Say that again?"

"Two of the episodes you wrote for the show," Zack explained. "That way, there's no problems about rights, credits, residuals, all that."

"Zack, wait a minute. Are you actually telling me you want me to go into a large room in Miami, Florida, where people are eating dinner, and reenact one of my old television shows?"

"Two. We call it *An Evening with Jack Packard.*"

"Those are TV scripts, Zack, they can't—"

"Very easily adaptable," he insisted. "The one on the yacht, remember that one?"

"It wasn't very good," I remembered.

"The nice thing about your modesty, Sam," he said, "is that it's so unforced."

"It still wasn't very good."

Outside my window a tan car with stars on its doors and a red and white Tootsie Roll on its roof came up and stopped. Two tan-uniformed Smokey the Bears got out and looked at the house through their sunglasses. "I'll have to get back to you, Zack," I said, and hung up as the Smokeys ambled toward the front door.

Nearly noon. Do sheriff's deputies eat quiche?

4

YES.

Oscar arrived some time after the deputies. I'd already told my story once, and Ken and Chuck and I were out looking at the battered Volvo. Oscar, having bustled over from his Daimler, was just demanding I go back to the beginning and tell the tale all over again when Robinson came out squinting into the sunlight and in his most exasperated manner said, "How many for luncheon?"

"Four," I said. "We'll eat out by the pool."

"Very well." He raised an eyebrow at the ex-Volvo. "Good God," he said, and returned to the house.

Ken grinned behind his sunglasses at the idea of having lunch with a TV star out by the pool, but Chuck frowned after the retreating Robinson, saying, "I've seen that fellow before."

"Not on a wanted poster," I assured him. "That's William Robinson, he—"

"He's an actor!"

"That's right, he used—"

Chuck snapped his fingers, delighted at his own powers of observation "I've seen him in the old movies on TV. He played snooty butlers and valets all the time."

"He still does," I said, which was a sort of a joke, except that nobody got it. The fact is, Robinson, who is now seventy-three, hasn't had an acting job in fourteen years. As that career wound down, he filled in the at-liberty spaces between roles by actually working as a butler or valet for various stars he'd met in films over the years. I didn't know him then—he was passed on to me six years ago and has been here, disapproving of me, ever since—but apparently for at least a decade he migrated between those two lives, being a butler for a while, then acting like a butler, back and forth. He's still *performing*, of course, still doing the lovable curmudgeon, the cranky old Arthur Treacher bit, and I doubt by now he himself knows if his English accent is real or fake.

But all actors get to live twice these days, the second time on the Late Late Show, where Chuck had apparently been seeing him. Grinning, shaking his head, Chuck said, "Only in L.A., huh? You want a butler, you get an actor that specializes in the part."

"I guess so," I said. "Shall we go around back? Robinson gets testy when I keep him waiting."

So we went around back. Ken and Chuck, being on duty, said no to white wine, while I said yes. I would also have a small bottle of San Pellegrino mineral water, a lunchtime habit I learned from my friend Anita Imperato back in New York. Oscar felt he could choke down a vodka martini. Ken and Chuck asked for Tab, and Robinson gave them a look of searing hate. Tab, with his quiche!

All of that out of the way and the four of us seated around the glass table on the shady side of the pool, Ken grinned at me and said, "Probably you think I'm dumb, but you know the one thing I wonder about in what's happened here?"

"What's that?"

"Why you wanted your attorney present," Ken said, and passed his boyish grin on to Oscar as well.

Oscar is a bald man on top with a wiry thick fringe of

astonished gray hair around the sides, sticking way out beyond his ears. He's in his mid-forties, and is essentially sort of baby-faced, but that bald head and halo of gray shrubbery make him seem as though he must be ancient, so the final effect is of an old baby. And one thing he's good at, as an old baby, is pouting. He pouted now, in friendly Ken's direction, saying, "Is there any reason, Deputy Donaldson, why Mr. Holt should not have his attorney present?"

"Wait a minute, Oscar," I said.

"It's a little unusual, that's all," Ken explained.

"That's right," I agreed, and leaned forward to tell them my story. But then I leaned back again while Robinson put down our drinks. *Clack, clack,* went the glasses of Tab in front of the deputies, and he announced, "Luncheon will be served immediately." Then he left.

I leaned forward again. "I don't know if you guys know this," I said, "but I was a police officer myself for a year and a half, back on Long Island."

They looked politely interested.

"If I remember the way the cop's mind works," I said, "it goes like this:'This fella Holt says somebody tried to kill him. He says he doesn't know who they were or why they were doing it, but it was four of them in two cars, very well organized, almost professional.' Now, if I was still taking the county's dollar, the first thing I would say to myself is, 'Maybe there's cocaine in this story. There's a lot of cocaine in these hills, a lot of cocaine stories being told around this neighborhood; this looks like a falling out among druggies.' That's what *I* would have said to myself."

They both smiled. I waited, but they didn't feel like making any comments at that moment, so I went on.

"I'm drug-free. I always have been, always will be. I'm a bit of a fitness freak, I guess, and there's things I wouldn't want to do to my body. So this is *not* a cocaine story, and if it is, they got the wrong guy."

Ken said mildly, "That's a very distinctive red car you've got there."

"That's right. And they hit on me very shortly after I got out on the freeway, which isn't that far from home. I figure they were staked out around the corner on Bellagio, and followed me."

Chuck said, "So you don't claim it was mistaken identity."

"I don't *claim* anything. Except that four guys put a lot of thought and effort into killing me, and the reason I asked my attorney to be present here is that I'd appreciate it if you put the same amount of thought and energy into finding out who they are instead of what possible thing I might have done to trigger it, because I haven't done anything."

"Sure you have," Ken said.

"What?"

"I won't know until you tell me."

Robinson interrupted at that point with quiche and cobb salad and cucumber slices in vinegar and water. I asked for another spritzer and Oscar felt he might do justice to another vodka-mar. Ken's and Chuck's Tabs were just fine. I said, "Robinson, is Mr. Cooperman's chauffeur being taken care of?"

"He is in the kitchen," Robinson said absolutely deadpan, "showing me how to make something called a Sloppy Joe." With a slight tilt of the head Robinson took himself off.

We ate a bit, and then Ken said, "Sam, I don't think we ought to start off on the wrong foot with each other. You figured we'd come up here and just see some crazy movie star—"

"TV star."

"It's all the same from my point of view."

"Okay. Sorry."

"You figured," he said, "we'd jump right to drugs as being what it's all about, and you're pretty sure it isn't drugs, so you wanted your attorney present to impress us a little."

"Without getting your back up," I said.

"That's what I'm working on," Ken told me, "not getting my back up. This is a very nice lunch."

"It sure is," Chuck added.

Oscar said, "I think Sam just wanted to be sure you fellas remembered he was the victim and not one of the perpetrators."

"Still and all," Ken said, putting down his fork and taking off his sunglasses at last and giving me a level stare from intelligent blue eyes, "as you pointed out, Sam, those people put a lot of time and effort and organization into that attempt. Now, when I went out to the car and called in just before Mr. Cooperman arrived, I learned a couple things."

I looked alert. Ken said, "That gold car you say you hit, or made it hit you, whatever it was. It did crash into the divider, and the two men in it were seen to run away. The vehicle is a Hertz rental, picked up late yesterday afternoon at LAX. The belief now is it was paid for with a stolen credit card."

"*Very* elaborate," I said.

"It was you they were after, and they were serious about it. You don't attract that much high-intensity input, Sam, you really don't, without having done *something* to catch somebody's eye."

"I don't know what it is," I told him. "That's the truth."

"I believe you. But if I were you, I'd think real hard on the subject. People who work with that kind of devotion at killing somebody maybe won't be discouraged just because they missed once. They might believe in that old saying."

"If at first..."

Ken nodded. "That's the one," he said.

I SPENT THE REST OF THAT odd lunch—just me and my West Coast lawyer and a couple of deputies—trying to think what I had done or said or seen anywhere in the world in the last few months that could have caused that big a reaction. Nothing came.

Of course, stupid though it may sound, I was also distracted by Zack's suggestion that I go do a couple of Packard shows on the dinner theater circuit. The idea was too ridiculous to think about, of course, but nevertheless I did think about it, and what I mostly thought was:

Which was the second script?

Okay, the one on the yacht, that could be cut down to one fairly simple set involving the wheelhouse and the lounge and the afterdeck, I could see exactly what Zack—or his genius, Danny Silvermine—had dreamed up for that one, but which was the second adaptable script? I had done a total of seven, all in the last two years of the show, and I just couldn't keep myself from thinking about them all, wondering which was the one Danny Silvermine saw me doing in front of six hundred people eating roast beef.

Well, I didn't manage to answer either of my pressing questions during lunch, and finished the meal still not knowing either which script or why kill me. Ken and Chuck offered police protection, which they knew I would decline and which I declined, so then they said I should keep in touch and I said I would. Ken wrote out a phone number and gave it to me, saying, "It's in there somewhere, Sam, their reason is inside your head. For your sake, I hope you find it."

"Me too. I'll phone the instant anything surfaces." I walked them around to their car, where Chuck grinned and said, "I just got to tell you, Sam, I was a real fan of yours. I watched your show all the time when I was a kid.

"Thanks, Chuck," I said with some kind of smile on my face. When he was a *kid*? The show's been off the air only three years!

Oscar stayed a while longer, to chat about legal problems. I'd be making a quick trip to New York tomorrow to appear for the defendant's discovery proceeding in my lawsuit against the New York-based comic book company that had used my "image and likeness" without payment or permission. Morton Adler, my attorney in the East, was actually handling the case, but Oscar was quite naturally taking an interest, so we talked. Instead of his normal third vodka-mar, he asked for coffee, saying, "Believe it or not, I'm going to a mosque from here, and there shouldn't be anything on my breath."

"Funny," I said. "You don't look Arab."

"Ha-ha," he said sarcastically, and pouted. "It's Al-Gazel, the new one they just built in Beverly Hills."

"And they have a Jewish lawyer?"

"They do not. They have an Italian supplier of copper sheeting, and there's some question now about who has to pay for all the security arrangements over there, and it is Mr. Catelli who is wise enough and lucky enough to have a Jewish lawyer."

"With nothing on his breath."

"Absolutely."

Finishing his coffee, Oscar gathered up his chauffeur—

a short stout man sated with Sloppy Joes—and departed for his mosque. Once I was alone I phoned my insurance agent to describe what had happened to my Volvo. She said somebody would come out to look at it, but it sure did sound totaled, and I could undoubtedly expect full replacement costs. "Except for the adaptations, of course."

"What do you mean? Why 'of course'?" Since I'm so tall, I usually have to have cars adapted to suit me; front seat mounted farther back, things like that. I said, "If you don't pay for *that*, it isn't full replacement."

She sounded dubious, saying, "I don't think the company will go for it, but let me see what I can do."

"Thanks," I said grumpily, and hung up, and it was then, while brooding about the minginess of insurance companies, that it hit me.

Ross Ferguson.

Had to be. Ross Ferguson and the tape he showed me last November in New York. He *hadn't* got out from under after all; he'd lied to me.

Ross Ferguson. The people who'd nailed *him* were after *me*.

If this were a television story, the first commercial would come along just about now.

THIS BEGAN THREE MONTHS EARLIER, back in New York. I have a townhouse there on West Tenth, and I like to spend the fall and early winter in the city, when the weather's at its best. I do my shopping, go to the theater, hang out with friends. I get to walk a lot, a thing that's impossible in L.A. I usually stick around till after Christmas, spend the holidays with my family out on Long Island, and then fly west with the first snow.

So it was November, I'd been in town a little over a month, it was late afternoon, and I was in the lap pool I'd installed in the basement, to keep my swimming muscles in shape while I'm in Big Town, when Robinson called over the loudspeaker-intercom from upstairs that Ross Ferguson was on the "blower" for me. "He says it's most urgent," boomed out his voice, resonating, bouncing back from all that pale green tile in the long low-ceilinged room. My lap pool is the only echo chamber in Robinson's life these days, and he makes the absolute most of it.

"Take a number," I shouted in the general direction of the mike on the far wall. "Tell him I'll call back in five minutes." And I swam underwater for a while, to keep from having to answer questions or make decisions.

Actually, it was eleven minutes later when I called Ross back—he was staying at the Hotel Pierre—I having in the meantime finished my laps, taken a quick shower, put on my blue terry robe, and come upstairs to the bedroom floor. There used to be an elevator in this four-story building—five if you count the basement— but I had it taken out during the conversion, much to Robinson's dismay.

Ross sounded his usual self—which is to say, a bit pompous, attitudinizing, self-centered—but according to his dialogue he was desperate. "I'm desperate, Sam. I have to see you at once. I can be there in twenty minutes."

"But I can't," I told him. "Sorry, Ross."

"Sam, I'm not kidding you, this is *urgent*."

I was in the bedroom, and my calendar was next door in my office, so I said, "Hold it a second, Ross, don't go away," put him on hold, went through into the office with its view over Tenth Street—the bedroom gets the garden and the interesting building-backs and the occasional shots of sunlight—and I sat at my desk, picked up the phone there, and said, looking at my calendar, "I'm free all day tomorrow. You want lunch?"

"Sam, please," he said, and this time I could hear an edge of something different in his voice. Tension? Fear? "I can't spend another night like this."

"Christ, Ross." I shook my head, though he wouldn't be able to see it. "The thing is, Brett's opening in a play tonight."

"Brett Burgess?"

"That's right."

"And noblesse oblige, huh?" Which was more like the Ross I was used to; unnecessarily nasty even while asking a favor.

"Ross," I said, "he's one of my oldest friends. He taught me what little I know about acting, just as you taught me what little I know about writing."

"Well, I'm in more trouble than he is. It's barely six o'clock; what time's the curtain?"

I sighed. "We're having dinner before," I said. "I promised. Look, Ross, if it's really that bad—"

"It's worse, Sam. Am I somebody who goes around crying wolf?"

"No, you're not," I had to admit.

"Okay," he said, and yelled, "*Wolf!*"

"All right, all right, there's a real wolf. I tell you what, after the show, I could probably get away, uh...how about midnight? Will you still be up?"

"I won't sleep at *all* tonight, Sam," he said.

7

BRETT BURGESS IS ABOUT MY AGE, not quite as tall as me, a bit broader in the shoulders and the jaw. We met soon after I went out to L.A., he being another young hopeful in that first agent's stable. (He gave Brett his name, too, just as he gave me "Sam Holt." I have no idea who Brett was originally.) Brett and I auditioned for the same or similar parts, we worked together just once as World War II German soldiers in a miniseries, and Brett moved over to a different agent very shortly after I made my own switch.

The difference between us is Brett never got a series. The other difference is Brett is an *actor*, always has been, has never had any other goal in life. In the early days he was very generous with his knowledge and experience, and I wasn't overstating by much when I'd told Ross that Brett had taught me whatever I know about acting. Brett has never looked down on me for being just a slob who drifted into his profession and right away grabbed the brass ring, but if anybody had the right to take that attitude toward me, it would certainly be Brett.

That's why Ross's noblesse oblige crack had stung, as he'd known it would. I always feel a little guilty toward Brett and at the same time—silly though it may sound—a little envious. It's true I made the money, got the fame, had what in anybody's lexicon has to be called success, but Brett is working. He's a working actor, he gets movie roles, TV roles, small parts in big plays and big parts in small plays, he's constantly stretching his muscles and practicing his craft, while what am I doing? Stitching back and forth in my lap pool.

Brett was opening that night in an off-Broadway theater near Sheridan Square, in an imported (and translated) Brazilian play called *The Two Colonels*. He was the second lead, the bad colonel. Our dinner date was for six-thirty at Vitto Impero, an easy walk over to the West Village. Anita Imperato, who has run Vitto Impero ever since she threw her gambling-man husband out seven years ago, had agreed to become a customer in her own joint for tonight and join us at our feast. "Don't talk about the play," she said as we all took our places at the round corner table in the back, where a bottle of Pinot Grigio and a big bottle of San Pellegrino mineral water already awaited us. "I'll want to see it for myself."

"You coming tonight?" Brett asked her as I opened the San Pellegrino and filled our water glasses.

"No, let's see what the critics say." Before anybody could respond to this flat-out contradiction, she signaled for Marcie the waitress and told us, "Angelo says the red snapper is terrific tonight."

Brett said, "What's tonight's pasta?"

Briskly shaking her head, Anita said, "Something with strawberries."

"In that case," Brett told the waiting Marcie, poised with her pad and pencil, "I'll have the tortellini." Brett believes in a carbohydrate charge before high-tension experiences like an opening night.

I had the red snapper, since that was what Angelo the chef liked at the moment, and Anita had a carpaccio appetizer and a salad, nothing more. She's a tall and slender woman, Anita, almost bony, and I think she keeps her shape because she's around food too much, and feels contempt for it. She's very good-looking, but doesn't care about that, and therefore doesn't dress or make herself up to enhance her looks, and so it's easy not to notice. Her face is a long oval, with features that are somehow both strong and delicate; a small but sharp nose, large acute brown eyes, and long very black hair falling in thick waves around her head.

Anita and I have had a thing together off and on over the years, but she refuses to take it seriously, so it's never developed into much. In the first place, she thinks it's ridiculous for the owner of a small-time Italian restaurant in Greenwich Village to be hooked up with a TV celebrity, and in the second place, she's one year older than I am, which is an absurd thing to care about, but she does. Also, she knows I have a girlfriend named Bly Quinn out on the Coast, though they've never met. "I'll just be your New York girl," Anita says with that crooked grin I like so much. "I'll just be here to see you don't lose your East Coast edge." And she gives me a kidney punch with her hard little sharp-knuckled fist.

Since Anita had started the meal by banning discussion of the play—a smart and thoughtful move on her part, I later realized—we talked instead about other things. Brett had changed New York agents again, *The Two Colonels* being the first fruit of the change, so we discussed that. Brett's girlfriend, Maria, who would join us at the theater and I would sit with during the show, was thinking of taking a job with a travel magazine, which would put her out of the country a lot—she was a photographer, had been taking pictures of food for *Gourmet* the last three years and was tiring of it—and this prospect of a constantly departing Maria was making Brett think about proposing marriage, so we worried that bone for a while, until Anita said, "Brett, is it your idea if she marries you, she'll give up her job?"

"Well—*that* job, I guess." He grinned. "She could still work, believe me, particularly if she wants to go on eating."

Anita shook her heath "Marry her to keep her home," she said. "No wonder I hate men."

"If that's the only reason I want to marry her," Brett said, "forget it." He has a nice, easy, self-deprecating grin and he leans his head forward a bit from his big shoulders, like a very amiable bear. Most of the time he's cast as a heavy—like the bad colonel in tonight's play—but twice I've seen him do commercials that brought out that other side of him, and I wish he could get to use it more. In one of the commercials he was teaching a boy how to put a lure on a fishing line, and in the other he was a friendly truck driver explaining motor oil to a kid in a jalopy.

Maybe one of the reasons Brett hasn't made it is that he's too nice to be a major heavy and too bull-like to be a major hero. Too bad, if true.

Anyway, I had walked over to Abingdon Square for dinner, and now Brett and I walked back east to the theater, where Maria was waiting for us out on the sidewalk. Brett kissed her and grinned at me, we both suggested he break his leg, and he went away to his dressing room while Maria and I had coffee in a place nearby. I told Maria, a skinny, bubbly, bouncy black-haired girl, that I'd heard about this new job possibility with the travel magazine, and she talked about it, but not with what seemed like particular enthusiasm. After a while I began to get the idea she had only considered the job as a ploy to get Brett to quit stalling around and propose. I wondered what Anita would make of *that.*

A few other people I knew were at the opening, including Bill Ackerson, Dr. William Ackerson, my East Coast doctor and Brett's, a show-biz buff who keeps the *Hollywood Reporter* and both *Varietys* in his waiting room. He always dates one or another of his young and beautiful patients; tonight's was a smiling blond singer apparently named Bunny. Assembling, we all milled about a bit—at that point, you never know if you're at a wedding or a wake—and then we went in to see the show.

The Two Colonels was intellectual-dumb, so concerned with its meaning and its political symbols that it pretty well left out character entirely and twisted its plot around to look like a wrought-iron fence. Afterward, we told Brett how terrific the play was and how wonderful he was in it—he actually had invested his role with more individuality and interest than had been written into it—and congratulated the rest of the cast and the director.

Bill Ackerson and his Bunny hopped quickly from the scene of the crime, but a group of us went out for drinks together afterward, the usual thing, actors hanging out together, coming down off the nervous high of performance. After a while everybody forgot I used to be the television hotshot and we all just talked together. It was very pleasant, and the next time I looked at my watch it was five minutes to twelve.

I hadn't thought about Ross Ferguson the entire time.

8

WHEN I WAS A TEENAGER, it was a big thing on the weekends to take the train into the city and wander around either Times Square or Greenwich Village. This great big exciting place, New York City, the center of the known universe, was practically our next-door neighbor, full of electricity and promise. We didn't know what the hell to *do* with it then, but at least we could enter into it and wander around and stare at it and pretend we were cool.

That wasn't so very long ago, but nevertheless things have changed a lot. New York somehow seems to have less promise than it did, or the promise is somehow now tainted with expectations of defeat. The electricity is still there, but with a stronger current of danger. Times Square has degenerated into some sort of subhuman pit, and all over the city there's less of a sense that rich and poor are breathing the same air. The drawbridges are up; the self-made millionaires aren't from Akron and Kansas City anymore, they're from Oman and Kuwait.

One of the few parts of the city that hasn't changed— or at least hasn't become unrecognizable—is Greenwich Village. That's why I live there, and why I feel comfortable walking in it late at night, and why it was so difficult to walk faster even though I was going to be late for my meeting with Ross Ferguson, who I could see from half a block away, pacing the buckled old slate sidewalk in front of my house.

I don't know where Ross Ferguson came from originally, but by now he couldn't be anything but what he is: a successful Hollywood writer. In his early fifties, with thick steel-wool hair that's all pepper and salt, he has a year-round dark orangy-brown tan, and in his native habitat he tends to wear silk shirts open to the waist—curly gray hair-clumps on his bronzed chest— and heavy necklaces of gold chain, and designer sunglasses on top of his head. He's been writing for more than twenty years out on the Coast, a few movies but mostly television, owns a piece of a couple of successful series, and lives up in the hilly part of Beverly Hills with a succession of wives and girlfriends. Actually, I think it's just girlfriends these days, his accountant having told him he can't afford any more wives—that is, ex-wives.

I know I've made him sound terrible, and in many ways Ross *is* terrible, but the odd thing is, he's also a very talented guy and fine craftsman. He was one of the three or four most prolific writers for *Packard*, and his scripts always gave us interesting things to do and think about, characters with more complexity than absolutely necessary and story lines that took unexpected but not unbelievable twists and turns. When I first sat down to try my hand at a *Packard* script, Ross was one of the three people I showed it to, and he was wonderfully generous and forthcoming in his response. If life hadn't made him a rich bronzed Hollywood writer, he probably would have been a hell of a teacher, and possibly a better and happier human being, though I realize it's stupid to make that kind of judgment about another person. Anyway, whoever he might have been, a fine writer and a fine teacher and a rotten apple is who he is, and who I was now approaching along the sidewalk on West Tenth at not quite ten minutes past midnight.

"Jesus, Sam! I thought something happened to you!" His expression was so tense, so worried, that I felt immediately guilty at being late. "I'm sorry, Ross," I said, "I really am. You know how actors get after an opening."

"More self-absorbed than ever," he commented, reverting to his usual self. "Hard to believe, I know."

"Well, I'm here now," I pointed out, guilt all gone. "Come on in."

The only lights burning inside the house were on the staircase, which meant Robinson had gone to bed, disapproving my late hours, no doubt. Ross and I came in and shut the door and I hit various light switches, saying, "You want something to drink?"

"Yes," he said simply. "I have a story to tell you, Sam, and then a tape to play, and they'll both need a drink."

"A tape?"

"Wait'll you see it." His eyes looked hollow, haunted, an expression I'd never seen on him before.

"I'm looking forward. Name your poison."

"Brandy."

"Fine. We'll go up to the office, in that case; the brandy and the VCR are both there."

"It's U-Matic," he said as we went up the stairs.

U-Matic? That's the professional level of tape, similar to the Betamax system but with a tape twice as wide. I've never seen that much difference in quality, but that's what the networks and the producers all use. My secret opinion is that the professionals use a different tape system because if they used the same system as the amateurs, how would they know they were professionals?

Anyway, I have players for all three systems, so that was no problem. Up one flight, we went into my office—the night-time view, across quiet West Tenth, is of low skyline and lit windows—and I opened the liquor cabinet while Ross shucked out of his topcoat.

Away from his native habitat Ross's clothing style

became a little uncertain. His tan topcoat was good quality, suggesting someplace like Brooks Brothers. His dark gray suit, fitting a little badly in the shoulders and seat, made him look older, and as though on his way to the funeral of a business acquaintance. The black tasseled loafers softened this image a bit, not much, while the pink shirt and the flowered tie were just crazy.

My office is a fairly large room, divided into two areas. Toward the front is a double-sided antique desk with green leather insert top; depending on my mood or what's going on, I can sit facing the room or the street. The chairs on both sides of the desk are identical; oak, with green leather seats and backs.

The rear half of the room contains more casual seating: a low short sofa, upholstered in soft cotton with an autumn design of branches and berries and fallen leaves, facing a pair of low overstuffed swivel chairs in a light brown. The back wall, opposite the windows, contains, in addition to a door to my bedroom, cream-colored shelves filled with books, VCRs, and stereo equipment.

Armed with brandies, we sat facing each other, me on the sofa and Ross nervously moving in little arcs back and forth in one of the swivel chairs. I said, "Cheers," and we sipped our Rémy, and I said, "What brings you east, Ross?"

"You," he said. "I had nowhere else I could turn, and your service said you were in New York, so here I came."

I put my snifter down on the oak coffee table between us. "You came all this way just to see me? No other reason? What's going on?"

He had taken a small paper bag from his topcoat pocket when we'd first come upstairs, which he now fidgeted with in his lap. From the shape I would have said it contained a U-Matic tape. Now he patted it and said, "First I'll tell you the story, then I'll show you this."

"Fine."

"Do you remember Delia West?"

I didn't. "Remind me."

"I went with her awhile, a year or two ago. She's the one who threatened a breach of promise suit. Can you imagine? In this day and age, a breach-of-promise? That's after her own lawyer laughed her out of his office when she tried palimony."

"I'm sorry, Ross, I don't remember this one," I said. "And she does sound like somebody I wouldn't forget."

"A killer," he said, and then looked startled. "Jesus," he said. "Language is coming up and hitting me in the face."

"Delia West," I reminded him.

"Yeah. She was married to a stuntman; he did some stuff on *Packard* in the early days. She split, divorced him, went to live with a lady psychiatrist for a while, then switched back to men, then maybe a year and a half ago she took up with me. We hung out for, I don't know, three, four months. She never actually did live in the house, you know, I'm not that stupid, so that was what went wrong with the palimony."

"Plus the shortness of the time," I suggested.

He knocked back some Rémy, a little more than if he were tasting it and enjoying it. He said, "Sure, that's why she switched over to breach of promise. Takes no time at all to say 'Will you marry me?' No conjugal domicile necessary before the wedding bells."

"*Did* you say 'Will you marry me?'"

"Are you crazy? My accountant would kill me! Oh, shit, there I go again."

"Ross, is there killing in this story?"

"Wait for it," he said, like any good writer. "The point is, Delia and I were done and over with more than a year ago. I'd let her stay out at the Malibu place when I wasn't there, and she had some sort of weird freaks in for a party; they fucked the place over good, and that was the last straw. Good-bye, I said, and she went to her lawyer, and it's been a life of writs and summonses and threats ever since.

"She's actually going forward with the breach of promise?"

"It's just a nuisance suit," he said, shaking his head. "My lawyer tells me she just wants to make enough trouble so it's easier to pay her off than fight her. I told him screw that, I'll pay you twice what I'd pay that bitch, so that's where we are. Or where we've been."

"Now we cut to the car crash."

He managed a shaky grin. "That's right, Sam," he said. 'Now we cut to the car crash." He finished his brandy and held out the glass. "Okay? Would you mind?"

Ross isn't a lush, I'll say that for him, so I got up and said, "Sure," and poured him a second drink twice as large as the first, a good third of the way up the balloon. This I gave him, and sat again on the sofa, and said, "Crash."

"Two weeks ago," he said, "I went to the Malibu place. I'd had a fight with Doreen—"

"Delia, you said."

"No, no, Doreen." At least he looked sheepish about it. "That's the new one," he said. "She *is* living in the house. So when we had this big ruckus a couple weeks ago, I went out to the Malibu place—I intended to go out there the next day anyway—and when I walked in, there was Delia, dead on the floor."

"Good God, Ross! Dead? That must have been terrible."

"It was."

"When was this?"

"Two weeks ago."

I was horrified and embarrassed "Ross, I never heard a thing about it."

"Nobody did." He grimaced, looking away, then took a deep breath and said, "She was murdered, Sam, and I'll admit it, I panicked."

"Oh, oh."

"I looked at her, dead. Strangled, you know? A murder victim, in *my* house. Jesus, a terrible sight, Sam."

"I'm sure it was." I'd seen a few victims of violence back when I was on the Mineola force, but this was Ross's story, so I let him alone with it.

He shook his head, stuck on the memory. "A terrible sight."

"What did you do, Ross?"

"I could see how it was going to be. Say I called the cops, tell them what I found, they come over. Delia and I did some public fighting while we were together, you know. More than once I said various wild things in restaurants and at parties and like that."

"Things like 'I'll kill you, you bitch,' for instance."

"You must have been there," he said with another shaky grin. "Also, there was the lawsuit going on. Also, I'd had a few drinks, it was late at night, she was in my own place in Malibu. What's anybody going to think? Sam, I put my old plot maven's mind to work on this thing, and I saw absolutely nothing between me and the electric chair but my own wits."

"No electric chair," I told him. "No death penalty at all in California, and when it was—"

"Yeah, yeah, I know, the pellet in the bucket, I wrote that scene myself five six times over the years. 'Rocco's forearm muscles tense, pulling on the straps.' But you know what I mean."

"You mean you turned it into a story," I told him. "A plot."

"Well, that's what I do, right?"

"You said to yourself, 'Here's the situation. The hero's innocent, but he looks guilty as hell. So what's the next scene?' " And as I said that, I saw what he'd done. "Oh, Ross," I said. "You didn't."

"I did."

"You hid the body."

"I *disposed* of the body. No corpus delicti around *this* bunny rabbit. I made the whole thing un-happen."

"That's bad," I told him.

He shook his head, grimacing at himself. "What can I tell you? It seemed like a good idea at the time."

"What did you do, exactly?"

"Took her out in the boat. She was still almost warm when I picked her up. The boat was anchored just off the beach. I carried her out to the dinghy, putt-putted out to the boat, went *way* out. It was after dawn when I came back." He looked portentous, and said a line he'd have put in a script: "I came back alone."

I looked at the tape in his lap. "Somebody taped you? Carrying her out?"

"Worse." At last he pulled the tape out of the paper bag and extended it toward me. "Take a look."

I stood up, took the tape, and hesitated. Ross was really looking bad; troubled, scared, out of his depth. I said, "Why me, Ross?"

"I know you. I like you. I trust you. Also, you used to be a cop."

"Years ago, on Long Island. I gave speeding tickets."

"Come *on*, Sam," he said. "We worked together on that show; we know each other. I know you've got a good mind; you're *really* not just another pretty face like those other clowns."

"Ross, is this the next scene in the story? You find the dead girl, you panic, you dispose of the body, all fine script material. Then what's the next scene? You go to your old pal Packard?"

He blinked. "I don't know. That hadn't occurred to me. Do you think so?"

"I'm not Packard, Ross. I never was. I'm barely Sam Holt."

"Look at the tape, Sam," he said.

So I put the tape in the machine and switched on the monitor, and after what seemed like a lot of snowy leader, all of a sudden we were looking at a fairly grainy wide shot, in color, of a living room. Low sprawly canvas-covered sofas, tile floor, a white free-standing fireplace with a mouth like the shark in *Jaws*. Lots of wide glass sliding doors. It appeared to be a night-time shot, without sound: I said, "That's your Malibu place, isn't it?" I had stayed there a few times, but I didn't remember it that well.

"Yes," Ross said as a girl appeared, wearing a bikini. Good, hard, skinny body, hard attractive face, mass of blond hair. "That's Delia," Ross said, as he himself appeared in a white jumpsuit open to the waist, chains swinging on chest, sunglasses on top of head. Both Ross and Delia were carrying drinks in short, wide, thick-bottomed glasses. They gave the impression they were a little drunk, and having an argument. The camera was stationary, not panning with them as they moved back and forth and talked and gestured as people do when they're a little smashed and trying to make some idiot understand their point of view.

Watching, I said, "When was this taken?"

"Wait for it."

So I waited. Nothing much was happening, just a couple of drunks mouthing off at each other. Then the Ross on tape banged his glass down onto the white plastic end table beside one of the sofas, and pointed at Delia in unmistakable anger. She apparently yelled something. He went over and grabbed the front of her bra between her breasts and yanked hard, and the material tore, and he flung the bra backhand out of camera range. She slapped his face. He punched her in the face and she staggered back, dropping her drink on the little white shag carpet near the fireplace. She was yelling, still angry, not yet scared. Ross waded in after her, punching at her head again. She put her arms up to protect her face and he hit her in the stomach, and when her arms shot downward, he put both hands round her neck.

From there on it got grim. They struggled, she went over backward, him on top, bearing her down, clutching to her throat. She kicked and writhed, she tried to scratch his face, pull at his hands, but nothing worked. I found myself tensing up, my stomach muscles clenching, my own throat feeling burned and sore.

The camera just kept watching. It didn't move. It didn't cut to later in the same scene. And it seemed to take a long, long time for Delia West to die.

At last the Ross on tape staggered back away from the body. He knelt on the floor, staring at her, then seemed to cry out, then turned away with his hands over his face.

Jump-cut. Extreme close-up. Delia's face. My *God*, how awful it looked! Tongue so thick and purple, jutting out. Eyes like joke eyes you'd buy in a carnival arcade, huge and round and covered with veins. Throat battered and bruised, *pushed in* in some horrible way.

I made a sound, backing away from the monitor. I could hear Ross swallowing and swallowing, very loudly.

I reached forward to turn the damn thing off, but before I got there the entertainment part of the show ended, and we went back to the snowstorm of black tape. I said, "Is that all of it?"

"Isn't that enough?"

It was. I hit Stop and Rewind, and turned to look at Ross. There was no sound but the whirr of the VCR.

Ross stared at me. His face was covered with sweat. He ran a hand over it, then drank brandy, then looked at the brandy snifter. He looked at me again. He said, "I don't have blackouts."

"All right."

"I didn't kill her."

Click. The rewind was complete. I said, "You mean that wasn't you?"

"I didn't kill her! Of course it wasn't me."

"Ross, it looked like you. *I* thought it was you."

"The basstards," he said, and grimaced at the blank monitor.

"Don't tell me about twin brothers, anything like that, all right?"

"This isn't a *story.*" He was mad and scared in equal parts.

I turned away from him, switched on the tape, watched the room appear, the girl enter, the seeming Ross enter. I pushed Freeze, and hunkered down to stare at that tiny Ross figure. After a while I saw the possibility. "All right," I said.

"Somebody who doesn't know me," he said. "Somebody like a cop, for instance. What's he gonna say?"

Stop. Rewind. I looked back at Ross. "Where'd this tape come from?"

"In my mailbox, yesterday. Not mailed, just put in there.'

"What did the note say?"

"You're right, there was a note." He reached into the crumpled paper bag and brought out a sheet of blank type-writer paper, folded in half. I took it, opened it, and read the words from newspapers Scotch-taped onto it: *We will be in touch. We will call ourselves Delia.*

"Did they get in touch?"

"No," he said. "I looked at the watermark on that paper, by the way, and it's the kind I use in my scripts. They think of everything, don't they? I could have done the note myself."

I said, "And they waited two weeks before they dropped the other shoe. Psychologists."

"Maniacs. But also magicians. I did not kill her, Sam."

"They left her for you to see. If you called the police, so much for that. But once you disposed of the body, they had you. Psychologists. They knew their man."

"Bastards, bastards, bastards."

I permitted myself a little smile, though there wasn't that much in view that was amusing. "They guessed you wrong in one way, though," I said.

"How was that?"

"They figured to let you stew two three days before they called. They figured you'd stick around, scared, getting more scared. They didn't know you had a famous criminologist pal named Packard, and that you'd go all the way to New York to see him."

9

IF I ACCEPTED ROSS'S STATEMENT that he hadn't killed Delia West, and for the moment I did accept it, then the big question was, how did this tape come into existence?

Fakery. Some sort of fakery. Had to be.

And the dead girl had had to be part of the fake. She'd gone into it knowing they were pulling a scam on Ross Ferguson, but the part she hadn't known about was that she would actually be dead at the end of the set-up.

Because that was definitely Delia West. We looked at the tape a lot more times that night, Ross and I—usually punching Stop and Rewind just before that awful final close-up—and there was no question in his mind but that the nearly naked woman we were seeing in the last moments of her life was Delia West. "I *knew* her, Sam, I knew her, and that's her."

"And is that you?"

"Jesus, Jesus." He stared at the monitor, his nose almost touching the screen. "He looks like me and yet he doesn't, you know? Jesus. Does he move like me?"

"Almost," I had to say. "Not quite right, for somebody who knows you. Do you actually have a white jumpsuit like that?"

"Sure. It's hanging in the closet in the Malibu place right now, or at least I think it is. That's where I last saw it."

"Do those look like your chains?"

"Sure, why not? There's a thousand out there all alike. Chains is chains."

We looked at the tape. We looked at the tape. We looked at the tape.

It was not the original, it was a copy, and therefore just the slightest bit blurry around all the edges. It looked like the tapes you see of undercover FBI men in sting operations, except it was in color and there was no date and time numeration along the bottom. Until the bit at the very end, it was one continuous long shot, with the full figures of the people visible throughout. I said, "Where was it taken from? Where in the room?"

"On that side. This side here, where we're watching from, is where I keep all my VCR and stereo stuff. The same as you've got here."

"You have a VCR camera out there, for U-Matic?"

"Sure."

"Where do you keep it?"

"Mostly on top of the machine, the VCR machine, just sitting there. Available, you know, if we want to fool around."

"Ross, might there be tapes out there of you and various people, maybe even Delia, doing *other* kinds of things together?"

He ducked his head, and managed to look at the same time embarrassed and pleased with himself. "A few," he said.

"They'd look a little like this tape here."

He looked at the monitor. The two people walked back and forth, arguing. His face fell: "Yeah, they would."

"So if somebody says 'How come this tape exists?' the answer is, you thought you and Delia were going to fool around a little, so you switched on the camera and then things turned nasty."

"Oh, shit," he said. He was working his way through my brandy. "Shit shit shit."

We looked at the tape. We looked at the tape. We looked at the tape.

I said, "You say Delia used to be married to a stunt-man?"

"Yeah."

"Well, she learned how to fake taking a punch."

He watched. "Shit, she is faking, isn't she?"

"This isn't where she got strangled," I said. "Look at her face."

"Oh come on, Sam."

"Ross," I insisted, "look at the tape. At the end of this we get when she's really dead, but look at it now. Her eyes aren't bulging out, we can't see her tongue. This is fake."

Jump-cut; no fake. I hastily hit Stop and Rewind, then Stop and Play. "Watch her, Ross, she's acting."

He watched, and this time I managed to hit Stop before the jump-cut. We looked at each other. He said, "They killed her afterward."

I said, "So the fake Ross wasn't in on the murder part either. He was just the guy who looked a lot like you, or could be made to look a lot like you."

"Jesus, these makeup guys now—"

"I know it. All these people needed was the Academy Guide, just turn the pages, looking at every actor's face until they find *you*."

"All right," Ross said. "We know how they did it. The question is, what do I do now?"

"You take this tape to the law."

He stared at me. "Are you crazy?"

"No. You've got to get out from under this thing, whatever it is, and the only way to do that is go straight to the police. Give them the tape, tell them what you've done, hope for the best."

"I can't deal with the *police!*"

"You think you can deal with these people? Whoever they are, they're very smart and they're very mean. You'd rather have them to deal with than the law?"

He thought about that. He said, sounding dubious, "I don't know what they want from me yet."

"If it was something you'd like, they wouldn't set up a scam this elaborate."

"But we don't know what it is."

"Look, Ross," I said. "You wanted Packard's advice? There it is. Take this problem straight to the cops. Show them how it's a fake."

"Come on, Sam, we're in the *business*, we can see how it could be done, but the *cops?* Tell them that isn't me?"

"Why not? Explain how it's done."

"They won't listen," he said.' "They'll have *me*, they'll have the *tape*, they'll have my confession that I disposed of the body. Or do I lie about that?"

"You can't. You have to give them the whole truth."

"And nothing but the truth." He brooded at the monitor, now dark and blank.

There was no longer any reason to look at the tape. I rewound it one last time, gave it and the note to Ross, and he put them away in the paper bag. We talked about the police some more, he remained dubious but said he'd think about it, and finally, around four in the morning, he left.

The next day I called Ross at the Pierre, and they told me he'd checked out, so the day after that I called him at home in Beverly Hills and his service said he was out of town, she didn't know where, didn't know when he'd be back, would be happy to take a message. He didn't respond to the message.

Three months went by. After the holidays Robinson and I returned to Bel-Air, collected the dogs back from Bly, and settled into our western life. Then last weekend I noticed in the TV listings a *Packard* rerun that Ross had written, and it reminded me, and I phoned him.

"Oh, hi, Sam! It's been a long time, kid!" He sounded chipper, happy, even frenetic.

"Not since New York," I said, to remind him.

"Say, listen," he said, lowering his voice, becoming confidential. "About that, uh, thing we discussed—"

"The tape," I said.

"*Jee*-sus! Sam, forget it, okay? Never mind it, I took care of things."

"Did you talk to—"

"Listen, Sam, I'm on my way to Warner's, we'll talk soon, okay? We'll take lunch." And he hung up before I could ask him anything more. And just three days later four guys I didn't know did their level best to murder me.

10

AND THAT'S THE POINT WHEN, following my own advice to Ross back in November, I should have gone to the police. Normally I would have. That deputy Ken had given me a phone number to call, barely an hour before, and if my suspicions had settled on any story other than Ross Ferguson's, I would have called Ken the instant I'd figured it out. But under the circumstances, as a courtesy, before talking to Ken I called Ross.

Or tried to. I got his service, who said Ross was "unavailable at the moment," which was not the same as being out of town. I knew what the phrase meant. Sometimes Ross is working furiously toward a deadline and doesn't want to be disturbed, so he tells the service to say he's unavailable. Once or twice a day he'll collect his messages, and decide for himself who he wants to chat with. I told the service, "Tell him it's Sam Holt, it's urgent, I need to talk to him about the tape."

"Yes, sir," she said, and took my number, and I went out to the kitchen, where Robinson was cleaning up after Oscar's chauffeur's Sloppy Joes. He gave me a look and not a word, but the message was absolutely clear: He couldn't see how he could go on accepting me as an employer if my circle of acquaintances was going to include people whose chauffeurs made such messes as this in *his* kitchen, a sentiment easier expressed in a look than a sentence, come to think of it.

"Sorry about that, Robinson," I said.

"Your vehicle and my kitchen," he said, with possible plans to forgive and forget. "May I ask what occurred to the Volvo?"

"Dodge'em cars. A deliberate effort to run me off the road and erase me out of life."

Robinson paused in his clean-up to frown at me in wonder and doubt and incipient anxiety. "Is that the *truth*?"

"I would never lie to you, Robinson," I said. I perched on one of the stools at the work island and said, "That's why the police were here."

"Then it's out of your hands. Good."

"Well, not entirely. In the first place, those guys are still running around loose, and I don't think they've changed their minds about me very much."

"Perhaps we should go back east," he said.

"Not yet. Because, in the second place, I think maybe Ross Ferguson is mixed up in the story somewhere."

"*That* fellow." Robinson had not much use for Ross, had been known to refer to Ross as a "flibbertigibbet." "An enraged husband, do you think?"

"Robinson," I said, "there are no enraged husbands anymore."

"Pity," he said. "It's a sadder world."

"Not for Ross." Except that wasn't true either, was it? I said, "Anyway, the point is, I need to talk to Ross and he's not answering his phone. So I'll go over there—"

"And reduce another car to smithereens? Not to mention your own self."

"I'll go out the back way," I told him, "and I'll take the wagon."

Robinson was dubious. "I think you should phone the police."

"I already talked to the police."

"I think you should not leave the house without sur-rounding yourself with policemen."

"Now you're overstating the case," I said. "It's a fif-teen-minute drive from here. What I want *you* to do, if Ross calls after I leave, is tell him I'm on my way over and he should let me in."

"If you get that far."

"Very funny," I said, although Robinson is not exactly one for making jokes. "I'll be right back," I said, and left him to his clean-up and his pessimism.

The battered Volvo in the sunlight was more daunting than Robinson's doom and gloom. I looked at it, looked away, walked on over to the five-car garage, and lifted door number four. Immediately, Sugar Ray and Max appeared, wagging their tails. Door number four, they knew, led to the big Chrysler station wagon, the only car in which they got the occasional ride. "Sorry, guys," I said. "Not this time." Still, they hung around, looking bright-eyed and hopeful and eager to be of service.

I went into the garage. To my left was the empty slot number three, where the Volvo used to live, before it died. Beyond that, in slot number two, was the Porsche that I mostly used when going up to my land in Oregon, and in slot number one was the two-tone tan Rolls that I almost never drove anywhere, not certain I could live up to it. Also, the space around the driver's seat was too small for me, and I'd been assured I would harm my investment in the thing if I started making structural changes. So there it sat, a thing of beauty and a toy forever, unused. (The fifth space was filled with the power mower, tools, sacks of cement and fer-tilizer, pool-cleaning equipment, and all the other usual stuff.)

The station wagon was my best bet for this trip because it was just about the biggest and heaviest passenger car on the highway; this here Country Squire could eat Impalas for breakfast.

I drove out the back way, Sugar Ray and Max smiling good-bye, and went down and around to Sunset, where I turned east, headed back through Bel Air into Beverly Hills, turned left again off Sunset, wound around and up through the increasingly steep streets, and eventually came to the stone wall and locked gate of Ross's half-timbered fake Tudor mansion, on the right. A well-known comedian used to own the place, and when Ross bought it, he kept all the security gizmos because they appealed to his dramatic side.

I stopped the Chrysler with its nose not quite touching the chain link gate and got out to go over and open the little door of the combination mailbox and call system. This was how the tape was delivered. I picked up the telephone receiver, pushed the button, and waited.

Nothing. Was he really not home?

Still with the receiver to my ear, I looked through the chain link diamonds at the slope of a somewhat shaggy lawn, the ornamental plantings, the blacktop drive, and the huge, sprawling pseudo-English house that was actually about the size of a normal English village. There was no one in sight. A small closed blue van was parked at the top of the drive: the poolman. The uncertainties of private enterprise were recorded mutely on the side of the van, just above the yellow letters reading POOL SERVICE. The original company name had been painted out in a different shade of blue from the van body, and the new name had been thickly and sloppily painted on in garish red: BARQ. Barq Pool Service. Terrific name. The owners' initials probably: Bill, Artie, Ray and Quincy.

If the poolman was there, Ross must be there, to have let the guy in. Irritated, I pushed the button again. Come on, Ross, don't be so damn coy. I wished for a moment I knew

Morse code, so I could spell out my name on this button, but then I realized Ross surely didn't know Morse code either. I tapped out a jazz sequence anyway, to see what would happen, and nothing did.

Was it possible he really wasn't home? Maybe he let the poolman in and then went out. Or maybe the poolman has his own key; that wouldn't be unheard of. All these houses in Beverly Hills and Bel Air and the other rich communities along the hills, they're all armed with walls and gates and electronic alarms and guard dogs and actual private security guards (of which I had been one for a while), and yet there's a constant stream of people going in and out of those houses all the time. The poolman, the gardener, the house cleaner. Appliance repairmen, painters, interior decorators. Plumbers, electricians, carpenters. Delivery men.

Everybody but Sam Holt, apparently. If Ross was there, he wasn't about to answer this buzzer, so at last I gave up and got back into the wagon. The street was too narrow for a U-turn, so I went on up to the next cross street, which, with a Dead End sign, climbed up to the right into pine woods, through which I caught a glimpse of something oval that gleamed like a yellow spaceship in the sun. To the left, this street descended toward Sunset and Bel Air and home, and that's the way I went.

But I felt frustrated, incomplete. *Had* Ross been there? It was possible, if the work was going slowly and the deadline was really close, that he'd leave the house entirely for a few days, get completely away from normal life and normal temptations, and when that happened, I knew where he always went.

The place in Malibu.

I drove on past my turnoff to the back way into the house. Malibu was half an hour farther west.

11

MALIBU IS A PECULIARLY LOS ANGELES sort of idea. A narrow strip of land along the ocean's edge, it is backed by steep, precarious hills, with most of the slender flat band between ocean and hill given over to a six-lane highway, generally without dividers, called Route 1. Stores and fast-food joints are shoehorned between the road and the hills, while restaurants and luxury vacation homes are lined up like houses on a Monopoly board between the traffic and the tides. From time to time the sea reaches out a crooked finger and plucks some of the houses away. From time to time one of the unstable hills falls over onto the shops and, occasionally, the highway itself. The whole place is insecure and transitory and ephemeral, and besides that the traffic is dreadful and the houses are too close together. And yet...

And yet.

Real estate values are through the roof. If you can talk about real estate in a place where at any moment the ocean may foreclose your house or a mountain fall on it or a runaway tractor-trailer dropkick it into the next wave, then the values are through the roof. If the wind doesn't take it.

The expensive houses are expensively furnished, as though it doesn't matter that all that leather and chrome and steel and high design and original oils and museum-quality statuary may be edifying the off-shore fish next week.

Famous names are on the ownership papers if not always on the mailboxes, and I admit I almost bought a place in Malibu myself at one time—the second year of *Packard*, that was—before my sensible Long Island upbringing saved me. It's the stars who grew up in Omaha and St. Louis who live in Malibu; if you had my background, with photos in *Newsday* every winter and spring of beach destruction from Fire Island all the way along the coast to the Hamptons, you, too, would find Malibu a nice place to visit, but you wouldn't want to live there.

Ross's place was a few miles north of where Sunset ends at Route 1; from his deck you can see the surfers farther north, up toward the point. After I made the turn, I stopped at a Dairy Queen on the right and phoned my house to tell Robinson I'd be a little longer than anticipated.

"I had gathered that." I could tell he was concerned about me, which he expressed by becoming more disapproving than ever.

"I'm just checking if Ross is at his Malibu place," I said. "He didn't call, did he?"

"No. There have been three calls, none from Mr. Ferguson. Mr. Novak—"

"Tell me all that when I get back."

"Miss *Quinn* telephoned," he insisted. Robinson likes very few people on this Earth, but he does like Bly Quinn, and at times acts as though his primary job is to protect her from the likes of me. So he wasn't about to let me off without hearing Bly's message, no matter what else might be going on.

"What did she have to say?" I asked, since he was going to tell me anyway.

"She wished you to be reminded of your dinner engagement this evening."

Bly cooks for me from time to time, a trauma for both

of us but somehow a necessary element in our mating ritual. "I didn't forget," I promised. "Seven o'clock at her place, I know."

"That's correct."

"Hold the other messages till I get back. I should be less than an hour."

"Or possibly an eternity," he said.

"How you lighten my day, Robinson," I told him, and hung up, and drove on to Ross's place, which from this side looked to be nothing but a weatherbeaten gray board fence hung with wrought iron numbers and a black iron mailbox. In a small break in the oncoming traffic I made the left turn and parked against that section of the gray fence I knew was actually the garage door.

No one answered my ring. The fact I was getting used to this didn't mean I liked it. I rang several times while traffic whizzed and roared behind me, and the silence from the house continued.

Well, this time I could do something about it. It happens Ross had loaned me his beach house a few times, so I know about the key hidden in the hollowed-out space behind the wrought iron number 3, which swivels from the one screw in its top crossbar. I wanted to know if Ross was actually here. If he wasn't, I wanted to look for some hint as to where he might be. And I suppose, if truth be told, I wanted to look at the scene of the crime.

The entrance door is fashioned to look like the rest of the fence, and the round black iron keyhole might even be, from a distance, a knot in the wood. I unlocked and opened, returned the key to its hiding place, and stepped through into the narrow gray-green space between the entrance and the actual house. Vertical boards on both sides hid the four-foot gap behind the fence, which Ross used for storage.

The house door, a more elaborate one with four small

diamond-shaped windows in it, was also kept locked, but this key was practically in plain sight atop the doorframe. I went on in and, before shutting the door, stood on the first of the many white shag rugs with which Ross had strewn his house—not fur or wool, some washable fake—and called, "Hello? Ross? Anybody home?"

Did a floor creak? Was there movement somewhere ahead? I listened, and heard only silence.

The house was two stories high, or low. I had entered on the upper floor, which contained the bedrooms plus Ross's office, with its own view of the ocean and its own small deck for when he needed actual sea air in order to gather his thoughts. Downstairs were the living room and kitchen and so on, with a wall of glass doors facing the sea and leading to the main deck, the width of the house, with broad bleacher-style plank stairs descending to the beach— or ocean, depending on whether the tide was in or out, the moon was full or new, the weather was malignant or benign. Also down on the lower floor, of course, was the murder scene.

It was with a conscious effort that I decided to look around upstairs first. If Ross were here, it would most likely be the office he was holed up in, and if he were away, the office would be the likeliest spot to find hints to where he might have gone. The murder scene could wait.

From the front door a broad hall with a skylight led forward past a couple of closed bedroom and bathroom doors to a wide opening in the right wall and then a double door at the end. The wide opening led to a free-form staircase which curved down and around into the living room. (It would have been just out of camera range to the left in that videotape.) The double doors led to the master bedroom, which led to Ross's office, so that was the way I went, glancing down the stairs at the living room on the way by opening the left-hand of the double-doors—the right was sort of a fake, fixed in place—and entering a cool dim bedroom with the shades drawn and a woman's blouse and jeans tossed onto the king-size bed.

The brightest spot in the bedroom was the doorway in the right wall, leading to Ross's office. I glanced at the clothing on the bed—could that possibly still be Delia West's things, after all this time?—then walked diagonally across the floor toward that farther doorway. Movement seen in my peripheral vision was me in the gray-tinted wide minor above the two dressers.

Ross's office was also empty, though considerably more sloppy than the bedroom. One of the sliding glass doors out to the deck stood open; would he go away and leave it like that? Outside there, the gray Pacific idled away, out and out, under a pink and orange haze.

Ross's desk was a U-shaped multilevel construct of his own design, which always reminded me of Habitat. Word-processor components, filing cabinets, an old black Remington manual office typewriter for both its nostalgic value and back-up use during blackouts, electric pencil sharpener, a madly complex telephone system, more gimmicks and machinery than the villain in a James Bond movie, and all of it covered with a messy mulch of paper—manuscripts, letters, magazines, memos, notes, postcards, reference books lying open, photostats, newspaper clippings, and who knows what all. I stood looking at it; in this jumble I hoped to find directions to Ross's whereabouts?

A sound. A definite sound from behind me. The bedroom.

I turned, trying to be fast and silent at the same time, and bumped clangily into Ross's desk chair, which rolled away to smack into a filing cabinet. So much for the element of surprise; I hurried back across the office and through the doorway into the dim bedroom.

Nobody. Nothing. No sound. And yet the room felt different, as though the dust molecules in the air still vibrated from someone's recent passage.

To my left a pair of louvered doors fronted the closet. I went over there, listened, reached out to grasp both handles, and abruptly pulled the two doors open. A girl wearing nothing but blue bikini panties lunged out at me with a knife, crying, "Get away from me!"

12

I GOT AWAY FROM HER, back-pedaling halfway across the room, holding my hands palm outward so she could see I wasn't armed. "Don't shoot, lady," I said. "I'm friendly."

The girl had come one quick catlike pace out of the closet, still pointing that blade at me, and now she looked sharply left and right, obviously searching for the rest of my gang. Then she stared at me again, and frowned. "I know you," she said.

"Of course you do." I tried an amiable grin, noticing that the knife wasn't actually a knife at all but a long, shiny pair of scissors, Almost as effective a weapon, but making a messier cut. Still, I was relaxing, because I knew I was about to receive one of the few valuable fringe benefits of celebrity—instant recognition and trust.

"You're— Wait a minute." She shook her head. "You're Packard."

"I *played* Packard," I corrected her, as I always do. "I myself am Sam Holt."

"Ross—Ross wrote for your show."

"Oh, I get it," I said. "You're..." Not Delia, that was the dead one. "Doreen. You're Doreen,"

Her mouth twisted. "Mentioned me, did he? Some nice little locker-room gossip?"

That was irritating. "Last November," I told her, "Ross

said he'd had an argument with the girl he was living with. Her name was Doreen. He came here. He didn't volunteer any more details about the relationship, and I hope you won't either."

She gave me a doubtful but cynical look. "Have I been put in my place?"

"I hope so. Will you put the weapon down?"

She looked at the scissors, as though surprised to see them, then tossed them onto the bed. Then she stared at the clothing lying there, down at herself, and cried, "My God, I'm naked!"

"I had noticed that." Now that she was unarmed I felt it safe to move, and where I moved was toward the hall door. "Why don't I go downstairs," I said, "and you join me in a minute."

"Sure. Sure." She seemed distracted.

"Is there anybody else in the house?"

"No, no. Just me. Just us."

"You want coffee?"

"Sounds good." So I went downstairs and primed Mister Coffee and then went into the living room to look at the place I'd last seen on videotape. I don't know why I thought there should be some sign, some evidence of what had happened. It had been three months, and of course there was no reminder at all. I went down on one knee, patting the shag rug where Delia's drink had fallen when the imitation Ross punched her. It had been washed, naturally.

"Lose a contact lens?"

I looked up, and Doreen was coming down the stairs, wearing the blouse and jeans from the bed. She looked fragile but tough-minded, the spunky girl in the sentimental movie about horses, or orphans. "Just patting the rug," I told her, rising. "I think the coffee's ready."

She frowned at the rug, but tacitly agreed not to make a point of it. We went into the kitchen and I poured the coffee while she got milk from the refrigerator. "Let's sit on the deck," she said.

We did. On this side of the house one was almost alone. Tall wooden fences echoing the style of the fence out by the road marched down the property lines on both sides, extending nearly to the sea. The traffic noise of Route 1 was either muffled by distance or absorbed within the constant shuffle and slush of the surf. Ross's boat, the *Go Project*, bobbed in the sunlight off shore. The dinghy was pulled up almost to the house and tied by a long rope to one of the deck supports.

Doreen was like Ross's women, and at the same time not like them. Physically, she was correct, being quite tall and thin, and she'd demonstrated earlier that she could curl her lip with the best of them. But her hair was brown instead of blond and she was somewhat younger than his usual style, probably under twenty-five. Most of Ross's women look like producers' ex-wives or the writers of best-selling sex novels, but this one looked like a UCLA student; possibly the daughter of a Santa Barbara dentist.

We sat together on the low wide chairs, half-facing each other and half-facing the sea, and I said, "I'm looking for Ross."

"I figured that out," she said. "What do you want him for?"

"I think he's in trouble," I said, "and I think *his* trouble is making trouble for *me*."

She almost said something, but then decided not to. I waited, giving her a chance to say it after all, then pushed a little. "Why were you hiding in the closet?"

She brooded at me. "Are you a good friend of his?"

"Ross? I think so. Why?"

She considered her coffee, but didn't drink any. "I think he's at his house."

"I called and got the service. I went there, and got no answer."

"Something's going on," she said.

"Sure. What?"

She shook her head. "I don't know a thing about it, Mr.— Do I call you Packard, or what?"

"Sam. Why *were* you hiding in the closet?"

She thought that over very hard, wanting to talk and yet not wanting to talk. Her manner was that of the hip unaffected urban kid, and it was impossible to guess what was underneath—maybe even more of the same. Finally she shrugged, and in a low voice said, "I thought it might be those guys back."

"What guys?"

She heaved a long sigh, shaking her head, staring out at the sea. "Shit," she commented. "Ross told me not to say anything to anybody. Shit, I don't even know anything."

"What happened?"

"What mostly happened," she said, "Ross threw me out of the house for a while. Not a fight or anything, he just said I should come live here for a couple of weeks, don't talk to anybody about it, and he'll give me a call when I should come back."

"And then some guys showed up. Who were they?"

"I don't know, some kind of foreigners. Arabs or Greeks or something. They talked some other language with each other."

I immediately thought of the guys in the two Impalas. "Tell me about them," I said.

"They came here night before last. Just walked right in, around ten o'clock. I was watching Channel Five news."

"Just walked in like me? They knew where the key was?"

"No, they came in this way," she said, gesturing at the ocean. "They had some kind of boat, I saw it when they left."

"They came and then they left?"

"There was more to it than that," she said, and grimaced at some annoying or painful memory. "They came in—I think they thought the house was going to be empty. They were mad that I was here, they argued about it a lot with each other. I yelled at them to get out, I'd call the cops, all the normal stuff, so they slapped me around a little bit and I shut up."

"Uh-huh," I said. What she was telling me here with this laconic narration was that until the three guys had come in from the sea, she had always thought she was as tough as her pose, or thought it wasn't actually a pose but the real Doreen. The three invaders had taken away her belief in her own unflinchable hipness, but hadn't given her any new mode to replace it. So now she was doing a Hemingway, being stronger in the broken places, except she was trying to do it before the broken places healed. My function then was to pretend she was successful.

She went on, not meeting my eyes directly, in the same flip unemotional style. "They asked a lot of questions, who was I, what was I doing here, when did I last see Ross, all of that, and then two of them stayed down in the living room with me while the third one went upstairs. I heard him on the phone up there."

"Calling Ross," I suggested.

"That's right. Because after a while he hollered down I should get on the extension. I did, and it was Ross."

"How did he sound?"

"Very scared and very happy. You're his friend, right?

You know how he gets when he doesn't know what's gonna happen next."

"Tap-dancing on the tightrope."

"That's right." She grinned a little. "I like that image. I can see him; that's perfect for Ross. Tap-dancing on the tightrope."

"What did he say to you?"

"He said the guys were all right, they were just looking for some stuff he needed, they were helping him in the research on some project."

"Uh-huh."

"Sure uh-huh. If those guys were research assistants, Colonel Qadafi's a band leader."

"What else did Ross say?"

"Stay stay stay. Keep my mouth shut. Only a few days more. Lova ya, honey, keep a tight asshole." She grimaced. "*That* was good advice anyway."

"Oh, yeah?"

She looked at me. "What do you think? Wherever those guys come from, there's two kinds of women, and the good kind stay under lock and key with their whole bodies wrapped in black cloth, maybe even their faces. I'm some Jewish-American tramp in shorts, not married, not a virgin, living with a guy old enough to play golf with my father. Are they going to pass this up? A chance to make a brief male statement about bad girls?"

"Okay," I said.

"After they finished searching the house, they ran me through a little basic repertoire, nothing kinky, and the only question is, at the end of it are they gonna let me live?"

"I can see how that would be on your mind."

She picked up her coffee cup, noticed that her hand was shaking, and put it down again. Watching herself do so, she said, "I kept thinking, if I show some response, do they kill me because I'm a whore, or if I show no response, do they kill me because I didn't give them a good time? I figured I'd rather go out a bitch than a whore, so what they got was already dead. And then they left."

"What time was this?"

"A little before one."

"Then what happened?"

"Nothing." She frowned at me. "You think I should have called the cops?"

"Not necessarily."

"Not necessarily," she echoed, shaking her head. "The guys were gone, right, they were finished. They didn't come for me in the first place. They were mad I was even here, they were just coming to check the place out. Besides which, if I call the cops, do I tell them these guys are friends of my boyfriend, or not?"

"Okay," I said. "But how about going someplace else? Until whatever Ross is mixed up with is over."

"No," she said. "I stay here, I'm obedient, after a while it's over."

"You hope."

"I hope. Ross phoned me yesterday, in the morning, around ten. All chipper and happy and how-you-doing-honey and it-won't-be-long-now. Was I okay? Sure, I said."

"You didn't mention the rape."

She sighed as though I were an idiot. "No," she said, "I did not place him in any impossible positions. Okay?"

"Okay."

"He called again this morning," she said. "Same time, same message."

I didn't want to tell her about the death of Delia West, but I did want her to understand somehow the seriousness and the danger involved here. "Doreen," I said, "something very bad is going on. Ross has let himself get in over his head, and now part of what's happening is, he's told these people not to hurt you if they want him to go on cooperating, and they promised him they wouldn't hurt you, and that's why he calls every morning to make sure. But what happens when the game is over, whatever it is?"

"I don't know," she said.

"Neither do I. But I do know one thing about the crowd Ross is tied up with; they aren't afraid to kill people."

"So what do you suggest?"

"Go somewhere else," I told her. "Call Ross in a couple weeks, maybe a month, see how he is."

She sighed, shaking her head. "I burned a lot of bridges when I took up with Ross. My parents were *not* amused. And I'm almost broke. There're a couple friends I could impose myself on, but then there's a whole lot of questions, and I'm lousy at making up answers. Besides, right now I think the danger's over, at least for the next little while."

"You have no idea what s going on," I told her, "so how can you say when it's over, or how dangerous it is? You're just whistling in the dark."

"In the dark is where I am, so I might as well whistle." She grinned at me. "What else is there?"

"Come with me now, to my house," I said. "Stay as long as you like."

She smiled, but in a wistful, troubled way. "You're something of a hunk, you know?" she said. "*And* you seem to be a nice guy, so normally I'd jump at the chance. But just at the moment, the absolute truth is, I don't feel very much like sex. I was just about to take my maybe eleventh shower when you walked in."

"I have a girlfriend already," I assured her. "In fact, I'm having dinner with her tonight, so you'll eat with Robinson." Then I grinned, looking at her. "I wonder what Robinson is going to make of you," I said.

13

SHE DIDN'T HAVE THAT MUCH to pack; it all fit in a zippered canvas bag which I carried out so she could lock doors behind us when we left. I waited in the sunlight out front while she returned the key to its hiding place, and then we walked together to the station wagon.

He had been hiding on the other side of the car, and just as we got to it, he jumped up into view across the hood and pointed something at us. I didn't even think; I just threw Doreen's bag at him and followed it in a long flat dive over the hood that ended in me banging into him around the waist and the two of us toppling over onto the gravel-covered ground.

"Look out!" Doreen shrieked, and I twisted away, looking back and up to see a determined-looking woman— skinny, mid-thirties, large glasses, severe hairstyle—reaching for me. She, too, had been hidden behind the car.

I rolled again, but it wasn't me she was reaching for, it was the thing the man had pointed at us. I made a lunge for her, but too late; she grabbed it by the strap and went running, while her male partner sat up and blundered into my way.

"God *damn* it," I said. The woman was pegging it up Route 1 like an Olympic entrant. I glared at the man, the two of us sitting on the sharp gravel next to each other like a pair of infants in a sandbox.

He grinned at me, a bulky balding blond-haired guy in sweater and chinos. "Gotcha," he said.

"What assholes you people are," I said, disgusted, and got to my feet.

Doreen had come around the wagon and was staring in bewilderment at both of us. "What was that all about? Is he— Are they part of it?"

"No," I said, while laughing boy clambered upright, brushing dust and gravel off his pants. "This is a photographer from the *National Enquirer*. Right?"

"Read all about it," he said cheerfully. "Bye now." And he limped off after the woman, who, with his camera, was long out of sight.

Doreen still didn't get it, and said so. "I don't get it."

"I made a police report this morning," I told her. "The *National Enquirer* always follows up stuff like that if there's a famous name involved, just in case it leads to something they can use. They have everybody's license plate numbers, they follow people, they're everywhere. Do you have a scrapbook?"

"I don't lead that kind of life," she said. "Why?"

"In a week or two," I told her, "you'll have a nice newspaper photograph of the two of us, suitable for framing, coming out of our love nest."

14

ROBINSON TREATED DOREEN EXACTLY like a stray cat I might have brought in on a rainy night—distant sympathy not quite covering a fastidious conviction that this creature is probably flea-ridden. In lieu of putting a saucer of milk on the kitchen floor, he took her away to one of the guest rooms, plied her with thick towels, and urged her to take a good long soak in the tub. In the meantime I phoned Bly to tell her I hadn't forgotten tonight's dinner and to ask her what the Arabic word was for "lightning."

The reason for this strange request was something Doreen had said on the way over. I'd mentioned the poolman's van having been in the drive when I'd made my failed attempt to find Ross at home, and she said, "The Steno girls? Maybe *that's* the whole secret; they were in there screwing."

"No, no," I said. "A pool-cleaning service."

"Sure. Steno Pools. Don't you know them?"

"I don't think so. Are we talking about the same thing?" She nodded, her expression cynical.

"It's one of our a very local kinda gimmicks," she said. "Steno Pools, the all-girl pool-cleaning service. They come around in their hot pants and halters and bend over the pool a lot, and nobody gives a shit if they miss a couple leaves. Ross has used them ever since I've known him, but I don't think he's ever actually scored with any."

"Well, he's stopped using them now," I said. "There was some scruffy van there from an outfit called Barq."

"Barak?" she asked, surprised.

So I spelled it, and then she spelled hers, and explained, "That's Hebrew for 'lightning.' My father made me learn Hebrew for three years, just in case I ever wanted to go live on a kibbutz, which tells you how much he knew me. Now every foreign language sounds like Hebrew to me. When those guys broke into the house back there, at first I even thought *they* were talking Hebrew."

"Well, 'lightning' would be an unfortunate name for a pool service," I suggested. "And it wasn't your Hebrew word anyway. It had that Q at the end."

"Like Arabic," she said. "A lot of Arabic words have Q at the end, and a lot of Arabic words are very similar to Hebrew." She grinned slyly. "They're both Semitic languages, you know."

"An Arabic pool-cleaning company in Beverly Hills," I said. "Sounds unlikely."

But the more I thought about it, and about the swarthy guys who'd been drop-kicking the Volvo, the more I wondered just how unlikely Barq Pool Service was. At home, after turning Doreen over to Robinson's flinty care, I looked in the Yellow Pages under Swimming Pool Svce. and was not surprised by Barq 's absence. Directory Assistance had never heard of them either.

That was when I remembered that Bly has, among her research tools, a book called *The Concise Dictionary of 26 Languages*. I phoned her and said I was looking forward to dinner tonight and then mentioned the *26 Language* book and asked her if "lightning" was among the thousand words therein. She went away and came back and said, "Yes. Number five forty-seven, in fact."

"In Hebrew it's *barak*, right?"

"What is this, a card trick on the phone?"

"No, just a little research help for a friend. Is Arabic one of your twenty-six languages?"

"Just a second." A faint rushing, as of batwings, was followed by her suddenly saying, in a stretched-out nasal voice, "*Naam.*"

"What the heck is that?"

" 'Yes' in Arabic. Number nine ninety-seven."

"Hilarious. What about number five forty-whatever? Lightning."

"Cat got your sense of humor? Here it is: *Barq.*" She spelled it.

"Thank you," I said.

"Do you know it's *éclair* in French? Isn't that wild?"

"Very," I said.

"Let's see, let's see. *Blitz. Bhiksem*, that's the Dutch. Do you suppose that's where Donder and Blitzen come from? Thunder and lightning? I *like* that!"

"Me too. See you at seven."

"Wait, wait, you've got me interested. It's *salama* in Finnish, or at least in Finnish delicatessens. Listen to this! In Japanese it's *denkoo,* so if you're in Japan and there's lightning, you turn around and say, 'You're welcome.'"

"Good-bye, Bly, I'll be there at seven."

"I'm going to look up 'thunder,'" she was saying as I hung up. Which is her great weakness and also her great strength; everything distracts her, but sooner or later she puts every bit of it to use.

Usually a conversation with Bly makes me smile, but not this time. I sat looking at the phone, remembering that scruffy van parked beside Ross's house. The old name painted out, BARQ haphazardly painted on.

Lightning pool service.

And who's going to be in the pool when the lightning strikes?

BLY QUINN IS GOING TO BE thirty any minute now, and is dragging her feet. She would much rather be a kid with promise than a grown-up to be judged on accomplishment, and of course thirty is the big milestone between what you're going to do and what you're doing.

She came from somewhere in Maryland's horse country to begin with, a smart, good-looking, athletic blond girl with a mean tennis forehand and a knack of knowing when people are lying. She went to New York to be a film student at *NYU*, dropped out, started writing brief ironic short stories, and became fairly successful at it, with appearances in *Ms.* and *Harper's* and small literary magazines and even once *The New Yorker*. A small press in Chicago put out a collection of her stories called *Hesitation Cuts*, which led to a producer hiring her as a staff writer on one of the prime-time soaps, to give an edge to the female villains, which was when Bly moved to Los Angeles. Her soap was one that didn't make it to a second season, but by then Bly had fallen in love with Los Angeles and television and her entire life. She had always looked like a California girl, and now she is one, without the slightest regret. She has become rabidly anti-New York, anti-East Coast, even anti-Maryland. If she takes some time off and leaves town, she goes to Hawaii.

These days Bly works steadily and profitably as a sit-com writer. She does the episodes in which the teenagers run out of gas and get home late and the parents misunderstand, and the episodes in which father makes dinner, and the episodes in which the new next-door neighbors turn out to be black or Russian or homosexual or the husband's now-married college girlfriend or a free-love religious cult or (more recently) Hispanic. She has a true genius for the lines that go in front of the laugh track.

Bly makes fun of what she does, of course, even though she's good at it, because she doesn't think being a mere craftsman is a high enough goal. Her reasons for struggling against that thirtieth birthday have nothing—or very little— to do with the usual fears of growing old, losing one's looks, running out of time, all of that. No; Bly now sees herself as a very promising person currently disguised as a sitcom writer, and I know—because she's made several oblique ref- erences to it—that she's afraid she'll wake up on her thirti- eth birthday to find it's no longer a disguise.

She lives over the hills in Sherman Oaks, just beyond the pale into 818, high on the slope with a view northward over the great flat desert of the San Fernando Valley, that rigid-grid waffle iron where little white stucco houses and big black Pontiac TransAms fry where oranges once grew. For some reason, I didn't feel like taking the San Diego Freeway for the second time that day, so I traveled a more circuitous route involving Beverly Glen Boulevard and some switch-backing among the ranch-styles-on-stilts up to Bly's place, a small peach-colored stucco house tucked into a fold of the hill up near the crest; only three houses were higher than hers, up toward the DEAD END sign.

Bly's house is actually bigger than it looks from the road, which is fairly common in these hills. The front shows a wide peach garage door and a broad expanse of little lou- vered windows, all under a flat white roof dotted with white stones. Behind the louvered windows is a small slate-floored porch Bly has converted to a library chock-a-block with all the books she'd had trucked out from the East, and beyond that and the garage is the living room, the full width of the house, with a gas-fired fireplace at one end. Beyond the living room the house narrows, so that its shape is like a lowercase *d*, with garage and porch and living room in the ball of the *d*, while kitchen, office, bedrooms, and baths are in the extended line. The last quarter of the area is dominated by her swimming pool, with glass door entrances from living room and office and master bedroom. Behind all this, on cunningly leveled land, is a tennis court, which she owns jointly with three neighbors.

She never locks her door. Does she think she lives in the countryside? I don't know, but she never locks her door, so I went on in, through the library and into the empty living room. Was she in the pool? A sensible place to be, and the lights were on out there, it now being seven in the evening, but no; when I went out from the living room, the pool, too, was empty.

The office. I looked through the glass doors and there she was, in profile to me, in a cone of light, typing away, looking fierce. She scorns her work afterward, but she's deadly serious about it when doing it.

Standing in her view, I took my clothes off. This being only February, there was a nip in the air, but I knew she kept the pool heated and cold air doesn't bother me at first. I had to be present in her peripheral vision, but she remained unaware of me, pounding away at her word processor, glaring at the screen. I waited, but the air *was* cool, so finally I leaned forward and knocked on the glass.

She looked up, frowning, deep in Mom and Junior's repartee, then saw me, looked startled, then grinned. I, too, looked startled, pretended I was flustered at having been found naked, and stepped backward, as though forgetting the pool was there. As I toppled over backward into the water, I saw her laughing, but when I came up, she was already typing again.

The warm water was delicious. With the underwater light at the deep end illuminating the entire long cream bowl of the pool, and the surface of the water steaming slightly in the cool air, I seemed to be paddling around in a great tureen of clear broth; and I was the only oyster.

About ten minutes later I heard the office door slide open and Bly, also naked, came quickly across the terracotta tiles and dove into the water. She looked beautiful under there, passing the light, bubbles sweeping around behind her in a comet's tail. She surfaced, we swam to meet in the middle of the pool, and kissed, and she said, "Thunder in German is *Donner*."

"Oh, poo," I said, and ducked her, and we played for a while, which became more serious at the shallow end, and then more serious yet on the shag carpet in the master bedroom; we didn't want to soak the bed.

Then it was time to see what, if anything, had gone wrong with dinner. Bly can do anything involving machines, from word processors to single-engine airplanes, and she keeps demanding that the machines in her kitchen behave themselves and act right. Sometimes they do, but more often not. She follows recipes, sets timers, sets heat, sets memory, brings in satellite electric pots and pans, and in theory what comes out should be edible.

I think maybe the problem is machines can't themselves cook any more than they can write sitcoms. I don't know how to tell Bly she has to give the stove as much creative attention as she does the word processor, or else give up the whole idea of cooking, so from time to time I permit myself to go through this trauma with her. So far she hasn't poisoned anybody.

Tonight's meal was on the better side, in fact, when we finally got to it, a chicken casserole with a nice California Riesling. We also shared a bottle of San Pellegrino, Bly having picked up that habit from me. We ate in the living room, seated on the floor on opposite sides of the glass coffee table, swathed in our terry robes and with an honest wood fire in the fireplace. Mostly during dinner we talked about Zack Novak's idea—or his brilliant friend Danny Silvermine's idea—for me to take Packard on the road.

"Do you want to do it?" she asked me. She was giving me the same kind of intense look she gives her word processor, so I knew I had her attention.

"I want to do *something*," I said. "I just feel Packard's a graveyard now. He made me, he made me what I am today, and he made me rich, but at this point he's also made me unemployable. Do I take this thing in the hope Zack's right, the new setting, even with the old character, will make me look more like a real-life actor? Or am I just going to confirm everybody's opinion that I'm Johnny One-Note?"

"If it's everybody's opinion anyway, what difference does it make if you confirm it?"

"Because I'm trying to change their minds. Also, if I go on the road for no money with a play, that argues against me still being the viable film star I say I am."

"So you want to do an Ilya Morometz," she said, nodding. "Stay on the mountaintop, think beautiful thoughts, and wait for God to give you the call. 'Rise, Sam Holt, and save Holy Mother Russia.' But what if the call never comes?"

I stared at her. "Who the *hell* is Ilya Morometz? Where do you get these allusions?"

"I make them up," she said, which might even be true, but I don't think so.

I said, "I have to give Zack an answer pretty soon."

She shook her head, tasted some food, and said, "It's still cold in the middle."

"It's fine." She was right, it was still cold in the middle.

"Oh, well. Sam, you play a character named Jack Packard and you have an agent named Zack Novak. Do you realize how *absurd* that is?"

"It just happened," I said. "I know, you'd never name your characters like that."

Bly was the second of the three people I'd shown my first *Packard* script to, and along with some very good advice she'd also given me a hard time about my characters' names because they weren't ethnic enough.

"Of course I'd name them like that," she said. "Zack Novak and Jack Packard. But I'd do it for comic effect."

"Thanks a lot. The question is, do I do this dinner theater thing or not?"

"No, it isn't," she said. "The question is, you don't want to do this dinner theater thing, so what are your reasons?"

I laughed at that, and we spent the rest of the meal working out my reasons. You can, too.

After dinner and wash-up, we sat on the sofa near the fire and Bly brooded at the flames, saying, "I'm not taking your problem lightly, Sam, I'm really not. I know you're stuck, but we all are, aren't we?"

"Maybe so."

"I've had some intimations of mortality recently," she said, and shivered, pulling the robe tighter around herself.

"The big three-oh, you mean."

"That too. But I was at a funeral last Friday, and it was such a waste."

"A relative?"

"No, an actor, he played an aging hippie car salesman sometimes on *Gandy and Son*. Not really a regular, you know, maybe four or six episodes a year. I liked to write for him, I could slip across some sneaky anti-Americanisms."

"And he died."

"Car crash, at forty-seven. Isn't that stupid?"

Thinking of my own almost car crash of today, at thirty-four, I said, "Very."

"Nobody knows how it happened. Middle of the day, good weather, on the Ventura Freeway way out by Hidden Hills, he just lost control of the car, went off an overpass into the roof of a store. Two people killed."

"He had a passenger?"

"Some friend of his who did makeup over at Universal."

I stared at her. "Makeup?"

She stared right back. "Sam? What's the matter?"

"Do you have an *Academy Guide*?"

"Sure. What do you need?"

"Your friend that died."

"Beau Sheridan."

"I want to see him."

"Okay," she said, and shrugged, and went away to her office, coming back with the volume of the *Academy Guide* that includes the male character people. She opened it, put it in my lap, tapped a photo, and said, "There he is."

There he was. All the union actors and actresses are listed in the *Academy Guide*, with photo and telephone contact and usually a list of credits. So here was Beau Sheridan, smiling into the camera, giving one of the better-known agencies as his contact, with a modestly short list of TV series on which he'd worked.

He didn't look that much like Ross Ferguson, but the potential was there. The high balding forehead, the wide-set eyes. The jawline was good. This was the fellow, all right.

"Sam? What is it?"

I sighed. "I wasn't going to tell you about this," I said, "because I didn't want you to worry, and I figured it'd all be over by tomorrow anyway. But now maybe I will. Maybe I'd like to know what you think of it."

She sat beside me, all eyes. "Tell."

I told: The attempt on my life, the conversation with the police. "Then I realized it had to do with a problem of Ross Ferguson's from last November."

"Do I know about this problem?"

"No. It was his secret, not mine, so I didn't tell anybody."

"I had to drop the aspic," she said, nodding.

I frowned at her. "Is that another reference?"

"Yes. *Dinner at Eight*. But never mind, tell me chapter two of this story. The Secret of Ross Ferguson."

So I did, and she said, "You've been keeping this inside you for three months? You've come over here, we've had dinner, we've screwed, we've driven up to Ferndale together, I've stayed at your place, and all this time you had this thing, this murdered woman in extreme close-up, and you never showed it?"

"I wasn't trying to insult you, Bly," I said, "or keep you out of my life or any of that. It wasn't my secret."

"Jeepers," she said, and turned to frown briefly at the fire, which was almost out. She nodded at the fire, and looked back at me, and said, "Okay, you're an actor. You acted the pants off me."

"Bly, it really wasn't my secret to tell."

"It is now. Once they start trying to run you off the road, it—" She stopped, wide-eyed, and looked at the *Academy Guide* in my lap. "Oh," she said.

"He couldn't have known what they wanted the tape for," I said. "They probably told him it was a birthday gag or something like that."

"And the makeup man, sure. But why now? If they did the thing— My God, that was months ago!"

I said, "I think it's because they're making their move now. They've been setting it up for a long, long time, but until they actually do whatever it is they have in mind, nobody's dangerous to them. But now several of us are."

"Did you talk with Ross about this?"

"I tried," I said, and told her about that part, including Malibu and Doreen. Under other circumstances she might have made a couple of fake-jealous jokes about Doreen winding up at my house, but now she just stayed silent and absorbed. At the finish I said, "I figure Ross'll phone Malibu again tomorrow morning at ten, to be sure Doreen's alive and well. This time I'll be the one to answer the phone."

"But what's he doing with them? You think he's made some sort of deal with them?"

"I'm pretty sure he has. But it seems to me he's wrong; once they're finished with him they'll kill him too."

"It's all so elaborate. And ruthless. What can it be *for*?"

"I haven't the vaguest idea."

"I bet you haven't called the police yet, have you?"

"Tomorrow," I promised. "After I finally talk to Ross, I'll call the police. I just think I have to give him one chance before I do."

"Chance for what?"

"Maybe he can still get away from them." I told her about the poolman's van. "If they're in there with him, maybe he can get out before the police arrive."

"Sam," she said, "I wish you'd call the cops right now."

"In the first place," I told her, "it's after midnight. In the second place, all I've wanted to do since this afternoon was have one phone conversation with Ross. After that I'll tell the police everything. Including the death of your actor friend Beau."

She looked at the Academy Guide and shook her head. "These are really bad people, aren't they?"

"They haven't shown any redeeming features yet."

We talked about the mysterious "they" a while longer, without accomplishing anything. Bly asked me if I wanted to stay over, but I felt I ought to be at my place in the morning to talk with Doreen before going on to Malibu, so a little after one I left, promising to phone her in the morning, after my conversations with Ross and the law.

It was just a little out of my way, and I stopped for only a second in front of Ross's house. A couple of lights were showing, not many. The van from Barq Pool Service was still there.

16

FROM MY BEDROOM WINDOW I could see Doreen in the pool, doing her laps, a lithe, slender fish the color of sandalwood in an inland topaz sea. Little playful clouds in a washed-out blue sky rolled in front of the sun from time to time, and whenever that golden light left the pool, replaced by gray, Doreen looked to me like a shipwreck victim, swimming hard, pursued by sharks.

It was a little after eight in the morning. I'd come home from Bly's just over seven hours ago, to find only the all-night lights on, both Robinson and Doreen retired, no notes or messages from Robinson on my desk, no further events in Ross Ferguson's problem, whatever it was. My flight to New York wasn't till one this afternoon, so I should have time for everything I had to do before then. I put on my blue swimsuit, grabbed a towel, and went out to the cool air, emerging from the house just as another cloud overtook the sun. Max and Sugar Ray came over for a brief morning chat and accompanied me to the pool, where I dove into the wavelets of Doreen's wake, and the two of us plugged companionably back and forth, grinning occasionally as we passed, neither of us wasting breath on words. The dogs watched us awhile, decided we were boring, and went off around the house in search of adventure.

Having started earlier, Doreen was finished first, and hoisted herself out to sit at the edge of the pool, breathing hard through her diaphragm and smoothing her hair down with the edge of her hand to get some of the water out. Sunlight alternated with cloud, and I worked my water loom back and forth, counting toward forty. As I did, I wondered how much to tell her about what was going on, and decided she didn't need to know any more than she already did. She was away from the Malibu house, just in case Ross's new friends were to decide she was a loose end to be tied up after all, and she was safe as long as she stayed here. Any talk about murders and attempted murders and faked videotapes might just make her nervous and unpredictable.

Forty. My pool has no shallow end, so I made it forty-one today, climbing back to the end where Doreen still sat, beginning to look cold. She'd taken her feet out of the water and sat cross-legged tailor fashion in a rust-colored bikini, watching me, occasionally rubbing her arms, shivering a bit whenever the sun went away.

"You should have gone into the house," I told her, and surged up out of the pool like a walrus, water geysering all around me. "It's cold out here."

"I'm fine." She grinned, looking very happy this morning, though cold. "It's great out here. I feel clean, brand new all over again."

"That's good." Standing, I gave her a hand and she came gracefully to her feet.

"All the badness is gone," she said. "I'm ready for a fresh start." She was still holding my hand, smiling at me.

Oh-oh. "I guess you got a good night's sleep," I said, as bland and oblivious as could be, gently reclaiming my hand. "You were already turned in when I got back from my girl-friend's house."

"You're right," she said, "it *is* a little chilly out here." And we went off to our respective rooms to shower and dress.

When *Packard* first hit big, I suddenly found all sorts of attractive women making themselves available, and for several months I said a whole lot of "Yes, ma'am." I'm afraid I even spoke aloud more than once that fatuous line, "A gentleman never refuses a lady." Whatever women had been to me before, they had now become an endless flow of birthday presents, to be unwrapped and played with and outgrown.

For a long while I didn't notice how I'd changed, but women did, and more and more of them walked away from me, avoided me. Women in business meetings, wives of friends, actresses on the show—they all treated me as an uninteresting piece of driftwood they noted in passing and had no use for. There were still plenty of women eager to climb into bed with me, many of them absolutely beautiful, but somehow they weren't the *best*. The interesting women had turned away.

It was when I met Bly that I finally paid attention to what had happened. I liked her from the beginning, and at first she was open and cheerful with me, but then that disinterest came into her eyes, and when I pursued her, she was polite but nothing more. I even tried to get our story editor to assign her a *Packard* script, though it was absolutely wrong for her; trying to buy her, I suppose. She turned it down, to the story editor's relief. When I started saying no to other women's invitations, it was as a kind of sympathetic magic: If I turned enough women down, Bly Quinn would come around. Of course, Bly wasn't watching and couldn't know about my abstinence and wouldn't have cared anyway, but nobody ever said magic was logical. In any event, the result of the abstinence was my discovery that all those women hadn't been going to bed with *me* at all. It was money or power or fame they wanted to have sex with, and I was merely the instrument; the tool, if you know what I mean. Everybody was using everybody, and the beds were actually empty.

Well, if I'm going to be in an empty bed anyway, I'd rather not have to make conversation, so I long since gave up the candy-store approach to sex. There are two women in my life now, which is probably too many, but I can't see how to say good-bye to either, and I have no reason in the world to make it three, not even briefly. Doreen was a good body and a cute face and a rather unformed personality, and it seemed to me our relationship was just about right as it stood. So I would go on playing stupid, and I would bring Bly back into the conversation whenever Doreen got provocative, and soon she'd grow bored with it, without anybody having been embarrassed

We had breakfast together in the appropriately named breakfast room, light green and pale yellow, with a view over the ornamental hedges and the lawn toward the back road in. Robinson served us correctly and, for him, pleasantly. He was undoubtedly aware that Doreen and I had not shared a bed, and so was prepared in a conditional way to accept her. (Robinson watches out for Bly's interests much more than Bly does.)

Over breakfast I explained about the quick trip I'd be taking to New York; just overnight, arriving back here probably by five tomorrow afternoon. I saw no necessity to explain the reason for it, the details of my lawsuit.

In any case, she showed no particular curiosity. "I thought I'd watch some TV," she said. "You got any of your old shows?"

"Some," I said, surprised. "But you don't have to please the host by watching his program."

"I'm interested. Okay?"

"Sure. Robinson will show you where it all is, and how to work it."

Outside, I once again had to disappoint Max and Sugar Ray, who came bounding when I opened the garage door in front of the station wagon. "Your job is important too," I told them. "You watch the house." They accepted that, though they were dubious.

As I drove down toward the rear gate, I glanced in the rearview minor at the house, and suddenly thought of Doreen in there, curled up on the sofa in the den, watching old *Packard*s. I connected it with that sheriff's deputy, Chuck, saying he'd watched the show when he was a kid. That would be true of Doreen, too, of course. Was she subtle enough to have done that on purpose, to make me feel old, as revenge for having turned her down?

Packard never had tricky ones like that to solve.

17

I WENT INTO THE MALIBU HOUSE as cautiously as yesterday, but this time it was empty. I was a few minutes early, so spent some useless time looking at Ross's video equipment and studying the murder scene before going up to his office, where I intended to take the call.

Before leaving yesterday we'd closed the glass door leading from office to deck, so now the room felt stale and stuffy. I slid open the door, went outside, and was looking at the *Go Project*, thinking how it was only a long-time fiction writer who could have been mouse-trapped in exactly this fashion—and how would they go about throwing their rope around an actor?—when the phone rang. I went back inside, sat at the desk, picked up the phone, and held the receiver to my ear, not speaking.

There was a little silence, like a comic-strip cloud balloon with a question mark in it, and then Ross's voice said, "Doreen? Baby?"

"Hello, Ross," I said. "It's Sam."

"Sam! Oh, my God!"

"Don't—" I started, but he did anyway. He hung up.

I phoned his house, and quit after ten rings. The son of a bitch was still playing hard to get. I sat at his desk, furious, looking out at his boat, thinking I'd like to go out there with a hatchet and punch a hole in the bottom of the damn thing, when the phone rang.

"Hello?"

"Sam, how you doin'? We were cut off, baby! What are you doing *there*, buddy boy?" He sounded manic, like the world's worst fake orgasm.

"Waiting for your call," I said.

"Uh." He ran out of steam very briefly, and I could imagine him at the other end, blinking rapidly, building himself up again. "Is, uh, is Doreen there?"

"I sent her east. She has school friends back there."

"Some pal. Saving her from the dirty old man, huh?"

"Something like that. Ross, I've been wanting to talk to you before I call the police."

"Police!" All the crap and flapdoodle went right out of him. "Jesus, Sam, what *for*?"

"Yesterday," I told him, "four swarthy guys in two cars deliberately tried to cream me on the San Diego Freeway. The cops told me if I could figure out why anybody'd want to do that, I should call them. I figured it out, but I wanted to talk to you before I made the call."

"Wait a minute, Sam." He sounded very serious. "Are you telling me somebody tried to *kill* you?"

"My guess is, some of your poolmen."

"No no no," he said, though not as though arguing with me. "We can't have *that*. Wait right there; I'll get back to you."

"Oh, I don't think so, Ross," I said. "For all I know, those guys are headed this way right now."

"But listen, Sam, I don't know what went wrong, I don't know who got— All right, somebody made a mistake, and I'm glad it didn't— You aren't, uh, banged up or anything, are you?"

"No, I'm not," I told him, "but my Volvo will never play the violin again."

"Look, uh, do you want to go home? I'll call you there."

"Come see me."

"No, I'll call you, I'll phone you, you say where, any-place you say."

It seemed to me important to get Ross away from his house and whoever he was sheltering in there, so I said, "Not on the phone, Ross. I want to see you and look at you and know you're all right. I want to be able to see your face when you explain things."

"I'm not sure I—" He dithered a minute, then sighed and said, "All right, I'll work it out, they can't— Your place?"

I didn't want that, not with Doreen there. I said, "No. You know where Zack Novak's office is, in Century City?"

"Sure."

"I'll meet you there at eleven."

"This morning? Sam, I might have to—"

"I don't want to give your friends time to set anything up," I told him. "Besides, I have a flight at one this after-noon. I'll be at Zack's place at eleven. If you don't show, I call the cops right then."

He sighed. "There's no reason for this goddamn thing to get out of hand," he said, more to himself than to me. "No reason to *kill* people."

I could have mentioned Delia West, but there didn't seem to be any point. "See you at eleven," I said.

18

"**T**HIS IS DANNY SILVERMINE," Zack said.

Of course it was. Five foot eight, round and soft of body, dressed with expensive informality in shades of tan, ingratiating smile trying to distract attention from android eyes, Danny Silvermine stuck out a ring-laden hand and said, "You been outta work too long, Sam. I hope we can make a team here."

"Uh-huh," I said. This was the result of my having phoned Zack from Malibu to ask for the loan of one of his conference rooms. Clearly, he'd immediately called this guy to come right over, and I wouldn't be astonished if it soon emerged that Danny Silvermine was also a client of the agency.

The corridor fluorescents gleamed off Zack's bald head but were absorbed in his impeccable dark blue tailoring. A tall cadaverous man who combined courtly manners with a full range of agent jargon, he liked to present to this California world a kind of smoothed down Savile Row façade. Now, he said, "I know you have to chat with this other fellow first, but Danny's right here in the office, we could take a meeting when you're done, Danny could open out his thinking on this."

"Or lunch," Danny said, and grinned as though he knew we shared already a lot of jokes and attitudes. "Not to be pushy," he said. That was the joke, and the attitude.

Having a guy tell me, ten seconds after we've met, that he doesn't intend to be pushy, makes me want to go away somewhere and think about something else.

"I'm flying out this afternoon," I said. "One o'clock, out of LAX."

Danny looked downhearted at that news, but Zack smiled and said, "Perfect. We can ride out together, talk it over in the limo."

"I have my car."

"Leave it," Zack said. "When are you coming back?"

"Tomorrow"

"I'll have you picked up. You know, Sam, the sooner we discuss this concept, the better."

"But it's at your convenience, Sam," Danny said, waving his rings to show he wasn't being pushy. "I am the handmaiden here."

Essentially, Zack was right, of course; the sooner we got into the discussion of Danny Silvermine's concept, the sooner I wouldn't have to think about it anymore.

"Okay," I said. "Just get me there by twelve-thirty."

"Absolutely," Zack said, and Danny said, "I really appreciate this, Sam."

"See you in half an hour or so," I said.

Zack said, "Sam, this other matter, you want me to sit in?"

"It's not work," I told him.

"I sure hope not," Danny said, smiling all the way back to his ears, fidgeting with his rings. "I don't want to lose ya before I getcha."

I said to Zack, "It's a personal thing, that's all, we need neutral turf. You know the guy, he's another client. Ross Ferguson."

"Ex-client," Zack said, but without bitterness. In this

business people change agencies too often for anybody to get scars.

"I didn't know that."

Zack shrugged and grinned, above the fray. "It is in Ross's nature to get divorced."

All of a sudden Danny was a small round creature with antennae. "A writer?" he asked, looking extremely casual and extremely alert.

I decided to be mean. "A hyphenate," I explained. "A writer-producer." Let Danny think there might be competition.

Danny smiled and smiled, having nothing to say. Zack told me, "We'll be in my office when you're done. Cindy tell you where you are?"

Cindy was the receptionist. I said, "Yes, in the little yellow room at the end of the corridor."

Zack shook his head with a sad but forgiving smile. "We like to think of it as gold," he said.

On that note we went our separate ways, the smiling Danny following Zack back to his office, me heading down the corridor toward the little yellow/gold room. All around me hummed the morning activity of CNA. If clients like Ross Ferguson tend to change agents a lot, the agencies themselves are usually also in a state of flux, though CNA had been in its present configuration for almost eight years. Back when I'd first signed with Zack, he was part of a much smaller outfit called Novak-McCarthy, but shortly after I got the *Packard* job that agency merged with two others, Career Representatives Associates (CRA, then, with a home office in London) and Allied Management, to form Career-Novak-Allied. All over town people changed CRA to CNA on their Rolodexes.

Over these last years McCarthy and a couple of the Allied people have splintered off to form their own management group, CNA bought out its London parent's interest, and another small agency called Tar-Gray was absorbed, but the essential CNA agency has remained more or less intact. They represent writers, actors, directors, producers, and a few composers; they put together talent packages for films and TV programs when they can; and on that inevitable day when a publicity-hungry Congressional committee starts to investigate the antitrust implications of the packager-agencies, I'm afraid CNA is going to be among the first under the microscope. I do smile sometimes at the mental picture of Zack Novak taking a meeting with a panel of unamused Congressmen on television, explaining to them that even though CNA gets a packaging fee only if it loads a project with its own clients, nevertheless there are no unfair trade practices involved. I've never mentioned the fancy to Zack; he wouldn't smile.

The room was yellow, dammit, gold has more brown in it than that. The other color in the room, in the carpet and upholstery, was rust. The conference table was wood-grain Formica, but I think the chairs were actual wood, at least in part. Posters of forgotten movies and TV shows graced the windowless walls, though not yet *Packard*; that poster was still out in the corridor among the shows that might still be remembered.

A yellow phone—not gold—was the only thing on the table, down at the far end. Leaving the hall door open, I took the seat at that end of the table, in front of the phone and facing the doorway. Removing from my shirt pocket the slip of paper on which Deputy Ken's phone number was written, I was smoothing it on the table when Ross himself appeared in the doorway, sunglasses on top of head, blinking, smiling on and off like a neon sign, and saying, "Don't tell me I'm late."

I looked at my watch: "Two minutes early."

"And under budget. I always make deadlines." Ross came in and shut the door behind himself. He was very nervous, covering it with panic. Glancing at the phone, and the piece of paper under my left hand, he said, "You really want to bring in the law, huh?"

"For both of us," I told him. "Ross, there's a difference between being overly imaginative and being stupid."

"Not always." His shirt, as usual, was open almost to the waist,, showing tanned skin, gray hair, and gold chains,. Fingering the chains, he came down the table, sat to my right, and said, "Sam, I've talked with the people. We understand each other now."

"You probably thought you understood them yesterday."

"They panicked, Sam," he said, demonstrating a goodly amount of panic himself. "We had a deal, everything was going along fine, they thought they had total security. See, I never mentioned showing you the tape, telling you the story."

"The truth will out," I suggested.

"God, I hope not. Anyway, the point is, when you called the other day, you started talking about the tape—"

"They were listening."

"Well, sure," he said. "That's part of the deal; they monitor the calls. They're involved in a very tricky operation, Sam, you just don't know."

"I want to know."

"Yeah, I was afraid of that." He bit his lips, drummed his fingers on the table, watched himself drum, then sighed and shook his head and showed me a face full of furrowed brow. "I can guarantee, Sam,", he said, "that you aren't in any more danger. You talked to Doreen, right?"

"Right."

"So you know I can make it stick. I'm not their *prisoner*, Sam, we've got an arrangement, a deal, and they *need* me."

"How long?"

"All the way through to the finish. Which is gonna be in just about a week from now. And the thing is, I told them to lay off Doreen and they laid off. Am I right?"

"So far."

"So now I told them to lay off *you*," Ross told me, electric with sincerity. "And they will. I gave them the whole story, how I showed you the tape and you gave me advice and all, and how you wouldn't go talk to the law because you're my friend, and all the rest of it. They bought it, Sam, they honest to God did."

"Tell me what's going on," I said.

"Aw, come on." He fidgeted in his chair, rapping his knuckles now on the tabletop. "Don't lean on me, Sam, okay? Accept it, they made a mistake going after you like that, and now they know it, and it won't happen again. You want me to pay for the Volvo?"'

I stared at him. "Pay for the Volvo? Ross, have you lost your marbles? You're playing around with *killers*, and you want to *stay* with them."

"It's almost over." Ross reached out and placed a trembling hand on my forearm. "Just wait for it, all right? Just trust me a little bit longer; I'll tell you the whole story when it's done."

A horrible suspicion crossed my mind as I looked at his straining face, and I said, "Ross, for God's sake. Do you see a *project* in this?"

His eyes slid away from mine. He said unconvincingly, "Who could think about work at a time like this?"

"You actually do," I said. "What is it, you see, a movie-of-the-week?"

That brought him back, with a sudden expression of scorn on his face.

"Television? You think all I know is television?"

"Tell me what you know."

He considered, his hand still vibrating on my forearm like an electric eel.

"Okay," he said, and lowered his voice. "Sam, this is big, this is very big. This is foreign governments, this is— What this is, it's a *book*."

"A book."

"A nonfiction book, from the *inside* of the whole experience." His eyes shone now with visions of sugar-plums and glittering prizes, panic all but forgotten. "A mammoth best-seller," he said. "Sam, it can't miss."

"If you're still around to write it."

"Oh, I will be," he said with total conviction. "I know how to deal with these clowns, Sam, I'm in that house like a lion tamer in the cage. It's tricky as hell, you don't have to tell me that, but I'm *doing* it."

"What's the story, Ross? What are they up to?" He withdrew from me; hand off arm, face closing up, body moving back against the chair, fingers touching the chains on his chest. "Don't ask me that, Sam," he said.

I lifted my left hand from the piece of paper and rested it on the phone. "Somebody's going to ask you," I told him. "Either me, or a deputy sheriff named Ken Donaldson."

He blinked, he blinked, he blinked. The chains clattered quietly in his fingers. The yellow windowless room in the fluorescent lighting seemed to grow steadily smaller. At last Ross sighed, and shook his head, and said, "I can tell you part, okay? Enough to get the idea. Okay?"

"Tell."

"What this is," he said, pausing to lick his lips, tap the table, play with his chains, glance toward the door, "this is a government, okay? Middle East, all right? There's a per-son, there's a very important person, you could call world-famous— Not an American, I promise you that, okay?"

"Tell," I insisted.

"I'm telling, I am. This government, they want this person for like a show trial, you know the kind of thing? So they can never get to him, there's always this extreme security around him."

"And you've invited him to dinner? Where do you connect with this, Ross?"

"He's going to be in a place, this person," Ross said. "There's a specific place he's going to be, a specific time, and from my property is absolutely the only way anybody could possibly get through the security. See, the land, you know, the land and then the other land."

"Next door, or behind you, or something."

"That's right. So when the person is *there*, they can go in and grab him, come back out through my place, take off. From there they get him out of the country and however they do it, I'm done; it's all over for me. They just need to be in my house a little while, setting up, getting everything ready for when they go in. And they need *me* to keep a normal front, you know? A regular appearance, so there's nothing wrong on this land that's right by the other land."

"And in order to convince you to cooperate in a kidnapping," I said, "they murdered three people."

He blinked at me, at a loss. "What do you mean?"

"Delia, to begin with."

"Yeah, yeah," he said, impatiently brushing that aside, clearly not liking to be reminded. "They had to have a real good hook in me, didn't they? And do you think I cry a lot over Delia?"

"They killed her. They didn't know her, or dislike her, or have anything to do with *her* at all. They killed a human being just so they could get a handle on you. And you want to be their lion tamer."

"I *am* their lion tamer! Jesus, Sam, I've been making a

it work, everything was fine, if you hadn't called and started talking about tapes on the goddamn pho—" But then he stopped abruptly, and shook his head, expressing irritation at himself. "No, forget that. Now I'm acting as though it's *your* fault. All right, these are very tough people, they're from the army and the secret police, you know, in that country, and they aren't exactly Boy Scouts."

"They're exactly murderers."

"And kidnappers, don't forget," he said. "And I'll tell you the truth, I haven't yet seen one of them phone home to his mother. But I can *handle* them, Sam, and it's just one more week, and I promise nobody's gunning for you anymore." He managed a shaky grin. "The fact is," he said, "now they realize you're not just some schmuck, you know? You're not that easy to kill."

"Thank you."

"So they know you're tough, and they have my guarantee you'll keep quiet until they're finished, and they need *my* cooperation, and they know if they took another shot at you and missed again, you'd have entire *armies* of cops swarming all over my place. So you're out of it; absolutely, completely, and totally out of it."

"Ross," I said, "maybe you have enough for the book now."

He stared at me. "What book? What have they done? A murder in the local papers, three days and it's over. When these guys make their move, it's going to be front page. Everywhere. Around the whole world they are going to make headlines, and those headlines are going to sell *my book*."

I sat back, trying to understand and believe this idiot. "Ross," I said, "you are a certifiable lunatic."

"Granted," he said. "But I know a commercial property when I see one, and I am *sitting* on one. And whether or not I am certifiable, it would take a close blood relative to certify me. You're a good friend, Sam, I came to you with this problem in the first place because I like you and trust you and I know you're a good friend. But you don't have the right to pull the plug on me on this thing.'"

"I know about a murder," I said. "Legally, I have to report it to the police."

"You've known about it since November," he pointed out. "You didn't report then, you don't have to report now. Nothing's changed. There was a little mistake, an error in judgment—"

"Jesus Christ, Ross!"

"That's what it *was*! And it's over, it's over, it's over! What do you want from me?" Then, struck by a sudden thought, he leaned closer and said, "Listen, how about this? I'll phone you every day. Twice a day if you want. Let you know how things are going, everything's all right. I don't phone you, that's when you bring in the cavalry."

"You're out of that house now," I told him. "I'd like you to stay out of it, stay away from it, let the law go in there and clean them out."

"And the book?"

"Oh, come on, Ross, you want it published posthumously?"

"Depends on the advance," he said, then shook his head and his right hand, saying, "Sorry, no, bad joke. All I can say is, I've told you everything I can, I'll make constant phone calls to you if you want, I guarantee you're not in any danger, and all I ask is you don't bring in the law just yet. Please, Sam. No cops, not before they make their move."

How could I agree to such a thing? It was completely crazy, wildly dangerous, and probably illegal. Ross clutched my arm, bent forward, staring at me, straining with every pore to force me to go along with his conviction.

But how could I? These people had already murdered three times. They had done their best to murder me. They were blackmailing Ross, planning to kidnap some world figure, and three of them had casually raped Doreen en passant. How could I just walk away from it, think about something else?

"Listen, Ross," I said. "I can understand the way you're thinking now, I see you're all full of this book idea, but these people aren't *research*. They're alive, and they're mean, and they'll kill you like blowing their nose."

"No," he said. "They need me, and I understand them. Sam, for Christ's sake, you always told me I was a good writer, you liked the scripts I did on *Packard*, you thought they—"

"What has *that* got to do with anything? This isn't *Packard*!"

"This is *people*." His palms were pressed flat on the tabletop, he was leaning toward me over them like a gymnast, as brittle as an ice sculpture in his intensity. "Sam," he said, "you've written stories, what the hell do, you think a story *is*? Is it just 'and then, and then, and then'? That's for the bricklayers! Stories are people, who they are and what they're doing and what they'll do next. If I'm any damn good at what I do, it's because I know the tools of my trade, and the tools of my trade are *people*."

"Oh, come on, Ross, how can—"

He made an abrupt hurling motion, pointing up and away to his right with a trembling rigid arm, as though aiming at some castle on the hill. "Those are *people* up there, Sam," he said, "and I know them, and I've been tiptoeing through them like Tippi Hedren in *The Birds*, and if you don't go making some fucking loud *noise*, I'll be all right!"

"Ross, this doesn't make any—"

"Let me tell you something," he said. The pointing finger came around to vibrate in my direction. "You blow the whistle here, I'll tell you what happens next. I'm out, you said so yourself, but Doreen is still in. If I don't come back, the very first thing they do is turn Doreen into cold cuts, and I am not kidding."

"The police could—"

"Bring the mayo. There's no way to stop it, Sam. There's no way to stop them packing that girl into a suitcase and *leaving*. *I* don't know where they'll go. *You* don't know where they'll go. But they can always find *us*, fella, and don't you forget it. And they'll *still* work out some way to do what they want to do. So what will you accomplish, except to kill three people, including yourself?"

"And your book."

"You're goddamn right, and my book!" he yelled. "I'm going through fucking *hell* in that house, and I want my reward at the end of it!"

"A bullet in the back of the head."

"That's up to me, Sam," he said. "That's *my* choice." How could I leave it to Ross's judgment when he'd spent his entire life proving he had no judgment? How could I trust him to really understand what was going on in his house?

He leaned farther and farther forward, his face straining toward me, eyes trying to burn inside my head and rewire what they found there. "Sam, Sam," he said, half-whispering. "I'll never get a shot like this again."

If I were to call the deputies, *could* Ross's friends be gone before they arrived? Probably. Would they do something atrocious to Doreen in revenge? Absolutely. Would they go to ground somewhere unknown and scheme some other way to pull their kidnapping? Of course.

If I did nothing, at least Doreen and Ross were safe for the moment, and we knew where to find those people. If I did nothing, Ross himself might finally get scared enough of the situation to come out and give the full cooperation that would be necessary; the name of the country behind this, the place where the attack was supposed to happen, the name of the intended victim. At this moment, if I called the deputies, Ross would clam up solid,

I sighed. I folded the piece of paper and put it in my pocket. Ross sat back, trembling, grinning from ear to ear, letting out long-held breath. "It'll be all right, Sam," he said.

It was already all wrong, and I knew it. "I could change my mind at any second," I said.

"You won't have to, Sam," he promised me. "From here on, from here on, it's a coast, all the way."

19

THE EXTERIOR OF THE LIMOUSINE was silver, with black windows and the license plate SSTAR 23, its owner (and the chauffeur's employer) being Star Car Service, with whom CNA has an annual contract. The interior was an egg carton for Fabergé eggs, each cup (or seat) lined with thick silvery blue plush, the floor and most other surfaces covered with hairy shag carpeting in the same color, so that riding in it was like being in a science fiction movie's idea of a symbolic womb.

There were four low roomy seats in the passenger area, two facing forward at the two facing back. The tiny refrigerator between the forward-facing seats was filled with splits of many different liquids, while the small TV screen between the rear-facing seats was dead black when not in use. The chauffeur's—I nearly said "pilot's"—compartment could be closed away by electrically raising either a clear glass or a black plastic partition.

Our arrangement in the limo lent itself to a discreet form of psychological pressure. I was in the right rear seat, left forearm atop the refrigerator, while the other two sat facing me, flanking the TV's square black doorway. Danny was directly opposite, demonstrating his respect by giving me lots and lots of legroom, his own legs twisted out of the way as though to say that mere producers don't need such things. The partitions between us and the chauffeur were left down, the space open, because, of course, none of us had anything to hide.

We had boarded this air-conditioned vehicle in the cool shadowed parking level of Zack's building, where it had been waiting for us near the elevators, and then we went out to the traffic and the bright day, muted by the sheets of black on side and rear windows. As we drove along, Danny talked and Zack talked and I tried to listen, but after my conversation with Ross—and particularly after what he had browbeat me into agreeing to—it wasn't easy. My eyes kept straying to the surrounding traffic on Santa Monica Boulevard and then on the San Diego Freeway, where no swarthy men peeled out of the jumble in Chevy Impalas.

Belatedly, it had occurred to me that I hadn't managed to tell Ross about the deaths of the actor and the makeup man. I'd started to, I'd said there'd been three murders, but then we'd been sidetracked by the outrageousness of his intentions and I'd never gotten back to it again. Would it have made any difference? Probably not. Ross, whose overdeveloped sense of drama had led him into this mess in the first place, could see nothing now but the drama—and the success—of the book he was going to write.

Why had I let him talk me into it? Was it because all he was asking me, as all I was asking Zack, was to be permitted to work? At some point in the discussion with Ross it had seemed to me that I didn't have the right somehow to keep him from his *career*, as though the job were more important than the life, as though threats to the life were irrelevant if the job could get done; like the German director Werner Herzog risking himself and his crew in South American jungles to get a movie made. Was all that as stupid as I now thought it? Did my identification with Ross's plight as a worker get in the way of my common sense? Should I renege on our agreement?

"Of course," Zack was saying, "Sam will have a clearer picture of all this once he reads the scripts."

"Oh, sure, sure." Smiling, Danny Silvermine looked at me and massaged his knees. "I hope you won't mind the liberties I took," he said. "Just to fit it on the stage, you know. But the heart of the material was already there, and I left that alone. It's not often you meet an actor who's a real natural writer too."

"It didn't feel natural," I told him. The world seen through the tinted glass beside me was blue-tinged, watery, but beyond Danny's compact head, beyond the dispassionate chauffeur and out through the windshield, the day was bright and washed-out and glaring, like an overexposed print. Lying in submarine shadow on the empty fourth seat beside me, beyond the refrigerator, were the two slender scripts, both in baby-blue folders imprinted in gold. *The Man Who Was Overboard* was on top. Remembering my earlier curiosity as to which was the other script Silvermine had thought adaptable, I reached over to pick them up, shuffled the bottom one onto the top, and read *Salute the Devil*. Oh, the military school. But how could *that* work onstage?

Zack and Danny Silvermine had both fallen silent, leaving only the soft sounds of tire-hum and air-conditioning, which I didn't at first notice. Putting down *The Man Who Was Overboard*, I leafed through *Salute the Devil* and saw how it had been done. That had been my first script, my very first attempt to write anything in fiction, and it was all talk from beginning to end. Later I'd learned more about letting action carry the story, but that first one was dialogue, dialogue, dialogue. Following the advice of my three mentors—Ross, and Bly, and Terry Young, my reporter friend in New York—I'd "opened it up" by setting all the talk in different places: on the rifle range, in the stable, among the cadets while they marched. What Danny Silvermine had done was shift all those scenes down onto only two sets, the senior cadets' locker room and the faculty lounge.

But wouldn't that merely emphasize what was amateurish and inept in the story? I leafed through this careful product of the word processor, with its justified right margins and eye-catching use of italics and boldface, trying to see at a glance if the result was better or worse or just the same, and then I became aware of Zack and Danny watching me, waiting. I turned back to the first page: *Salute the Devil*, by Samuel Holt. I said, "You didn't give yourself a credit."

Danny giggled, either from nervousness or relief, impossible to tell. "Oh, I figured we'd work that out," he said. "Whatever you want, it's fine with me. My ego isn't involved in that part, Sam."

But can you be a good writer—or even a good rewriter—if your ego isn't involved? I didn't ask that question, merely dropped the script back onto the other one and said, "I'll have to read them, of course."

"Oh, of course!"

"But at first glance it looks as though you've done a good job. I wouldn't have known how to redo *Salute*."

"It was all there," Danny assured me, leaning forward, spreading his hands. "You provided the substance, Sam, I just noodged it around a little."

Zack said, "Sam, if you decide to proceed with this, I'll tell you something right here in front of Danny. He's a detail man. If you go on the road with him, he'll get the details right."

Danny squirmed with pleasure, like a puppy. "It's what I love to do, that's all. Provide the setting, let the artist be free to create."

Everybody in Los Angeles is an artist. To meet a producer who claimed not to be an artist was refreshing, and made me warm to him. "I'll read them," I said.

"That's all I could ask, Sam. I want you to know I appreciate it."

Zack said, "Next week, Sam, you'll give me a call?"

"Don't rush the man!" Danny cried, hurrying to my defense, demonstrating how he'd behave if we went on the road together in a more meaningful way than in this limousine.

Beyond the chauffeur, out in the glare, the huge green sign announced MANCHESTER BOULEVARD: LAX was near.

"I'll read them on the plane," I said. "Then take a few days to think it over."

"Of course," Zack said.

"So next week's no problem," I said. "Early next week."

"That's fine, fine."

"I *really* appreciate this, Sam."

We all smiled together in perfect harmony, we were polite, Zack was pleased and avuncular, Danny was effusive, and the chauffeur slowed for Century Boulevard.

20

UNLESS REQUESTED OTHERWISE, airlines prefer to preboard infants in arms, unaccompanied minors, people in wheelchairs, and celebrities; it makes it easier to maintain the passenger flow. That's why I was surprised to find someone already in the window seat next to mine when I came onto the L-1011 with three children of divorce and a resigned-looking Oriental couple bearing twins in arms. My fellow preboarders turned right toward coach when they entered the plane, I turned left, and there he was, my seatmate, the pre-preboarder.

My first impression of him, a hard-bodied man in his fifties wearing a dark blue pinstripe suit, was of a top-ranked corporation or divorce lawyer, but such a man wouldn't be preboarded like this. A senator? That seemed possible until I reached my seat and he turned to look at me, when I saw that he was European. Foreign, anyway.

I don't know how to define that idea, how this mongrelized melting pot of ours has managed to come up with a distinctive American look—or several distinctive American looks, I suppose—but we have, and this fellow was none of them. His coarse pepper-and-salt hair was cut full, emphasizing its waviness in a dramatic way I thought of as Italian. There was nothing unusual about his suit and vest and maroon-figured tie, but the white shirt's collar points were too long and narrow, giving him to my American eyes a vaguely untrustworthy look. Similarly, his mouth was thin-lipped, almost colorless, and looked unused to smiling, while his cheeks were rounded, almost puffy, noticeably so in his otherwise hard-boned face, suggesting something alien in his normal diet. (Americans tend to go puffy lower in the face, sagging down onto the jawline.) The skin of his face was leathery, tanned by sun or wind and faintly pocked with some childhood disease. His eyes were small and darkly brown, and they glanced at me in brief disinterest before returning to the airline copy of *The Economist* he was leafing through.

My luggage consisted entirely of one attaché case containing Danny Silvermine's scripts, other reading matter, materials concerned with the lawsuit that was taking me east, and a beautiful green silk sweater I'd found in a shop in the Rodeo Collection, as a present for Anita. Since there's so very little of the materialistic about Anita, she's hard to shop for, so I wind up buying whatever reminds me of her, regardless. This Italian sweater reminded me of Anita's eyes; whether she ever wore the thing or not was up to her.

My seat, as usual, was 2-C: nonsmoking, aisle, on the north side of an eastbound plane to avoid glaring sunlight. Dropping *The Man Who Was Overboard* onto this seat, along with a yellow legal pad and a ball-point pen, I stowed my attaché case in the overhead bin, told the stewardess I'd like the orange juice, thank you, without the champagne, and settled myself down to wait for New York.

The only flaw in preboarding is the long, long wait before the plane takes off. While we were still on the ground, my seatmate went steadily through every bit of reading matter in *The Economist* and then turned to another of the several airline-copy magazines he'd stashed in the seat pocket, another advantage of preboarding, getting to pick first through the available magazines. He chose *The*

Atlantic next, beginning with the puzzle at the back, which he slowly but inexorably filled in, in ink, with long pauses while he brooded into space, searching out the answers.

And I read *The Man Who Was Overboard*. When I finished, I'd made barely half a dozen notes, and those were mostly perfunctory. Danny Silvermine had done his job well, keeping most of my dialogue, bridging and explaining scenes that couldn't be transferred from film to stage. If you accepted the original premise, that this was a story worthy of recycling in another medium, Danny had done a clean and craftsmanlike job. My only problem was with the original premise. Was this script as tired as I thought it was, or was I the only one so totally weary of Packard and all his works?

Deciding a double dose might help answer the question, and the plane still not having taken off—though first class was now about two-thirds full—I got to my feet, retrieved the attaché case, switched scripts, put the case away, and sat down with *Salute the Devil* to see my seatmate frowning at me. "I beg your pardon," he said with an accent that wasn't quite English, "but have we met? Forgive the intrusion, it's simply that you look familiar."

The person who knows he knows me but doesn't know why is fairly common, particularly now that *Packard* is fading into history. Something told me this man would not have been a regular viewer. I said, "I'm an actor; you've probably seen me on television."

"Oh, is that right?" He seemed pleased, though the thin-lipped mouth didn't exactly smile. "Where I live," he said, "I see mostly cassettes. Is your work available on cassettes?"

"In a limited way," I said. "I was on a series for a while called *Packard*."

He nodded, politely trying to remember the name. "Would that be a detective show?"

"Yes."

With a brief headshake he said, "Then, forgive me, I would be unlikely to watch. I am a detective myself, you see, and the difference between television and my own experience..."

"Yes, of course." When American cops tell me such things, as sometimes happens, I always assume it's a kind of snobbery, but wherever this fellow came from, police work was undoubtedly *very* different from the American TV version.

"On the other hand," he went on, musing, tapping the nearly complete *Atlantic* puzzle with the tip of the pen, "I can remember being amused by *The Rockford Files*."

"The class act," I agreed.

Dipping into a vest pocket, he came out with a white card, which he handed me, saying, "May I introduce myself? Hassan Tabari."

The card was expensive stock, the lettering a smooth and faintly Oriental script. His name was in the middle of it, and in the lower right were two lines that read, *Minister of Justice, Principality of Dharak*. I said, "Dharak. I'm sorry, I don't think I..."

He was amused, and now he did smile, with closed lips. "We know nothing of one another's worlds, I see. We are one of the emirates between Saudi Arabia and the Gulf."

"Where they're bombing the oil tankers?"

His expression became grim and angry. "Disgraceful," he said. "*There's* a crime for you, but no detective work involved. Unarmed neutral ships are bombed and strafed, innocent sailors slaughtered, and the murderers defiantly announce themselves."

"Iran and Iraq."

"Precisely." He turned his left hand palm upward. "And who is to arrest them?"

"No one," I agreed.

"There are so many outlaw states in the world." He was coldly furious, a strong man frustrated. "And too many, I'm afraid, in my own neighborhood."

We were interrupted then by the stewardess doing the safety announcements as the plane at last was towed back away from the gate and taxied itself out toward its runway. As one stewardess read the drill over the sound system, another one with a fixed smile stood at the front of the cabin, showing the safety card, demonstrating the operation of the seat belt and life jacket and oxygen mask. When at last she was finished, I turned back to Hassan Tabari and said, "By the way, my name's Sam Holt."

The name meant nothing to him; in some ways a relief, in some ways disconcerting. Extending his hand, he said, "I'm pleased to meet you."

His hand was firm, leathery, dry. I said, "Are you on your way home?"

"No, only to New York, to talk with our U.N. Mission. I was in Los Angeles conferring with the police there about a pair of my co-nationals who had behaved badly. I was permitted to question them to see if there were implications for me at home. Fortunately, there were not." His expression almost sly, he said, "It would appear they received their ideas about bank robbery from television."

Until he'd said that last part, I'd half-believed the co-nationals he was talking about were the people who'd tried to run me off the San Diego Freeway, the ones Ross was tied up with. It would have been a ridiculous coincidence, but if coincidence didn't happen in this world, we wouldn't need a word for it. However, the lions Ross saw himself as taming weren't bank robbers, and they weren't—unfortunately—in the hands of the Los Angeles police.

In any event, I now understood why he'd been boarded ahead of those who normally go first. A government minister from a strife-torn corner of the world who had just been visiting with the police in Los Angeles would have somewhat more than the normal clout.

He said, "And you? I see you're reading a script. On your way to an acting job?"

"I wish I was," I said, and told him briefly about the lawsuit against the comic book company.

Again he was amused, though distantly. "You must forgive me," he said, "if I think your problems not entirely...serious."

"In comparison with the Mideast, you mean."

"In comparison with life."

"Life is an accumulation of details, isn't it?" I asked him. "Police work is, I know."

He bowed his head, though still amused, saying, "I am properly chastised. You're right, the details must be attended to. Whether we are doing our laundry or changing the world, the point is that it must be done. But still, that is a script," he added, pointing to *Salute the Devil* in my lap.

"Yes, it is."

"And so it is in some way work, and must be done, and I must not keep you from it. I shall return to my own very engaging puzzle, which does not *have* to be done, which is its charm."

He nodded to me, with his near smile, and as the plane at last lifted off the runway, he neatly filled in one more word of his puzzle. I opened *Salute the Devil* and read, but aware of a nagging uncertainty: Which of us, in that last exchange, had been put down?

21

BECAUSE THIS WAS A DINNER flight we had the movie first, Hassan Tabari obediently lowering his window blinds at the stewardess's request, but then switching on his reading light, having consumed *The Atlantic* by now and moved on to *Scientific American*, in which at last he showed some selectivity, not devouring it all, skipping over the article on insect larvae. In the meantime I had finished both of Danny Silvermine's scripts and had decided to show them to Anita while I was in New York, because maybe I was the wrong person to say whether or not they worked, whether or not the basic idea was a good one, whether or not Packard was still viable. The movie was a pretty poor comedy I'd already seen parts of on cassette, but I watched it anyway, feeling lazy and disoriented, needing distraction from my two problems. Danny's scripts were problem number one, and, of course, Ross was problem number two. (The lawsuit responsible for this trip got hardly any of my attention at all.) It might have been easier to limit my fretting to Danny Silvermine if it hadn't been for the presence of Hassan Tabari. Because of the part of the world he came from, and because of the pool company that called itself *Barq*, he couldn't help but remind me of Ross, about whom I had done absolutely nothing of any use, with the single exception of getting Doreen away from him and his friends.

The movie, as all bad things do, came to an end. I removed the headset, and was trying to decide which of Tabari's magazines I would ask to borrow when the man himself raised his window blinds, put down *Scientific American*, and said, "The person who performed the role of the doctor in that film is Lebanese, you know."

"Oh, really?" I tried to remember the actor's name; it had been a smallish part, about the size my friend Brett Burgess gets hired for. "I hadn't known that," I said. Nor had I been aware of Tabari at any time looking at the screen.

"His mother was French," Tabari explained, "so he took her name when he became an actor. Westernizing, you see."

"Ah."

"So," he said, shrugging, "we are not all bombers of defenseless sailors, hijackers of innocent tourists."

"All Arabs, you mean."

He considered the term, and rejected it. "All Moslems," he decided. "After all, the Iranians are not Arabs, as they never tire of announcing. The dispute is religious rather than racial. In fact," he said, suddenly voluble, shifting position so he could face me more comfortably, "I sometimes think the internal Moslem struggle is infinitely more important than Arab versus Jew. That one is merely about territory, but the war within Islam is for the soul of the world."

To have such an overblown hyperbole come from so restrained and self-controlled a man at first startled and then amused me, which must have shown in my face, because he cocked an eyebrow at me and said, "Do you think I over-state the case?"

"Slightly," I said.

"Perhaps," he agreed, and nodded, and said, "but only very slightly. We control the world's energy for the next century. We shall decide whether or not the machines of western civilization turn. Don't you think we will have some say as to what that civilization looks like?"

"It's possible," I admitted.

"The fundamentalist sects," he said, "have captured Iran, taken control of Libya, assassinated Sadat, helped to destabilize Lebanon, performed terrorist acts against you of the West, and are creating great trouble and concern in every moderate Moslem nation. Even Saudi Arabia is not as proof against the virus as it appears."

This was far from any area of expertise I might claim. I said, "We can see the struggle's going on, all right."

"But who are these people in white nightdresses, eh, slaughtering one another?" The twist he then gave his mouth could not have been called a smile. "The Jewish lobby in this country makes no distinctions among Arabs," he said, "and therefore America does not, and that us a very bad mistake."

"I'm really not up on all this," I said, wondering how to get back out of this conversation, and deciding the thing to do was find a need to visit the lavatory.

Tabari leaned back, shaking his head at himself, as though aware he'd gone too far, made me nervous. "I'll say only this," he told me. "Our fundamentalists are to us a more violent form of what your fundamentalists are to you. The sort of people who a generation ago forced the famous Scopes monkey trial and still today try to keep evolution out of your schools. The kind of people who bomb abortion clinics. In America these people are merely an irritant, one point of view among many at the fringes of a strong center. In my part of the world there is no center, there are only the extremes. You would not like a world, Mr. Holt, that would please some of our imams."

"I'm sure I wouldn't."

"I have no idea, of course, what your contacts with Arab Moslems have been— "

"Actually, none that I know of," I said.

He affected surprise. "None at all? Are you sure? For instance, there's a great deal of Arab money in your American film business now." And he gestured at the script of *Salute the Devil* in my seat pocket.

Trying to imagine Danny Silvermine as a front for Arab money made me smile.

"No," I said. "So far as I know, this is the most extensive conversation I've ever had with an Arab."

"Well, well," he said, seeming to relax a bit, "what a heavy responsibility I bear, representing a quarter of the world to you in my one person. I'm afraid I've been a bit too intense to make a completely good impression."

He had. "Not at all," I told him.

"In my position," he said, "you must understand, I have dealings with these fanatics from time to time; they tend to dwell in my mind."

"I can understand that," I said.

"I am Minister of Justice in Dharak," he reminded me, "sworn to uphold our law. But these fanatics have no use for civilized law. They believe only in a cold and rigid law of their own devising, which they blame on God."

"Hard to deal with."

"They cannot be dealt with at all," he said with great intensity. "They can only be guarded against, rooted out, isolated, defanged. Being a policeman in smalltown America is nothing like this, I assure you."

"I believe it," I said, and then was glad to be interrupted by the stewardess wanting to open our tray tables in preparation for dinner. It made for a distraction that permitted me to keep from letting Tabari see that he'd made a mistake.

Being a policeman in smalltown America. But that wasn't *Packard*—a show, in any case, that he claimed not to have seen. That could only be my own pre-acting job on the force in Mineola. This was *not* coincidence.

This was something to do with Ross.

22

HAD TABARI ALSO NOTICED his mistake? Hard
to tell. He didn't at once pick up the thread of conversation,
and in fact neither of us had anything to say during dinner.
He ate some sort of vegetarian thing that looked mostly like
a large scab, and I ordered, as I always do, the
chateaubriand, because that's prepared on the plane and is
likely to be a bit less awful than the other choices. Neither
Tabari nor I had liquor, he asking for ginger ale and I club
soda. He ate everything on his plate, including the roll and
both crackers, while I just picked at my food, since I'd be
eating a real dinner later on with Anita. Beyond his sharp-
featured puffy-cheeked face the sky was already graying
toward twilight, though it had only been one in the afternoon when we'd started. But we were flying away from the
sun, losing three hours; it would be nine at night when we
arrived in New York. A February night in New York; I shivered, thinking of it.

But what I mostly thought about was Tabari. Who
was he really? What game was he playing? And what
should I do about it? He was important enough to have
arranged to be put in the seat beside me and boarded
before every other passenger; so was he actually who his
card claimed him to be? And if so, what sort of principality or emirate was this Dharak? He had spoken pas-
sionately against what he called "outlaw nations," but

121

was that merely blowing smoke, the devil claiming to be an angel?

If his approach had been more direct, I would probably have been far less suspicious. But he had come to me under a cover of lies. Still, thinking back over our conversation, I couldn't figure out what it was he wanted. He hadn't seemed to pump me at all, or even to be particularly interested in me. He'd given vent to some dubious political statements, that was about it.

Should I brace him, tell him I knew this was no chance meeting? My instinct told me not to, that nothing would be gained that way. He'd simply deny it, of course, look at me as though I were crazy, ask me what I thought he was up to. And what would I say next, since I hadn't the slightest idea what he was up to? Either I'd wind up telling him about Ross or I'd fade away into silence; and I was definitely not going to tell *anybody* about Ross.

The only advantage I had, it seemed to me, was that possibly Tabari didn't know he'd made that error. So, for the rest of the flight, I'd be polite and noncommittal, I'd chat with him and listen carefully to what he said, and try to figure out what he was up to.

Except it didn't work that way. Tabari had apparently lost all interest in conversation. When the meal was over—I had coffee, he had more ginger ale—he actually offered me a choice of the magazines he'd squirreled away (I chose *The Atlantic*) and went back to his *Scientific American* to read about insect larvae after all.

We had another hour before landing. Full night spread across the world outside the windows, I leafed through *Salute the Devil* once more and had another cup of coffee, and Tabari folded his hands and closed his eyes. The pilot announced that we were crossing over Allentown, Pennsylvania. The "Fasten Seat Belt" sign went on. The "No Smoking" sign went on. The pilot told us the time in New York—eight fifty-seven, Eastern Standard Time—and the weather—twenty-one degrees, cloudy, some chance of snow by morning. The plane juddered as the landing gear was lowered. The pilot told the stewardesses to take their seats. I decided to follow Tabari when he left the plane.

23

ONE OF THE MANY CONTRASTS between my New York and Los Angeles lives is that in L.A. I have four cars—or did, until one of them became It in that game of tag—while in the East I have none. Usually in New York my own feet or a taxi will do, but for special occasions I have an account with a small limousine and car rental outfit on West Fifty-sixth Street. My usual driver is a heavyset white-haired Irishman named Ralph, and he it was who stood waiting beyond the revolving doors at the end of the long walk from the plane. I saw him, and nodded, and saw Tabari behind me reflected in the glass of the doors, carrying over his shoulder his black garment bag.

I had made my good-byes brief—Tabari hadn't suggested a later meeting, or a shared ride to the city, or any of the continuations I'd been expecting—and had made sure to get off the plane ahead of him, moving as quickly as possible among the other passengers. When I reached Ralph, therefore, Tabari was visible but was some distance back down the corridor, having been forced through the same channel as the rest of us. Ralph grinned at me, pointed at the attaché case, and said, "Will that be it, then?"

"Yes. Ralph, there's a fellow behind me, probably just coming through the doors, about fifty, hard-faced, three-piece pinstripe suit, carrying a garment bag. See him?"

"It's the well-dressed thug you'd mean," he said, looking over my shoulder.

"That's the one." I moved toward the exit, and Ralph moved with me. "We'll keep in front of him here, but then we'll follow him. I want to know where he's going."

Ralph grinned at me. "So Packard rides again, does he?"

"Come on, Ralph," I said. "Don't make fun. And as we go outside, glance back and see if he's gone off to get any checked luggage."

The automatic door opened, letting frigid air in and us out. Ralph hitched up his overcoat, head turning left and right to ease the collar. "No," he said. "Your fella's coming right along behind."

"Good. Brrrr! Where's the car?"

"Just to our left here."

I was in the casual jacket and slacks I'd worn for my meetings with Ross and Danny, and the pilot had not been wrong about the temperature. I strode at a swift but dignified pace across the pavement to the limo parked by the No Parking sign, and clambered into cozy warmth, Ralph shutting the door behind me. This car was merely a stretch Cadillac with good legroom, a pair of jumpseats, and ordinary upholstery. Only the tiny refrigerator echoed SSTAR 23.

As Ralph went around the rear of the limo to the driver's door, Tabari came out of the terminal and paused. A slender young man in a cloth cap and gray overcoat approached him, carrying another coat over his arm. They greeted each other as master and servant, and then the young man took the garment bag, handing Tabari the coat. It was heavy, of black wool, with a black fur collar. From its pocket Tabari pulled a dark fur hat, shook it, and put it on. The young man, carrying the garment bag over his arm as he'd carried the coat, led him off to the right, and as he walked, Tabari took black leather gloves from the other pocket.

Ralph got behind the wheel, shut the door, and nodded at Tabari and the other man. "That'll be the fella from the maroon Sedan de Ville," he said. "I noticed him before, with the diplomat plates."

"We follow him."

"No problem at all," he assured me.

The young man held open the rear door of a maroon Cadillac, and Tabari slid in. Ralph shifted into drive, and we eased forward. He said, "Want me to stay in front till we're beyond the airport?"

"No. It's possible he'll be going to another plane, or an airport hotel, or almost anywhere."

"Would I know who this fella is?"

"No more than I would," I told him. "I was preboarded, and he was already there, in the next seat. He pretended he'd never heard of me, pushed a conversation, and then let it slip that he knew I was an ex-cop."

"Planted there. *National Enquirer*, do you think?" Ralph was a constant reader of the *Enquirer*, and from time to time would bring me up-to-date on the rather rackety life I led in those pages.

"Not this time, I don't think," I said. "I don't know what it's about at all, that's why we'll follow him."

The maroon Cadillac pulled away from the curb, and Ralph moved us out after it. Leaning forward, I could see the red, white, and blue New York State diplomatic corps plates: DPL and a set of three numbers. Unfortunately, snow and grime obscured all three numbers. Another coincidence?

There was a stop sign where the feed from the airline building's arrival area led into the main airport road. The car ahead stopped, its red brake lights gleaming. Ralph said, "We've had a good amount of snow, as you can see."

Dirty mounds of gray snow topped by a layer of black soot flanked the roadway. Again I remembered my last limo ride, through glaring sunlight, five hours before.

The maroon Cadillac's brake lights winked off, and the car moved smoothly out into a very light flow of traffic. Ralph pulled up to the stop sign, stopped, and a black Buick Riviera on the main road came to a halt directly in front of us, no more than a yard from our front bumper, blocking our exit. "Well, Jesus, Mary, and Joseph," Ralph said, and honked his horn.

The Buick's interior light went on. The driver, a bundled-up middle-aged man, was alone in there, studying a roadmap. Ralph honked again, and lowered his window to shout a few unfriendly comments into the cold night, and the man in the Buick just kept frowning at his roadmap. Cars behind us honked.

It was only a minute, maybe a minute and a half, but it was enough. Tabari was gone. Then the man in the Buick looked up, saw us with complete astonishment, switched off his interior light, and drove on. He had ordinary New York State plates, gone too fast to be read.

Ralph eased forward and gave me an ironic look in the rearview mirror. "Your friend didn't want to be followed, did he?"

"Apparently not."

A little farther on we saw the Buick turn left away from the airport exit, on a loop that would take him back deeper into JFK. We didn't follow him. What was the point?

24

T WAS EASY TO AVOID TALKING with Anita about Ross's problems and my strange seatmate on the plane; I held up my end of the conversation instead with Danny Silvermine and the comic book lawsuit. I hadn't told Anita last November about Ross, when he'd showed me the tape, and I saw nothing to be gained by opening that story now. In the first place, I was still ambivalent about my own part in it, and didn't want to have to justify my continuing silence, my agreement not to go to the police. In the second place, Bly's reaction when I'd finally told her had been enlightening; she hadn't cared at all to know I'd kept a secret from her so successfully for so long, even though the secret had nothing directly to do with her. Maybe the rule is, if you've succeeded in keepin,g a secret, don't spoil your record.

There were still several tables of customers in Vitto Impero when I got there at quarter to ten, coming directly from JFK. Anita stayed at her post at the cash register and I sat by myself at the round corner table in the back where we'd had dinner with Brett Burgess the night his play opened. (It had closed again long since.) Marcie the waitress brought me a number of things Angelo the cook thought would restore me after my journey, and I washed it all down with San Pellegrino and Pinot Grigio, taking my time, because by my own body clock it was barely seven in the evening.

When the last of the regular customers left, Anita came over to sit with me and help finish the wine. I told her then about Danny Silvermine, and she asked to see the scripts, which were in the attaché case on the empty chair beside me. I handed them over and finished eating while she skimmed *The Man Who Was Overboard*. My meal and her reading were finished at the same time; Marcie took away the plates, I said no to coffee, and Anita said, "What's the point?"

"Exactly," I said.

"You already did this, right?" She tapped a sharp fingernail on the script's blue cover. "I mean, you already wrote it, you already played it."

"That's what I keep thinking," I told her. "But on the other hand, it's work, isn't it? It's doing something as opposed to doing nothing."

"So do something else."

"I've been trying to, honey."

"No, I mean with this guy Silverman."

"Mine, Silvermine. In what way, do something else?"

"Write a play," she said.

I just looked at her. She finished her wine and said, "You want more vino?"

"No. What do you mean, write a play? Write *what* play?"

"Whatever you want to appear in. Maybe another detective story, where you're not Packard, but it's still the same kind of form. Maybe you could be the murderer."

"Wait a minute," I said. "Write a *play*? I'm not a writer!"

Another fingernail tap on the scripts. "You wrote these."

"For television!"

"They're still plays. Silvermine—is that really his name?—he just changed them over for the stage, that's all.

Dialogue, plot, characters, it's all the same, and here's two times you already did it."

"But—" I was stymied by this brand new way of looking at things. I said, "But that was just *Packard*, I already knew the setting and the characters and the whole thing. I had people to help me—"

"People could help you," she said. "What if you went to Whatsisname and said, 'Look, I don't want to do Packard anymore, but I'll write you a brand new original play and star in it, and you can promote it as Sam Holt, the star of *Packard*.' I mean, you're saying the guy's gonna pay peanuts anyway, it's just a stunt for dinner theater—"

"Yeah, but—"

"But," she said, "why wouldn't he say yes to a whole new original *play* on the cheap? You'll let him have it for no advance or anything, the same deal as if he used these *Packard* scripts. In fact, *he* could help you; he's good at this kind of thing. Do you like the guy?"

"Well, actually, he makes my flesh crawl," I said. "He's one of those people where you can't say exactly anything he's done wrong, but he just tries too hard or something, and he comes over very creepy."

"So you wouldn't want to collaborate."

"No."

She shrugged. "You could do it on your own. You did it before."

"But I don't have a story, I don't— I wouldn't have the first idea how to write a play."

"You'd figure it out. What about that writer friend of yours?"

Did she mean Bly? Neither of my lady friends makes much mention of the other. Warily, I said, "Who?"

"The guy who did the scripts for your show, helped you—"

"Oh, Ross!" But now I was doubly wary. Did Anita know? How was that possible? "What about him?"

No, Anita didn't know. She said, "He could help you, show you the format, explain how it works. The same as he did on these," tapping the scripts again.

"I could ask him," I said doubtfully, because who knew how much longer Ross would be around to ask anything of. And as I said that, I found myself wondering if Ross's story could be a play. The double on the videotape. *Instant Replay*, was that a title? Was there any way to show that on a stage? Who would I play? Maybe Ross himself.

But that was awful, to turn a friend's trouble into a story to advance your own career. Trying to turn my mind away from the idea, I said, "I'll think about it, anyway. It just might be the solution."

Anita grinned. "Ask me anything," she said.

"Okay. What are you doing after dinner?"

"Going to bed with you, I believe," she told me.

"Your place or mine?"

"Well, we're here."

"And your place is all shut up," she pointed out. "Will you stay the night?"

My meeting on the lawsuit wasn't until ten in the morning, and my New York place was, as Anita had said, closed up. Robinson was still back in L.A. "Love to stay the night," I said.

As it turned out, that was a very lucky choice.

25

ANITA OWNS THAT FOUR-STORY-HIGH corner building on Abingdon Square, facing the little park full of preschoolers by day and homeless drunks by night. The restaurant, Vitto Impero, takes up the ground floor, with two apartments on each floor above, Anita's being in the rear one flight up, accessible either through the public hall and stairway or via the circular staircase up from the restaurant's kitchen to her living room.

The apartment itself is odd in one respect; it has no kitchen. Anita has the restaurant, of course, one flight down, and in any event she has such little interest in food that for her a kitchen would be a severe waste of valuable space. For ice and mixers there's a small refrigerator built into the cabinetry in the outer part of the bathroom. What used to be the kitchen, at the rear of the apartment, is now the bedroom, complete with working fireplace and two sets of french doors leading out to the terrace. When she'd bought the house, there had been merely a tarred roof back there, created by the ground floor's being twelve feet deeper than the stories above, but now the space was duck-boarded and, in summer, full of plants. In February the potted plants were inside, crowding the bedroom, and the larger planters outside were merely dead earth streaked with aging snow.

I wasn't due to become a New Yorker again until

April, so this was an oddly askew twenty-four hours. When I've been in California awhile, living there seems comfortably open and relaxed, and New York feels awfully cramped, whereas after I've adjusted to my East Coast life, it seems snug and cozy, while L.A. looks disjointed and barren. I was in my western mind right now, and wouldn't be back here long enough to adjust, so I simply tried to ignore the fact that Anita's circular staircase was so awkward and narrow, that her entire apartment was small enough to fit in half my garage out in Bel-Air, and that, with summer's plants brought inside, her bedroom was so crowded I didn't dare stretch without looking first to see what I was going to hit.

I was still on California time as well, meaning that my body clock thought it was barely nine P.M. when we went to bed, and not much later than ten when Anita said, "Enough."

She didn't mean sex; she meant the conversation that had followed sex, she bringing me up-to-date on the goings-on of mutual friends, people like Brett Burgess and Dr. Bill Ackerson, who would drop in to the restaurant from time to time. We'd been talking about Bill Ackerson's habit of dating his beautiful show biz patients, and how all his girls seemed to be equally pretty and vacant and interchangeable, with names like Muffin and Bunny, when all at once Anita's eyes glazed over, her head tolled back on the pillow, and she said, "Enough."

"Are you pooping out on me?"

"You say you want to get up at eight," she pointed out, "and that's seven hours from now."

"Oh, all right."

So we turned off the light and Anita curled up against my right side and went immediately to sleep, while I lay awake for some time longer, looking at the faint gray rectangles of the french doors, with New York outside. The city never sleeps. Neither do I, I thought, refusing to turn my head the other way to see the illuminated numbers of the digital clock.

So strange to be here in this fashion. I'd been with Bly yesterday and I'd see her again tomorrow, and here I was with Anita. My two lives are usually more distinct and disparate than that, me spending months or at the very least weeks in one place or the other, adjusting gradually.

But what else should I have done? If I'd gone home to Tenth Street instead and hadn't seen Anita at all, or if I'd just dropped by for dinner and then gone home to sleep alone, she would have become very annoyed, and I wouldn't blame her. But it was this hit-and-run aspect of the thing, the wham-bam-thank-you-ma'am, that made my odd life suddenly stand out for me in unusually stark relief.

In every part of my life, it now seemed to me, the story was the same, I was neither one thing nor the other yet both. I was neither a New Yorker nor an Angeleno, but I was both. I was neither Bly's fella nor Anita's, but I was both. I was neither a true star nor a has-been, but somehow I was still both. What frequently seemed to me a good and rich and rewarding life now seemed, in this wakeful February night in Manhattan, merely a life of well-controlled vacillation. "Indecision is the key to flexibility," read a sign I'd once seen over a producer's desk; it was meant to be a joke.

As time went on, and the dim light through the french doors didn't change, it was almost a relief to find myself fretting about Ross Ferguson instead, and what might or might not be happening in *his* life during my absence. God knows I hadn't been particularly useful or brilliant on that front so far, and yet I couldn't help the feeling that my being away, even for this short a time, would make things worse. I shouldn't have left; I should have insisted on a delay in the discovery proceeding. I should be there when Ross and his lions do whatever it is they plan to do.

Eventually, the grayness of the french doors blurred, and I slept.

26

THE NEXT MORNING I THOUGHT I saw Tabari in the back of a cab. I'd left Anita's place, weary but awake, at eight-thirty, walking across the Village toward my house, surrounded by overcoated people hurrying to work through the cold and the dirty remnants of snow. As I waited for the light at Sixth Avenue, the cab passed me, headed uptown: It was gone before the image sank in, and I couldn't be exactly sure it was Tabari I'd seen, but I was less than a block now from home, and if it really had been him, I wouldn't call *that* coincidence, either. I'm going to find something at my house, I thought, and walked a bit faster.

I was right. I saw the two police cars and the ambulance from half a block away, and as I neared the house, its front door opened and two dark-uniformed men came out, awkwardly carrying by its straps a body bag.

Who? *Robinson* flashed through my mind, but, of course, he was home in Los Angeles with Doreen.

There was no one in residence here. Except me. The body bag was carried over to the ambulance, and I went up the stoop to talk to a uniformed cop in a parka standing guard outside my closed front door. He gave me an extreme fisheye as I came up, not recognizing me, clearly believing I was a reporter or worse, and before I could say a word he told me, "Nothing's going on, pal, just keep walking."

"Well, no," I said. "I live here."

He frowned, but then his suspicion switched to astonishment. "Jesus Christ, it's you!" he yelled.

"Always has been."

I would have brushed past him to talk to whatever higher-ranking person might be inside, but he preempted me, turning, pushing open the door, yelling into the house, "Sergeant! It's him! He's back!"

"Could I go in there?" I asked.

"Just a second." He didn't make a big show of blocking the doorway, but it wouldn't have been easy to get around him. And standing still, wearing over my California clothing only the light topcoat which was all I'd had waiting at Anita's place, I became aware of just how cold it actually was.

I said, "What's going on here?"

That surprised him for some reason. "You tell me," he said, and a woman's voice behind him said, "Okay, let him in."

The cop moved over and I crossed my threshold to find in my hallway a short woman of about thirty with extremely pale blond hair and a round, snub-nosed face. She was wide-hipped, in black slacks and a bulky rose-colored sweater, with her badge ID clipped to the sweater above the left breast. "Sergeant Shanley," she introduced herself.

"Sam Holt," I said. There was some sort of sharp a metallic odor in the air, faintly familiar.

"I know who you are," she said, sounding impatient, but mixed with some kind of excitement—not at meeting a TV star, something else, something similar to that sharp odor. "So you got away from them, did you?" she said. "That's great. Come on in here and tell us all about them."

27

SERGEANT SHANLEY WAS VERY disappointed when it turned out I hadn't been kidnapped after all. It made the case both less interesting and more puzzling. If those guys hadn't made off with me, what the hell had they been after?

Once it was established that I'd spent last night somewhere other than at home—Sergeant Shanley gave me the look of a den mother catching a cub scout cheating with his knots—I at last found out what was going on around here. I have two alarm systems in this house, including a silent alarm that phones the precinct farther west on Tenth Street. At seven-ten this morning that alarm had gone off, and the first patrol car to respond had been fired upon. Back-up cars had arrived, shots were exchanged, four panes of glass in my living room windows were broken, and the residual smell of gunfire was what I'd noticed when I'd first come in.

After a while no more firing had come from the house, and the police had approached it to find the front door jimmied open, the other alarm system short-circuited, the rear door to the garden standing open, and the house apparently empty. At that point they'd found out the name of the owner—me—and called my house in Bel Air, where Robinson, awakened from sleep at what was for him five in the morning, had naturally told them I was in New York.

Thus they'd decided it was a celebrity kidnapping and that I'd been taken away out the back.

In the meantime a normal search of the house had produced a dying man in a second-floor closet. The police return fire had apparently got him, hitting him in the lung. Abandoned or forgotten by his friends, he had hidden away in the closet, and now he was drowning in his own blood. He'd carried no identification and was already terminally unconscious when he was found. An ambulance had been called, but the man was dead before it got there, and was being carried out when I arrived; a swarthy white male, approximately twenty-five years of age, with black hair and black moustache, wearing ordinary workclothes except that the shirt was French.

It was clear this wasn't an ordinary burglary; the police estimated half a dozen men inside my house during the gunfight. Nothing appeared to have been taken, nothing searched or disturbed except as a result of the breaking in and the shooting. It had been reasonable to assume a kidnapping. But if it wasn't a kidnapping, what was it?

That was Sergeant Shanley's question, and I was sorry I couldn't help her. That is, I was sorry I *could* help her but wouldn't. Because this had to be Ross's friends again, of course, up to who knew what. Maybe kidnapping had actually been their idea, in which case it was a damn good thing I'd stayed with Anita last night. (It was anyway, it always was, but this added a reason.)

And what did all this mean about my friend from the plane, Hassan Tabari? Had that been him in the taxi, leaving the scene of the crime? Was he a part of the group around Ross? What had he wanted from me on the plane, anyway? Every day, it seemed, when it came to Ross and his tame lions, I knew less and less about more and more.

Once I was filled in I asked permission to call Robinson, who would be very worried right now. "I'll be right here," Sergeant Shanley told me, and I went upstairs to call from the office.

They hadn't been upstairs at all, or at least there was no trail left, unlike the first floor. Only the dead man, who'd left a few blood drops along the way, nothing more. I phoned Robinson, who so forgot himself that he actually sounded pleased to hear from me: "Where *are* you? Are you all right?"

"I'm fine, I'm at the house."

"But the police—"

"Yes, they're here. I spent the night with Anita."

That changed things. Robinson's loyalty to Bly Quinn is so total that he can't bring himself to think anything good of Anita at all. When we're in residence in the East, he's stony-faced and monosyllabic every time he's in her presence, and now there was a sudden distinct chill in his voice when he said, "Yes, I might have known."

"Poo," I told him. "You *should* have known. How's Doreen?"

"Asleep," he said, still chilly. "It's quite early here, you know."

"All right, Robinson, I just wanted to tell you everything's fine."

"Well, hardly that," he said, then decided to forgive me again. "Thank you for calling."

"Sure," I said, and broke the connection, and phoned Walter, the contractor who's overseen all the work I've done on this place. I told his answering machine about my broken windows, jimmied door, and spoiled alarm and asked him to take care of it before a whole lot of people moved into my place in my absence. Then I phoned Morton Adler, my New York attorney, and told his secretary I might be a few minutes late for the discovery proceeding, but would get there as soon as possible. Then I went back downstairs to chat with Sergeant Shanley, whose first name was Maureen, though she didn't encourage me to use it.

A second plainclothesman was in my living room now, a gloomy narrow-shouldered fortyish man introduced as Clifford. After how-do-you-do he said absolutely nothing, but merely sat and observed while Sergeant Shanley and I talked.

During my years on *Packard*, the absolutely most frequent problem we had with scripts could be summed up in the question, "Why didn't he call the police?" A story line that would seem perfectly reasonable and acceptable when the writer pitched it in the office would crumble in your hands once it had been laid out in a script, and you could see the only reason for the protagonist not to call the cops was that it would end the story right there. And *particularly* if in the story line somebody were trying to kill the protagonist, the question would always be "Why didn't he call the police?" Sometimes the writer would find another way to do it, but more often than not it would turn out to be a script we couldn't use, though, of course, having assigned it, we had to pay for it.

I remembered all that now as I sat down to talk with Sergeant Shanley and Clifford. People had broken into my house at an hour when they might have expected to find me home, which meant they had plans for me I wouldn't like, whether kidnapping or murder or whatever. I didn't even have to call the police; they were right here. So why didn't I tell them what I knew?

Here's what I could have said: "A writer friend of mine is being blackmailed by a very brutal ruthless gang of people, but he wants to stay with them because he thinks he can write a best seller about them. He squeezed a promise out of me not to break his story prematurely.

Knowing that I'm aware of them, they did try to kill me once, but failed, and now the story is they'll leave me alone because of the promise I gave my friend. They planted a guy on the plane coming in with me yesterday, though I'm not sure why, and I think I just saw that same guy this morning. I don't have any idea why they broke into this house. I've discussed this situation with sheriff's deputies in Los Angeles and have lied to them and with-held information."

Which was the very first sticking point, even before my absurd promise to Ross. I hadn't called Ken and Chuck, the deputies in L.A., once I'd figured out the truth because I'd wanted to give Ross a chance first to get out from under. It had grown from there, each step temporary, each one seem-ing like the right thing to do at that particular time, until by now I'd dug myself a hole that was going to be very tricky to get out of.

What if I told the whole story—or as much of the con-fusing mishmash of a story as I knew—to Sergeant Shanley, here in New York? One of her first moves would be to get in touch with Ken Donaldson and Chuck Nulty out in Los Angeles, and that would put their noses out of joint a whole hell of a lot. I'd lied to them, I'd stymied their investigation, and now I was going three thousand miles away to tell the truth to cops in *New York*. There were a number of serious legal difficulties Ken and Chuck could make for me if they wanted to, and they would definitely want to.

So. At each stage along the way there'd been a different answer to the question, "Why didn't he call the police?" and now we'd probably reached the most ridiculous reason of all: I wasn't telling the police the truth because I hadn't told the police the truth.

And Sergeant Shanley, in her own way, was as sharp as

Ken and Chuck. She said, "The house has been empty how long?"

"About two months."

"And you just came back to New York last night?"

"Yes."

"Was this a spur-of-the-minute trip," she asked, "or planned?"

"Planned for about three weeks," I told her. "I'm involved in a lawsuit; and I had to come back for the defendant's discovery proceeding."

"What lawsuit?"

So I told her about the unauthorized use of Packard in drawings of my own recognizable person, and our ongoing suit, and she wanted to know everything I knew about the comic book company. Clifford took notes while Shanley kept watching my face both during her questions and my answers. Finishing with the lawsuit, she said, "I understand you were a cop yourself once, out on the island."

"Mineola, year and a half, mostly auto patrol."

"So how does this thing look to you?"

"You mean the coincidence?"

She grinned. She wasn't a pretty woman, but there was a buoyancy and a quickness to her that were appealing. She said, "The day you come back to town, this one house in the whole block is hammered."

"The comic book company didn't send people to hit me, if that's what you think."

She raised an eyebrow. "They didn't? You're sure?"

"They aren't a fly-by-night outfit," I said. "They've been around for years. They're very cheap and schlocky, bottom of their market, but they're businessmen, not mafiosi. At any one time they've probably got two or three ongoing suits; they settle as late as they can for as little as they can. What we're doing here is tying them up and costing them money and letting all the *other* schlock outfits know we won't be messed with."

"So it's just a coincidence, is that right?"

I shook my head. "You'll have to ask the guys that did it."

She didn't like that answer; it smacked of the smartass. Compressing her lips, she said, "How many people knew you were making the trip?"

"Dozens. Household, friends, agent, lawyer, I don't know how many people. It wasn't a secret."

She nodded, thinking it over, and then said, "How long you plan to stay?"

"I have a seat on the one P.M. flight back."

That startled her. "Today?"

"The only reason I have to be here is to be questioned by the other guy's lawyer." I looked at my watch. "Forty minutes from now."

"Where?"

"Graybar Building, next to Grand Central."

"We'll get you there," she promised. "If we needed you, could you stick around a little longer, a few more days?"

"If absolutely necessary," I said. "But I'd rather not."

She nodded, and finally glanced at Clifford, who closed up his notebook. Shanley said to me, "If you don't mind, while I make a couple phone calls, I'd like you to go over the house with Clifford, see if anything's been taken or tampered with."

"I haven't noticed anything missing."

"Or tampered with," she repeated. "This floor and your office are clean, but we don't know what those clowns had in mind, do we? Maybe all they wanted was to rig a booby trap somewhere."

"Oh." That hadn't occurred to me.

"So let Clifford open everything first, all right?"

"Absolutely," I said.

Clifford rose, so I rose. Shanley said, "Okay if I use your phone?"

"Of course."

Clifford led the way out of the room and up. We started at the top of the house and worked our way down, Clifford being brief but efficient. On the way up he'd murmured, "I used to like your show," and I'd said, "Thank you," but that was the extent of our chitchat. And from top lumber room to bottom lap pool, we found nothing. The mess the invaders had made on the ground floor, the few drops of blood from the dying man (who'd done most of his bleeding internally); that was it.

Shanley was off the phone when we met her again in the living room, Clifford looking at her and shaking his head. Shanley said to me, "You got a limo coming?"

"I was planning to grab a taxi over on Sixth."

"We'll drive you," she said.

"Thank you."

"That way we can talk in the car and you won't be late." She gave me an opaque look and a flat smile. "And if anything occurs to you," she said, "we'll be right there."

28

SHANLEY KNEW SOMETHING was wrong, that was clear enough. I could tell she believed I was probably in a position to give her more than I had, but she didn't push it. They had other lines they could work from: the corpse of the one invader, whatever fingerprints the others might have left behind, whatever trail through backyards and other buildings they'd made in their getaway, whatever witnesses might come forward who'd seen them either coming or going. She didn't have a handle on my back, and she knew it, so she wouldn't waste time or embarrass herself by trying to get me to tell her things I apparently wanted to keep to myself.

But if she ever did get a handle on my back, I could expect Sergeant Maureen Shanley to give one hell of a yank. That was understood.

Their car was a battered and rusty pale green Plymouth Fury, unmarked on the outside but with police radio and other equipment on the inside, including a red flasher that could be suction-cupped to the roof when needed. It wasn't needed this time; we were making good time up Madison Avenue and around Forty-sixth Street to Lexington and down to the Graybar Building. The sky was dirty white with unfallen snow, but the streets were mostly clean. Shanley drove, with me beside her and the silent Clifford in back, and she assured me they'd keep a policeman on the door of my house until my guy Walter had come to repair the damage.

Both sets of lawyers, mine and the comic book people's, had offices in the Graybar, my guy Morton Adler on the twenty-third floor and their firm on twenty-nine. I met Morton in his office, and while we waited for an elevator I told him about the attack on my house during my absence last night and the cops' suspicion that the comic book people might have been behind it. Morton expressed amusement his usual way, by smiling shyly at the floor and nodding several times, and then the elevator came and we joined the three widely various people already in it, and rode on up.

Morton, a short and stocky man in his mid-fifties, with a neat round head crosshatched by thin but still black hair, looks mostly like a social science professor in a college somewhere within the city—maybe in Brooklyn. He moves slowly, and reacts thoughtfully, and knows an astonishing number of things. He doesn't have the smoothness and easy affability of Oscar Cooperman, my lawyer on the Coast, but New York doesn't much prize smoothness and affability anyway; a combination of traditional learning and quick street smarts is the winner here, and Morton has it.

Coming out of the elevator on twenty-nine, Morton said to me, "Slip that in."

"What?"

"The police suspicion," he said as we walked down the corridor. "Don't make a major point of it, and don't act at all as though you thought there was anything to it. Just slip the story into one of your answers, that your house was broken into last night, there was gunplay with the police, one fellow's dead, and the police took a great interest in our lawsuit." He nodded at the floor, chuckling to himself. "They'll become very nervous," he said.

"But they didn't do it," I pointed out. "They're innocent."

"That's why they'll be nervous," he told me. "They won't have the first idea how to deal with innocence."

29

IT DID MAKE THEM NERVOUS, too, and was probably responsible for the proceeding being rather shorter than anticipated. The company's legal position was that *Packard* was no longer a commercially active property but had fallen into a commonality of use, like cartoon characters based on W. C. Fields or a trenchcoated Humphrey Bogart, or like that ubiquitous smile face in a yellow circle that shows up everywhere. Our contention was that *Packard* was still actively in syndication and earning profits for its owners— including me—whose income would be put at risk if we didn't protect our rights.

As to *Packard* being a moribund creation, my job was to testify that I was still identified in the public mind with the character—God help me, that was true enough—and that it was still potentially a current vehicle. Furthering that idea, I somewhat unfairly brought out Danny Silvermine's scripts, explaining the idea of presenting them as dinner theater without expressly stating that I intended to do any such thing. This item pleased Morton and distressed the opposition almost as much as the invasion of my house, and when the two attorneys questioning me—decent, methodical men, doing their mundane nit-picking job—decided they'd had enough, Morton chuckled his way down the corridor from their offices, nodding at the floor, and saying, "A very nice touch, those little plays. Brilliant idea."

"They happen to be legit," I told him. "Though I'm probably not going to do them."

Slowly, he shook his head at me, an elfin sparkle in his eyes. "Sam, Sam," he said. "Why don't you let me go on thinking of you as brilliant?"

"Because I wouldn't be able to maintain it," I said.

Ralph and the limo were not due to pick me up until eleven forty-five, an hour away, so Morton suggested we go down to the bar in Grand Central for a celebratory Bloody Mary, since he now believed the opposition's attorneys would soon convince their clients to settle the case instantly, before it cost them any more wasted dollars. I said that sounded like a fine idea.

We had to stop by Morton's office first, for him to touch base with his secretary, and while we were there I said, "Morton, I bet you could help me with something."

"Something new?"

"Very new. I want to know if there's actually an emirate along the Arabian Gulf called Dharak, and if so, is there a Minister of Justice there named Hassan Tabari. And if both exist, what do we know about them."

He gave me a puzzled look. "I cannot begin to think of a context for you in which such a question would arise."

"And yet, there it is."

He studied me a few seconds longer, realized I didn't intend to explain my interest, shrugged his acceptance, and said, "Well, come in, let's see what we can find out."

Morton is one of four partners in this small but good firm, and he won the Sloppiest Office award for so many years in a row, it was finally retired; or maybe it's in his office somewhere, under something. Now, while he went nodding and thinking to sit behind his desk, I removed from a chair three newspapers, a law book, some mail, and two copies of a contract, put them atop the mountain of stuff already on the library table, and sat.

"Well," Morton said slowly, tapping his cheek, "there is one fellow I know. I know him socially, his summer place is up near mine, in Danbury. Near Danbury. He's South African, something with the United Nations, employed there, I think in public relations. He might be our man."

"I knew you'd know somebody."

"Let's not be hasty," he warned me, and turned to brood briefly at the telephone. He can be maddeningly slow, Morton, but eventually it all works out. Now, having assured himself that he remembered what a telephone was for and that he knew how to operate it, he reached forward to lift the receiver. Punching out the number, he leaned back in his swivel chair and studied me owlishly over the receiver while he waited, finally saying, "Tony Georgens, please." Then he waited again, nodding, looking at me, tapping his desktop with his free hand. This was a longer wait, and then he said the same thing again, "Tony Georgens, please," this time adding, a few seconds later, "Morton Adler." A short wait and he said, "Tony? Morton here. I'm fine, thanks. Tony, I have an old friend in my office who has a question you just might be the man to answer. His name is Sam Holt. Yes, that's the one, I'll put him on."

So saying, Morton leaned forward, extending the receiver to me, the coiled cord sweeping a small avalanche of papers to the floor. While Morton clucked at himself and went down on hands and knees to rescue it all, I said into the phone, "Mr. Georgens?"

"I was a *huge* fan of *Packard*," said an English-accented voice. "One of the very few intelligent shows on the air. I was devastated when it went off."

"Well, thank you very much."

"I don't suppose you were, though," he said. "Time to go on to other things, eh?"

You bet; and past time. "That was mostly it," I agreed. "How can I help you?"

Red-faced from effort, Morton was getting off his knees and back into his swivel chair, papers rescued: I said into the phone, "I understand there's an Arab country called Dharak."

"Ah, yes," he said. "One of the noncrucial Trucials."

"Their Minister of Justice is, I believe, called Hassan Tabari."

"If you say so."

"You wouldn't know him."

"I wouldn't know anyone on the domestic side. I do know their fellow at the U.N., not very well."

"Well, uh…" I didn't know exactly how to present the problem. "What kind of country is it?"

"Dry, I expect," he said. "Sandy. Small. I'm not sure what your question is."

"Neither am I, I guess. I think I want to know, well, their politics?"

"They are Arabs," he said, "and OPEC members. They are anti-Israel but pro-Western. Essentially, they link themselves with Kuwait more than with anybody else."

"So they're— what is it called? Moderates."

"Ahhh," he said as though this were a very prickly word indeed I'd just sent down the telephone line to him. "Moderates. Within the Arab context, yes. They are opposed to the fundamentalists in Lebanon and Iran and Libya and so forth. They like western movies and western clothing. On the other hand, they still have public whippings for various crimes, their women are limited to being household objects, and they haven't forsworn the clitorectomy."

"Okay," I said. "I think I have the picture. Thanks a lot."

"Any time," he assured me. "And when you come out with a new series or a movie or whatever you're doing, be sure to tell Morton, so he can alert me."

"I definitely will," I promised, and hung up, and said to Morton, "A nice fellow."

He nodded. "Why," he asked me, "don't you want to tell me the reason for your interest?"

I looked at my watch. "My driver will be here in fifty minutes," I said.

He sighed, shook his head, got to his feet, then paused to frown at me again.

"Just promise me one thing," he said.

"If I can."

"That it isn't love," he said. "Promise me you aren't considering running off with this Minister of Justice's daughter or some such thing."

Laughing in surprise, I said, "That much I can promise. And now, come on, I need that drink. I just found out my *lawyer* is a romantic."

30

A NICE YOUNG GIRL in the airline's blazer was about to preboard me, when my name was paged on the public address system. "Pick up the white courtesy telephone, please." I said to the airline girl, "That's me. Where's the white courtesy telephone?"

"Over here."

It was behind the check-in station, mounted on the wall next to a fire extinguisher in a little niche behind glass. I picked it up, listened to buzzing and a click, and then a female voice said, "May I help you?"

"I think so," I said. "I'm Sam Holt, you just paged me."

"One moment, please."

I waited. Beside me, the airline girl's smile was losing some of its crease; she looked at her watch, then pretended she hadn't. So far I was still a preboarder, and the regular boarding was being held up.

The same voice came back. "There's a phone call for you from Los Angeles. The gentleman is named Ross Ferguson. Will you talk with him?"

Ross? What was so urgent? What was happening? "Yes, I will," I said.

"Hold on, please, we'll switch him. If nothing happens in a minute or two, hang up, and we'll call you back at that station when we've reconnected."

How perilous she made it all sound. "That's what I'll

154

do," I agreed, and there was a click and silence. I turned to the airline girl, saying, "This is a phone call from L.A. Maybe you shouldn't wait for me."

Which gave her an opportunity to look overtly at her watch. "No, that's fine, Mr. Holt," she said. "We still have plenty of time. When your call is done—"

Ross's voice said in my ear, "Hello? Sam?"

"I'll be over there by the door."

"Fine. Thanks." The girl walked away, and I said into the phone, "Ross? What's up?"

"Listen, Sam," he said. He sounded tense but zapped up, convincing himself he was on top of things. What he was on top of, in fact, was the tiger. He said, "There's a question here."

"Yeah?" His friends had a question, was that what he meant?

He said, "When you flew back there yesterday, uh, who was in the seat beside you?"

"Why?"

"Sam, do you mind? Is it a big *secret*, for Christ's sake?"

His control was beginning to crack. "I'm wondering the same thing myself," I told him. "He said his name was Hassan Tabari, and he's supposed to be Minister of Justice in someplace called Dharak."

"How come he was in that seat?"

"Why don't you ask your pals? I think the thing was a set-up, but I don't know what the hell *for*."

"What did you talk about?"

"'Not much, that's why I can't figure out why he wanted to be there. He mostly read magazines, did the whole puzzle in *The Atlantic*. He told me he'd been talking with the L.A. police about a couple of his countrymen—what would they be, Dharakians?"

"Who gives a shit, Sam? What about them?"

"He said they'd been charged with bank robbery in L.A., and the reason he went out there was to find out if it connected with anything at home. He said it didn't. And he was coming to New York to talk with his guy at the U.N., I don't know about what."

"Why do you say it was a set-up?"

"They preboarded me. In fact, Ross, these people here would very much like to preboard me *now*, so if you could figure out why you're calling, I'd appreciate it. Anyway, they preboarded me, and he was already there, ahead of everybody. When it turned out he was an Arab from some dinky little Gulf state, I figured it had to be connected with your buddies somehow. Why, what's happening? A falling out among the troops?"

"Sam, you just don't know the situation here."

"That's true. I wish I did know it. Is there anything else?"

"Hold on."

The lion tamer went off to get instructions from his lions. I smiled across at the airline girl, giving her an encouraging nod and holding up one finger: just one minute more. She smiled back, also nodding, letting me know everything was just fine and she'd really appreciate it if I'd get my ass in gear.

"Thanks, Sam." Ross again. "Have a nice flight."

"You too," I said, but he was gone.

31

WHO WAS TABARI? I brooded that question most of the flight back. I had no seatmate at all this time, so I sprawled my legs over the entire area, ignored the movie, picked at the lunch, drank a lot of club soda, and tried to fit Tabari into the picture.

Ross had told me the Barq people represented a Middle East nation, that they were there in his house because it would give them access to a place where a person would be that they meant to kidnap and take back home for a show trial. Maybe that was the truth, or maybe Ross just thought it was the truth, or maybe Ross was lying to me and the scheme was something else entirely. But if it were true, would the Middle East nation be Dharak? And was Tabari a part of the scheme, or was he allied with the person they meant to kidnap? A Minister of Justice would be very involved in a major political show trial.

But would a "moderate" nation engage in murder quite as casually as these people? Even if in many ways Dharak was a backward and brutal country, the description Morton's friend had given me just didn't fit the style of Ross's companions.

So maybe the person to be kidnapped was from Dharak, but the kidnappers were from a different, wilder place, fundamentalists planning to put a moderate on trial in a public way. Judging by that strange phone call just now from Ross, Tabari wasn't an ally of those people after all; it seemed as though it worried them that I'd been talking with the man. So maybe he was on the good guys' side, if there was a good guys' side. Or maybe I didn't know enough of the story to figure out good guys from bad. Can't tell the players without a program.

All I accomplished, finally, in the five-hour flight, was to muddle my brain entirely, so that I was glad when it was over and I walked out to three P.M. California sunlight, the topcoat from Anita's place over my arm, the attaché case in my other hand. At the end of the ramp down which the passengers were shunted were several chauffeurs and messengers holding up pieces of paper or cardboard with handwritten names; among them stood a tall, light-toned young black man in tan suit and yellow shirt and brownish figured tie, showing a piece of letterhead stationery with the word *Holt* written on it. I went over to him, saw that the letterhead was from CNA, and said, "I'm Sam Holt."

"Yes, sir," he said, grinning, happy with life. "I recognized you. I'm Toby Packer from the agency, I have your car."

"Fine."

It was my station wagon, which I'd left at CNA yesterday when I took the limo instead with Zack and Danny Silvermine. Toby Packer led me to where he'd parked it in the loading zone outside. Rank does have its privileges. I said, "Can I give you a lift back to the office?"

"Not if it's out of your way, sir."

It was, but what the hell. "Get in," I said. On the drive to Century City, Toby Packer cheerfully told me about himself. He was a recent UCLA graduate—film school, I guessed, though he didn't say so exactly—working as an assistant agent with CNA, but clearly with larger plans for the future. A very smooth kid, he worked me with assurance and aplomb because, as we both knew, the day might come when he would be in a position to hire me or represent me or negotiate with me. At this early stage of his career, the best thing he could do with every meeting was try to leave a good impression.

I dropped him off at the agency, then headed home, deciding to go in the front way this time, just to see who, if anybody, was hanging around. Joggers thumped along the verges of Sunset Boulevard, most of them emerging from the lunar city of UCLA off to the right. Do joggers realize that what they are doing is acting out both escape and, through their treadmill style, the impossibility of escape?

Leaving them, I made the left turn through the servants' entrance arch into Bel Air, slowly traveled the various Bellagios, and turned into San Miguel without seeing anything suspicious at all. No one seated in a parked car, no pool-company truck—or any other commercial vehicle—stationed with a good view of my house or street, nobody walking their dog back and forth over the same route. Not even any joggers.

At the end of San Miguel stood my rough stone wall and chain link gate, which opened to my buzzed command. Sugar Ray and Max came bounding downslope to greet me, and I stopped to let them into the car. They enjoy climbing back and forth over the seats, wagging their tails, bumping into each other and into me. I let them do it on the property, but they know they have to settle down once we're on a public street. With them gamboling and frisking, I drove on up to the house, put the station wagon away, reaffirmed to the dogs our good relationship, and went into the kitchen, where I found a very worried-looking Robinson. "I don't know if I did right," he said.

I looked around, but I already knew from his expression that it didn't have anything to do with this kitchen, that

it was something more serious than a problem with lunch—
one too many quiches, or whatever. It wouldn't be that.
"Tell me about it," I said.

"Miss Doreen seemed to think there was nothing
wrong," he said.

"Doreen?" I lifted my head, as though to hear her
somewhere deeper in the house. "Where is she?"

"Well, that's the problem. She's gone."

32

IT SEEMED ROSS HADN'T BEEN deceived after all by my saying I'd sent Doreen east. She'd received a phone call around ten this morning, which would be just after Ross had talked to me at JFK. Then she told Robinson she'd be leaving soon, someone would come around to pick her up. They arrived half an hour later, a pair of tough guys so thuggish that Robinson began to have his doubts, but by that time it was too late. They were on the property, Doreen was packed, and she was willing to leave with them. From Robinson's description, they were more of the crowd from Barq Pool Service, though they'd arrived in an ordinary automobile.

"It was brown or green or something like that," he said, getting a little pettish. "Does it make any difference?"

"None," I told him. "You didn't have any choice, so don't worry about it."

"I *didn't* have any choice, and I *do* worry about it."

So did I. In the first place, I didn't like it that any of those people had been on the property, and in the second place, I was pretty sure Doreen had made a mistake going back to Ross, which was where I assumed she'd gone.

So I phoned him, and got his service, and left a message: "Tell him it's Sam Holt, and he has fifteen minutes to call me back before I make my other phone call."

The fellow at the service was dubious: "I'm not sure I'll hear from him that soon, Mr. Holt."

"Well, that's his problem, isn't it?"

It was barely five minutes later that he called back, sounding worried and innocent. "Sam? I thought we had everything worked out."

"Doreen," I said.

"Hey, buddy, what do you want with *her*? Aren't you and Bly still pals?"

"The last time *your* pals saw Doreen they gang-raped her."

A little shocked silence, then, "No, come on. Sam? Where'd you get that idea?"

"From her. She said she didn't tell you because she didn't want to put you in any impossible situations."

"Sam, buddy, I could wish you had the same attitude. I mean, maybe, talking to you, she was dramatizing for effect, you know what I mean?"

"Are you saying she lied to me, Ross?"

He sighed, long-suffering. "Sam, listen. Whatever happened in the past—and if that's true, what you said, I feel rotten about it, I really do—but whatever happened in the past, it's the past, it's over and done with; there won't be anything, anything else."

"Why do you need Doreen there?"

"I told the troops that was gonna upset you, I *told* them."

"Why do you need her, right in the middle of the trouble?"

"Because she's a loose end, Sam," he said, exasperated. "Because *you* took her away, and the guys here know it, and that means maybe she knows as much as you do, without promising to keep her mouth shut. So the best thing is, she comes and shares my bed and board again for a while."

"Let me talk to her," I said.

"Christ on a crutch, Sam, you're making me sorry I ever asked your help in the first place!"

"Ross, let me talk to Doreen."

"You don't have to, dammit. What are you gonna do, try and talk her into leaving? Ask her if she's got enough towels? She came here of her own free will, Sam, you've got to know that. Ask your man Robinson."

"Let me talk to Doreen."

"Next week. After this is all over, we'll all have a nice celebration dinner, the four of us, you and Bly and Doreen and me. You want Chasen's, or you want Ma Maison?"

"I want to talk to Doreen."

"Sam, I won't let you upset her. Just forget the whole thing," he said, and hung up.

The bastard. The stupid, arrogant, self-centered bastard. Why did Doreen go back to him? Was it because I turned her down yesterday morning? Maybe she was embarrassed, or irritated, or just simply bored. The *Packard* tapes must have been fairly cold comfort.

Now, wait a minute. *I* wasn't the heavy here, the villain making all the trouble. That was Ross, who should have known better than to draw the girl right back into the very middle of all the trouble.

Answers to questions never seem to come to me when I concentrate on them and rack my brains. Now, thinking about Doreen, not thinking about New York at all, I suddenly saw why those people had broken into my house and what it meant about which side Tabari was on.

Tabari's presence troubled them; therefore he was on the other side. It troubled them enough to have them make Ross phone me even before I got on the plane, to find out what was going on. They'd been listening in, obviously, and what would have happened if they hadn't liked my answers? Would the plane have blown up? I wouldn't put it past them.

But that would have been their *second* effort to find out what was going on. You could trust these people, every time, to shoot first and ask questions later. Their first idea had been to break into my house while I was asleep and ask me, as the British say, with menaces. Only when that hadn't worked had they gone for the gentler route.

They *liked* to be activists, these people.

I prowled my house, restless, my mind a jumble of Tabari and Doreen and Ross and the people from Barq and some unknown person who was to be kidnapped and put on trial somewhere in the Middle East.

Was Tabari the person to be tried?

Entering my bedroom, I stood by the window and looked out at the pool, gleaming in sunlight. A brief cloud went over, and then there was sunlight again.

Doreen, swimming back and forth in that water out there, a lithe fish in the sunlight, fleeing from sharks when the clouds came by.

I sat on the edge of the bed. With one hand I reached for the phone, while the other hand opened the bedside table drawer and pulled out that folded piece of paper.

Ken Donaldson's phone number.

33

TOOK NOTES WHILE CHUCK simply watched my mouth as I talked. It was four-thirty in the afternoon, and we sat out on the lawn in the sporadic sunshine, the house spread whitely on one side and the land dropping away toward Thurston Circle on the other. Max and Sugar Ray, having been assured by me and by their own sense of smell that the deputies were all right, lay on the grass beside us, listening, hoping for something nice to happen. Neither Ken nor Chuck interrupted me, and when I was finished, Ken said, "I must admit, Mr. Holt, I have trouble figuring out how your mind works."

I didn't like that retreat from California first-nameitis. I said, "What do you mean?"

"You're saying you lied to us. You're saying you lied to the New York police. You're saying you covered up a murder. Two days ago, when all you wanted to report was an attempt on your life, you insisted on having your attorney present. Today, when you want to confess to three felonies, maybe more, you're willing to talk to us alone."

"When this all started," I said, "I wasn't sure you'd take me seriously."

"If you'd told us all this, we would have."

"I didn't make the connection, not right away. Ross showed me that tape over three months ago."

Chuck said, "Sir, do you believe there was an actual murder on the tape?"

"Not exactly," I said. "I think the scene was faked, but the girl at the end was very dead."

Chuck nodded. "And you believe the man on the tape who looked like your friend wasn't your friend."

"That's right. I'm pretty sure now he was this actor who just died, Beau Sheridan."

Ken said, "Is there a phone I could use?"

"In private?"

He smiled thinly. "If I needed privacy," he said, "I'd go to the car and call in. In fact, I'd prefer you present."

"Sure," I said, and raised my voice: "Robinson!" When he appeared in the back doorway I called, "Could we have the phone, please?" He nodded, and went away.

While we waited, Chuck said to Ken, "I'm trying to think who's coming to town next week." To me he said, "He told you it was next week, right?"

"He said everything would be over just about a week from now."

"Tuesday or Wednesday, next week." Chuck frowned at his partner again. "Anybody special you can think of?"

Ken shook his head. "This town is always full of big names. That doesn't narrow it."

"Middle East," Chuck said. "Arabs or something, from Sam's description. Maybe they're after Omar Sharif." I was pleased to hear my first name being used again.

Robinson was coming across the lawn with the cordless phone, an item he held in his fingertips to express the disdain he felt for all innovations since about 1952. (Except Cuisinart—that he likes.) Putting the phone in the center of the table, he said, "Will there be anything else?"

"San Pellegrino," I told him. "You gentlemen want Tab?"

"Sure," said Chuck. "Thanks."

"I'll try that water of yours," Ken said. An adventurous sort.

"Certainly," Robinson said, and went away as Ken picked up the phone and dialed.

Chuck said, "Sam, tell me about your pal's house. Who's his next-door neighbor?"

"I don't really know. He's up in the hills in Beverly Hills, a big house, big houses on both sides, some rough ground out back. Hilly, upslope. I don't know how much of it is his, or whose land is next to him up there." I gestured in the direction of Thurston Circle, saying, "Like here. I own a kind of triangle of land down that way, and I couldn't tell you exactly who my neighbors are. You see that Russian olive?"

"That tree down there on the left?"

"That's a couple feet the other side of my boundary line. I have no idea who owns it, maybe that gray house down there, or maybe somebody back up this way on Bellagio."

Meantime, Ken was on the phone, talking quietly, and now he said, "Hold on," and turned to me, saying, "Delia West. Was she married or single?"

"Divorced, I think," I said. "She used to be married to a stuntman."

"Was West her married name?"

"Yeah. He was Eddie."

"Was?"

"No, not like that," I said. Robinson was coming out with our liquids, on a tray, in two bottles and a can, with three ice-cube-filled glasses. "So far as I know he's still alive. I just meant I haven't seen him since the show went off the air."

"All right. Was it Edward? Edwin?"

"Sorry, I don't know. His guild could tell you."

"Thanks," he said, and went back to his conversation on the phone as Robinson arrived and poured for us all. He didn't mind Chuck drinking Tab so long as no food of his own preparation was involved.

"I guess it's like the hostages," Chuck said, watching Robinson pour.

I frowned at him. "What is?"

"The Americans in Iran, that whole bunch held hostage. They got out, they came back, they wrote a lot of books about it. Probably that's what your pal is thinking. All he has to do is make it through the rough part, then write a book."

Robinson went away again with the tray. I said, "That's why I almost didn't call you guys, I didn't want to queer Ross's pitch."

Chuck nodded. "A lot of people think that," he said. "They've got a friend, gonna sail his homemade balloon across the Pacific, gonna make just one million-dollar deal with the Colombian drug importers, gonna spray-paint their name on the inside of the polar bear cage. Their friends know they shouldn't do it, but friendship says you gotta leave the guy alone. Ken and me, we're the ones scrape them off the pavement."

I suddenly remembered a few parallel incidents from years ago, back when I was on the force in Mineola. "What a waste," we'd say to each other while the body bag was carried out. "And his pals knew about it. Why didn't they stop him? Why didn't they call us ahead of time?" I was wincingly aware of what Chuck was trying to tell me, and I had absolutely nothing to say.

Ken hung up. He said, "There is no missing persons on anybody called Delia West. The deaths of Beau Sheridan and Michael Olsztyn are considered a straightforward one-car vehicular accident."

"What would they have called my death, yesterday?" I asked him.

He grimaced. "Yes, of course," he said. "That part of the Ventura Freeway where they bought it is raised about fifteen feet above the surrounding area. They were in a Honda Accord belonging to Sheridan. Some bigger heavier vehicle could have just sideswiped them off the highway and through the chain link fence."

"And by the time they land— They crashed through a store roof, didn't they?"

"A 7-11."

"So by then," I said, "the car's so mangled, there's nothing to show what happened to it up on the highway."

Ken drank some of the San Pellegrino. "Very pleasant," he said.

"Refreshing."

"Yes." He was distracted. Putting the half-full glass on the table, he said, "It's time to go see Ross Ferguson. You'll come along, won't you?"

34

THEY LET ME LEAD THE WAY in my own car, for which I was grateful. I'm always uncomfortable in the backseat of a patrol car, where I was a few times, when *Packard* did location shooting. Maybe it's the drop in status, I don't know. The people in the front seat of a patrol car own it, they are native to that world, they have assurance and authority, whereas the people in the backseat are civilians, they're witnesses or victims or whatever, who don't really belong. Having at one time been one of the people in front, I just don't like being the guy in back.

I was in the station wagon again, and this time I'd brought the dogs along, which made them very, very happy. Max, ladylike, sat smiling on the front seat, looking at me sometimes and otherwise studying the world beyond the windshield, while Sugar Ray stood in the cargo area staring out the rear window to be sure the deputies didn't get lost. Once we left Sunset Boulevard and started curving up through the twisty streets of Beverly Hills, Sugar Ray could no longer keep his balance and had to drop onto his stomach, but he still kept an eye on the police car behind us.

"You guys wait here," I said as I parked next to Ross's streetside stone wall. The dogs were used to that command, and made no effort to follow me. Both stood now, and watched through the window.

The first thing I noticed, when I got to Ross's gate, was

that the pool-company van was gone. Or it could merely be out of sight, tucked away in the garage.

Ken and Chuck, having parked behind me, walked over and also looked through the gate. "Big house for a writer," Chuck said.

"Producer-writer," I told him. "Ross has a piece of a couple of series."

"Well, that's not bad."

Ken said, "We got more information on the way over. The reason Sheridan and Olsztyn were together in Sheridan's car, they'd been hired for some sort of job."

"Oh, yes?"

"Not regular movie or TV work," he went on, "not according to Mrs. Sheridan. It was some private job, almost like home movies. She didn't know much about it. But the interesting thing is, Mrs. Sheridan says her husband told her it was the same people he and Olsztyn did some work for last fall."

I said, "Does Mrs. Sheridan know who the employer was?"

"No. Last fall they were paid in cash, so they wouldn't have to pay taxes or union dues."

"And so there'd be no record of the employer," I said.

Ken gestured at the house. "Let's talk to your friend."

"We can try, anyway."

I went to the side of the gate, opened the callbox door, picked up the phone, and pushed the button. I didn't really expect an answer, and was just turning to suggest to the deputies that we try some other method of getting in when there was a click in my ear and Ross's voice said, "Hello?"

"Ross," I said. "It's Sam. Let me in."

"Goddammit, Sam, now what are you up to? After Doreen some more?"

"I want to talk to you, Ross."

"We've talked. We made a deal. For Christ's sake, won't you just sit *tight* until—"

"We have to talk again," I told him. "I have a couple of policemen with me."

There was a quick little intake of breath, and then a brief silence. I could imagine Ross looking like Orson Welles in *The Third Man* when Joseph Cotten told him he'd gone to the police. What was it Welles had said? "Unwise, Holly, unwise."

What Ross said was, "I'll be right down." And there was another click.

I hung up, shut the door, and said, "He's coming down here."

Chuck looked irritated. "He won't let us in," he said.

"Let's wait and see," Ken said.

"I can smell it," Chuck insisted.

So could I. You never entirely forget what it feels like to be a police officer entering someone else's home, where your power and authority are at the most tenuous they ever get. People who want to be mulish and make difficulties can do so there, on their own ground. And why wouldn't Ross want to be mulish and make difficulties?

"Is this him?" Ken asked.

I looked, and it was. Ross never made any attempt to look as though he belonged with that big fake English house, so when he came down the steep driveway in thonged sandals and white jogging shorts and an open Hawaiian shirt of many colors and large dark sunglasses and his usual chains, he didn't look as though he could possibly live in that great Tudor mansion up there behind him. He mostly looked like a remittance man, the owner's raffish cousin, here for a not entirely welcome visit.

He was smiling, but edgily. "Sam," he said as he reached the gate, "what have you done now?"

I said, "Ross Ferguson, these are Deputy Donaldson and Deputy Nulty."

Ken said, "Mr. Ferguson, could we come in for a moment?"

Ross turned the edgy smile his way, saying, "What for? I'm trying to get some work done here."

"We hope you could help us," Ken said.

"With what?"

Chuck said, "Mr. Ferguson, wouldn't it be more civilized to talk without this gate in our faces?"

"Not necessarily," Ross said. "Officers, I have the greatest respect for the law, but I have to tell you, I don't want to take time away from my work—I've got a deadline coming up here, and I don't want to take time away for a lot of nonsense."

Ken said, "Why do you assume it's nonsense?"

"Because you're here with Sam." Ross turned to me, strain lines on his neck, eyes invisible behind his dark glasses. He said, "This is Doreen again, isn't it?"

"You know what it is, Ross."

He turned back to Ken. "Do you know about the collision Sam had the other day?"

"As a matter of fact, we do," Ken told him.

"Well, *I* think," Ross said, "I'm no shrink, but if you want my opinion, it shook him up. Sudden reminders of mortality, all that. He's mixed the whole thing up with a little spat my lady friend and I had, and his theories were getting so wild that when he went away to New York, Doreen came back to *me* rather than put up with it anymore."

It was difficult to keep silent, but I managed. Ken and Chuck were the pros here. It was Chuck who said, "This lady friend—Doreen?—you say she came *back* to you."

"She spent two nights at Sam's house. Didn't he tell you that?"

Ken said, "Where had she been spending her time before then?"

"With me," Ross said.

Chuck nodded at the house up the slope. "Here?"

"For a few months. Then we had a very stupid quarrel and she moved for a while down to my other place in Malibu. That's where Sam found her. Some *National Enquirer* people were hanging around, and he got all upset, saw conspiracies everywhere, and got Doreen so spooked, she went to his place. I ask no questions about how they spent the night, Doreen is over twenty-one, but by this morning she was beginning to think maybe he'd flipped, maybe after all this time he thinks he really is Packard, the great private eye, and he's off to solve mysteries where there aren't any."

"You're going too far, Ross," I said.

He pointed at me a finger that trembled slightly. "*You've* gone too far, Sam, dragging real policemen into your fantasy conspiracies. Making trouble for me—if we weren't such longtime friends, I'd be up at the house right now calling my lawyer to sue your ass from here to China."

Ken said, "Mr. Ferguson, is your lady friend at home?"

"Sure. Why?"

"Maybe we could go up and chat with her, she could confirm your story."

Ross looked exasperated, but then he turned and bellowed, "*Doreen!*"

We all looked up at the house, and there was a dramatic pause. The tiny sound I heard was Ross tapping his foot against the blacktop of his driveway, the sandal doing a muffled *slap-slap*. Then there was movement on the small porch at the near end of the house, and here came Doreen, very slowly, down the drive. She was in sneakers and blue jeans and a short-sleeved high-necked pale blue sweater; somewhat overdressed for the day, but not for the people presumably inside the house. She, too, was hiding her eyes behind large dark sunglasses, but her mouth was strained and sullen and obstinate.

"Come on, Doreen," Ross called, waving an arm to hurry her. "Don't take all day; you know I've got work to do."

It was hard to say what her eyes were doing behind the glasses. Looking at me? At Ross? At the deputies? She said, "Go ahead and work, then. Who's stopping you?"

"Sam is still at it," Ross told her. "For all I know, he told the cops I'd murdered you."

"Only Delia West," I said.

He pretended not to hear that, but I saw him flinch. He said to the deputies, "You have questions? Here she is."

"Mr. Ferguson," Ken said, "I'll ask you again to cooperate. Please let us in so we can conduct this conversation like grown-up human beings."

"Absolutely not," Ross told him. "That just stretches the whole ridiculous thing on for hours. You'll have to go to a judge and get a warrant, and no judge would listen to what Sam has to say and *give* you a warrant. I don't even have to stand here and talk to you."

Chuck said, "Miss, who else is in the house right now?"

Doreen's shoulders twitched. She said in a low, unwilling voice, "The cook and the gardener."

I said, "Not the pool cleaners?"

"No," she said, lower than before.

Ross said, "Doreen, did *National Enquirer* people follow Sam to my place in Malibu?"

"Yes."

"Did it rattle him?"

"He fought with the photographer man, knocked him down."

Ken said, "We're not interested in the *National Enquirer*, Mr. Ferguson." That having seemed to me irrelevant, I hadn't mentioned the *National Enquirer* to the deputies, and I was glad they weren't interested in being sidetracked by it.

"All right," Ross said to Ken. "You don't care about the *National Enquirer*. I don't care about *any* of this. Doreen, did Sam fill you full of conspiracy theories?"

"Yes." Barely audible.

"Did you come back here of your own free will?"

"Yes."

"Do you want to go back with Sam?"

"No."

"All right, then." Ross glared in triumph at the deputies and spread his hands. "*I* can't think of anything else to talk about. Good day to you. And Sam," he added, turning his glare in my direction, "when you're in your right mind once again, I may accept your apology." With that he took Doreen by the elbow and they both headed back up the driveway toward the house.

We watched them go. What else was there to do? "Shit," I said as Ross and Doreen disappeared onto the porch. A door slammed up there.

"Well, goddammit," Chuck said.

What an anticlimax. I'm sure the deputies felt it, but I felt it much worse. All of my agonizing over whether or not to call the police, and once I did, what happened? Nothing. A fizzle.

Ken said, "His pals are still inside there, that's for sure."

I said, "You still believe me—good. Thanks for the vote of confidence."

Chuck said, "Are you kidding? Deceit came off that man like body odor."

Ken said, "I'm trying to figure out what sort of complaint you could sign that would get us in there."

Chuck said, "What about, you say he's harboring the people who deliberately tried to run you off the road? Or the ones who broke into your house back in New York?"

Ken shook his head. "Where's his evidence, his probable cause? It's too thin for a judge; Ferguson is right about that part."

I said, "I remember, years ago, back in Mineola, there'd be a situation, nothing to do, and somebody would turn to us, we were the cops, we were the last resort, and they'd say, 'Do something, why don't you do something?' I'm having to bite my tongue to keep from saying the same thing to you guys."

"We'll talk to the B.H. police," Ken said, "ask them to keep a special lookout in this neighborhood. We'll hope to figure out who their target is, the middle of next week, though I'm not hopeful on that. But Sam, you say you've been in our position, so you have to know as well as us what we mainly have to do now."

"Yeah, I do." I looked through the chain link gate at the house, silent and closed. "You have to wait for somebody to break a law," I said.

"That's right."

I shook my head. "I shudder to think," I said, "what law that's going to be."

35

THE DEPUTIES LEFT FIRST, while I took time to give Max and Sugar Ray a walk. I suppose I was hoping that once the official police presence had departed, either Ross or Doreen would come back out to talk to me, but of course they didn't. What would they have to say? Ross had convinced Doreen to go along with his story, and without her to corroborate my version there was just no evidence of wrongdoing on Ross's property, and therefore no way for the deputies—or the Beverly Hills police, this would actually be their jurisdiction—to force their way past the gate. I'd played my last card, I'd effectively closed off communication for good with both Ross and Doreen, and I'd accomplished nothing.

"Come on, guys, let's go home. We've done enough for one day."

Once again, rather than do a lot of backing and filling, I drove on uphill from Ross's house to the next intersection. I was about to turn left there when I noticed that same glint of gold way up to my right that I'd spotted the last time. (*That's* gold, Zack, I thought; your conference room is definitely yellow.) It was some sort of large shallow dome farther uphill, seen obscurely through a filter of scrub pines and other weedy trees, and what it looked most like was the first sight of the flying saucer in a science fiction movie.

Oh, come on, I told myself. The situation with Ross

was ridiculous and melodramatic enough already, I didn't need extraterrestrials as well. But curiosity had me now, and I was in no hurry to get home and face the fact there was nothing left for me to do about Ross, so instead of turning left, downhill, toward Sunset Boulevard, I turned right and drove up past the Dead End sign to see what that golden dome was all about.

One curve from the intersection and I couldn't see it anymore, but it was definitely still up ahead somewhere. A second curve, still climbing, and all at once there was a guard shack and a barrier ahead.

It was exactly like a border post on a small road between two European nations. A small square wooden building painted light green stood beside the road. A long pole, banded in red and white, lay across the road at just about hood height. A black and white police car—Los Angeles County, I thought—and two blue sedans and a white van were parked in a blacktop area behind the little building. As it all came into sight, two uniformed men—one in blue, one in brown—emerged from the building, looking at me through their reflecting sunglasses and resting their right hands on the gunbutts at their sides.

I took my foot off the accelerator, and the Chrysler immediately slowed. Max put her front paws on the dashboard, the better to lean forward and look at this interesting thing, while Sugar Ray climbed over from the storage area to the backseat and stared forward, with the alert expression that means he's thinking of barking.

"Cool it, fellas," I said, and moved my foot toward the brake. There was something just too tense about those guys. I don't ever want to put any officials into the position of having to apologize to my next of kin, so I was prepared right then to stop, shift into reverse, and go back where I came from.

Except that just as I was tapping the brake, one of the uniformed men made a down-patting motion, obviously telling me to stop right there, to go neither forward nor back. So I complied, and even shifted into park. The dogs watched, tensing up a bit themselves, sensing the atmosphere, Max with her nose actually touching the windshield, Sugar Ray edgily moving back and forth on the rear seat, trying to get a better view.

One of the men stayed where he was, well back, in front of the car and a bit to the right. The other one moved off to my left and then came forward. They both kept their hands on their guns.

I pushed the button and my window lowered all the way. Sugar Ray immediately stuck his head into the space, close enough to my left ear to hear him snuffle. "Sugar Ray!" I said sharply. "Sit down!"

They both sat on their haunches, reared up on their stick-straight forelegs, watching with utter intensity.

It was a police uniform this one wore, dark blue, with silver badge. His belt was loaded down with all the gear of a cop; in addition to the gun, there was a walkie-talkie, a large notebook, a pair of handcuffs, and several small black leather pouches. As he approached I said, "Yes, officer?"

"May I help you, sir?"

Never has that question been asked with less good will. The only time I could remember myself ever being that tense on duty was once back in Mineola when a guy had gone berserk and murdered the three people in his immediate family plus two neighbors before barricading himself into his house. My partner Doug Walford and I were the first to respond to the squeal, and when we got out of the patrol car in front of that ordinary suburban house on a hot humid summer day, with a middle-aged woman in a sundress lying facedown dead on the lawn, I felt just about the way this cop here looked.

I'm an actor? Never have I tried so hard to act innocent. "Just taking the dogs for a drive, officer," I said. "I saw that dome up there, wondered what it was."

"Private road from here on, sir," he said. He had made sure to glance at the floor in back, ignoring Sugar Ray.

"There's no sign down at the corner."

"No, sir, there isn't. Just a dead-end sign."

"I suppose that keeps most traffic away," I agreed. "Except rubberneckers like me." I stuck my head partway out the window, wondering if I could see the dome from here. "Mind telling me what that is up there?"

"You could make a U-turn right here, sir," he said. "Just back around, and you can continue on your way."

For an Easterner like me, L.A. cops do seem to over-dramatize a lot, but that's their style and they didn't ask me for a review. "Okay," I said, smiled at him as falsely as he'd been calling me "Sir," and prepared to back up.

"Wait a second," he said.

Now what? I looked back at him, and he was frowning at me. "Aren't you—?""

Good—the salvation once again of having a known face. Taking off my sunglasses so he'd be sure he was right, I said, "Sam Holt. I used to play Jack Packard on television."

"I thought I recognized you." It was astonishing how thoroughly he'd thawed, all at once. He even cracked a small smile before turning to his partner and calling, "It's okay." The partner nodded, but didn't move, and his hand stayed on his gun.

"Sorry to make trouble," I said, put my sunglasses back on, and shifted into reverse.

"That's okay, Mr. Holt. And listen—" I shifted into park, and listened.

"We're keeping it quiet," he said, "to keep the civilians out."

"Uh-huh."

He leaned down, putting both hands on the window-sill. "It's that Arab church," he told me confidentially. "The mosque they just built."

I remembered my lawyer Oscar Cooperman saying something about a new mosque, and he representing a supplier for it. I said, "Why such total security for a church?"

"They've had some threats, I guess," he said. "About a month ago, when they were still building it, some guys tried to get in with a truck supposed to be filled full of Sheetrock; it was full of dynamite instead. Suicide mission, gonna blow up everybody and themselves along with it."

"Good God. Who were they?"

"I dunno. Some other Arabs. They get tough when they're mad at each other." He grinned a bit crookedly. "When we see a car we don't know," he said, "we get a little antsy."

"I guess so. Sorry to shake you up," I said. "I'll take the dogs for a run somewhere else."

"Good idea," he agreed, and with that lack of irony that I'll never entirely get used to in California, "Have a nice day," he said.

36

WELL, NOW I KNEW WHERE the lightning was supposed to strike.

Ross Ferguson's property was on the east side of his street. Up at the next intersection to the north I'd turned right, eastward, into that dead-end road, with the golden dome at the far end of it. Somewhere back up in those scrub woods on the hills there would be an invisible line separating Ross's property from the land belonging to the mosque.

Barq Pool Service—*lightning* in Arabic. And an effort had been made a month ago to destroy that mosque with a suicidal truck bomb. Oscar Cooperman had told me how tight the security had been during the mosque's construction.

This was what Hassan Tabari had been referring to on the plane, the incredible polarization between the fundamentalists and the modernists in the Arab world, with the terrorists and the fanatics here and there in control, with oil money to pay for their adventures.

Oil money to pay for setting Ross Ferguson up. Delia West thrown away as casually as any of the innocent bystanders they'd taken with them over the years. Official or semi-official support and expertise from fundamentalist governments, using spies and secret police well-trained by either the United States or Russia. All the time in the world to make their preparations, money no object and humanity nonexistent.

Who was coming to the opening day ceremonies that the *lightning* people planned to kidnap? A religious figure? A political figure? There was oil money on both sides of the Islamic religious war, and that was undoubtedly oil money being spent up there on that mosque, so would their target be some billionaire sheikh, to be held for ransom to finance more terrorist acts?

On the drive home Max and Sugar Ray soon settled down into their usual traveling mode of eager expectancy. I talked to them, my voice soothing, but what I told them was what I thought Ross had gotten himself— and Doreen, and to some extent me—tied up with. Religious maniacs. Armed professional terrorists. A religious war with roots on the other side of the world. People whose language and ambitions and desires and fears and code of ethics Ross Ferguson couldn't begin to understand. The lion tamer.

I drove in the front way, seeing nothing out of the ordinary. Would Ross's friends put me back on their hit list now that I'd reneged on the agreement, or would they forget me now that I'd proved ineffective? I wouldn't know for a while, would I?

The Volvo was gone. Max and Sugar Ray expressed their pleasure at the outing by racing madly off across the lawn, nipping at each other's shoulders, and I went into the house to ask Robinson about the Volvo and if there was any other news.

There was. "Your friend Ross Ferguson telephoned." It was just after five o'clock, and Robinson was seated in front of the television set in his little lounge in the el of the kitchen, watching the early news. "About five minutes ago," he said.

"He did, did he?" I was both surprised and annoyed; no good could come of another conversation with Ross.

"He said not to attempt to reach him back; he would try here every fifteen minutes until he caught you."

"Okay. Anything else?"

"Miss Quinn telephoned about an hour ago. She, too, will try again. Nothing else of moment." He wanted to get back to the lead story on the news.

I said, "The Volvo's gone."

"Ah, yes. Just after you and the police officers departed"—he wouldn't call them "deputies," as sounding too much like a western movie— "an examiner arrived from the insurance company. I studied his credentials with a great deal of care, I assure you."

"I don't doubt it."

"And he was as claimed. He examined the auto inside and out, started the engine, drove it back and forth, and expressed astonishment that anyone inside the car at the moment of impact could still be alive."

"Well, the impact was spread out over a period of time," I said.

"In any event, he agreed that the vehicle's useful life was at an end, and filled out several documents to that effect, one of which you will find on your desk. Before departure he informed me we need no longer keep the vehicle on the premises, and so I scanned the Yellow pages and found a person willing to take it away. A junk dealer, he's called. He asked me how much money we wanted for the car, and I told him if it could be removed today, no money need change hands at all. Frankly, I had thought it would be up to us to pay for the removal."

"So he came and no money changed hands."

"Exactly. He, too, left a document, which you'll find on your desk, and instructed me to inform the Department of Motor Vehicles by mail of the car's final disposition. That I have not as yet done."

Because his day's work was finished, of course, except for dinner, and he wanted to be left alone with his TV set. "Thank you, Robinson," I said. "I'll be on the phone now for a while." Not that he cared. With his remote control device he'd already turned the volume up. Various religious sects in Lebanon were killing one another.

The news is supposed to stay on the other side of the television screen, not break through into our private lives.

I left the kitchen and went through the house to my office, where the view out the windows over the lawn showed the late afternoon gathering itself for the rush of February's twilight. The little clouds that had been roaming the sky all day like a strayed flock were now gathering together, massing into fat regiments, and the lawn and shrubbery looked colder than I knew them to be. Max and Sugar Ray galumphed by, without politics or religion. I sat at the desk and called Deputy Ken's number.

He wasn't there, so I left a message, and then took a chance that Oscar would still be in the office, and called him.

Still in the car, I meant; he was. "Oscar," I said as the phone zizzed and brrrd in my ear, "do you *live* in that car?"

"What?"

"WHERE ARE YOU, OSCAR?"

"Wait a minute. Sunset Boulevard!"

"Where on Sunset?"

"Just passing the Beverly Hills Hotel."

"Heading which way?"

"What?"

"East or west?"

"Uhhh...toward the ocean."

Toward me, in other words. "Oscar," I yelled, "stop by a minute on your way!"

"What?"

"Come by for a drink!"

"That I heard!"

"Good." I broke the connection, dialed Robinson in-house, and when he answered I said, "Put some noshes together; Oscar Cooperman is stopping by for a drink."

"With his chauffeur?"

"Maybe he won't be hungry," I said, and the regular phone rang, and I switched over to it, saying, "Hello?"

"Sam, I'm disappointed. I'm very disappointed."

It was Ross, of course.

I said, "Ross, I don't want to start listing your mistakes because I wouldn't have time for them all, but you shouldn't have dragged Doreen back into it."

"She came back of her own free will," he said, "as she told those two Smokeys you brought around."

"What are you calling for, Ross?"

"First, to tell you I'm disappointed in you."

"Noted."

"You've done your best to fuck up *Fire Over Beverly Hills*, but you failed, so although—"

"What was that?"

"The *book*. Oh, that's right, I didn't tell you before, that's the working title. *Fire Over Beverly Hills*."

"You have a working title."

"Of course. You know that I always put some sort of title on every project right at the beginning so I can start a file, and if I'm discussing it with somebody, at least we have a name for what we're talking about."

Ross was dealing with murderers and terrorists and religious fanatics, he was in this thing several miles over his head, and I suppose it was a kind of instinctive defensive gesture to try to make it familiar and reasonable, to turn it into something he might be able to handle. So he'll start a file, he'll come up with a working title. He probably even had preliminary notes, in a folder.

In fact, come to think of it, the whole idea of turning this incident into a book might have been a defensive move, a way to survive the terror and uncertainty by having a *plan*, by having it all be aimed toward some purpose of *his* rather than theirs. He was a kind of kidnap victim himself, or hostage; in an equivalent position anyway, dependent on those people, coerced by them. It was very common for people in such a situation to work out complete though fanciful scenarios about their own plans, their reasons for going along, their relationship with their captors.

There was no point saying all this to Ross. He would almost certainly reject the idea, but if he accepted it, what good would it do? The moment for him to get out from under, I was beginning to realize, was gone. So I said, "All right, you're disappointed in me because I put your project at risk. What was your other reason?"

"To tell you I talked to the other people here. About you. I'm still your friend, Sam, despite everything. I hope you realize that."

"Of course I do."

"Well, the people here, they were very irritated by you, I hope you understand why."

"And?"

"You *do* understand why?"

"I'm fucking up their book too."

"You sure tried," he said, ignoring my irony. "But I told them, and it's true, now they're safer than ever. The cops have been here, I showed them how the American law works; a man's home really is his castle in this part of the world, it'll take a *lot* to make the law come back and risk humiliation all over again."

That was true, unfortunately. I could only hope my discovery that the new controversial mosque was Ross's next-door neighbor would be enough for Ken—and his superiors, and a judge—to take some action, but I had my doubts.

I said, "All right, Ross, I tried to end it and I failed. Now what?"

"Nothing," he said, and the in-house red light on the phone lit up. "That's the other reason I'm calling," he went on. "There won't be any efforts to shut you up or anything; you're in the clear. All right? I argued your case, pal, believe it or not, I argued very hard for you."

I sighed. "I believe you, Ross. I even appreciate it. It can't be easy, with a mob of religious nuts. Hold on a second." I pushed the button and said to Robinson, "Is that Oscar?"

"Yes."

"Give him a drink and some finger food. I'll be right out." And I switched back to Ross, saying, "Sorry, Robinson was buzzing me." But there was nobody there; he'd hung up.

37

OSCAR, LOOKING PLEASED and prosperous, stood by the glass doors at the back of the living room, gazing north at the hills. A vodka-mar was in his right hand, a pâté on a cracker in his left. He smiled across the room at me, saying, "I always find your place so restful."

"That's because it isn't moving."

His smile forgave me my frivolity, and he looked out the window again, saying, "What a spectacular view."

It is. The house was designed as much as possible to give discrete separate views from each section, with the best panorama saved for the living room. Facing north-northeast, with Japanese pines on the right to screen the garage and guest house while trellised vines on the left hide the pool area, the window wall of the living room opens onto a vista up into the Santa Monica Mountains. The tumbled bumpy hills alternate bare brown steeps with scrub-covered easier slopes, and only one or two barely visible rooftops up near the crests serve as a reminder of Man. Except for those, and the frequent white lines of vapor trail across the sky above the peaks, the scene is virtually what it was before the Europeans migrated west. "And only man is vile," I said.

"For which, speaking as an attorney, I am grateful." Oscar came reluctant but smiling away from the view, saying, "You're not your sunny self today. That car attack still depressing you?"

"Probably."

"Is that what you want to talk about?"

"Not exactly," I said. "I want you to tell me about that mosque you were going to visit the other day."

He frowned. "In connection with what?"

"It's in Beverly Hills, isn't it? Up a dead-end street? Looks like a golden flying saucer up at the top."

"Very true," he said. "Why?"

"I can't remember the name of it."

"Al-Gazel. Why?"

"You said there was a lot of extra security connected with the place. Why's that?"

Oscar's cheerful baby face was marred by a pout of exasperation. "Sam," he said, "I do not answer any more of your questions until you answer at least one of mine."

"The people who knocked my car all over the road is what," I told him. "I think they're connected with the people Al-Gazel's security is all about."

Frowning, Oscar put his drink down on the coffee table near us, beside the plate of canapés and my as yet unopened bottle of San Pellegrino. "Is this a coincidence," he asked, "or am *I* going to be batted around the freeway as well?"

"Oscar," I said, "how many attorneys have been involved with the construction of Al-Gazel? From the beginning."

"Architect's plans through completion? Hundreds."

"All from the Los Angeles area? Most of them tending to be in three-piece suits, male, smooth fellas, expensive? Not the kind you'll find down around the Second Street tunnel?"

He laughed, and picked up his drink. "And one of them will also be your attorney. All right. Why do you think what you think?"

I sat on the sofa and busied myself with opening the San Pellegrino and pouring, while I figured out how to word what I wanted to say. "A friend of mine got himself mixed up with these people," I said. "I think they plan to do something at that mosque next week."

"Good luck to them," Oscar said without alarm. Seating himself in the chair to my right, he said, "A water beetle couldn't get into that place without reciting name, rank, and serial number."

"My friend's property adjoins theirs. That's why these people forced him to cooperate."

"Still won't help." Oscar studied the plate of nibbles and chose one. "Robinson is a wonder," he commented.

"Why won't it help?"

"I'm not going to tell you *all* the security they have around that place," he said, "because in the first place I don't know it all. But I do know the perimeter is one hundred percent safe."

"Why? A fence? Guard dogs?"

"Microwave," he said.

All I could think of was ovens. "I don't follow."

"It's like a more sophisticated electric eye," he said, "but it's a very low-level sound wave."

"I've never heard of it."

"No reason for you to. No reason for me to, either, except on this job. It can't be used everywhere because some people claim it has bad side effects, everything from make your dog nervous to give your child birth defects, but it can be used in remote areas like the woods out behind the mosque, and that's where they're using it."

"Okay."

"My client, Mr. Catelli," Oscar said, "got a letter at the beginning of the job saying his crew shouldn't wander away back there because of the microwave alarm system. It's sophisticated enough to tell the difference between a human being and a rabbit, and they're using it with closed-circuit

TV. If your friend leaves his own property, climbs over the fence, and takes a stroll toward the mosque, no alarms go off, nothing like that. But when he goes through the microwave field, several feet inside the fence, a TV monitor in the guard room at the mosque turns on, and there's your friend on television."

"Ah-hah."

"At night it's infrared."

"The wonders of technology. Somebody tried to drive a truckload of dynamite up there last month, you know."

He looked mildly interested, not particularly surprised. "Did they? I hadn't heard about that, but they're doing a good job of staying out of the news. They're trying to keep the whole thing as quiet as any twenty-seven million-dollar mosque in Beverly Hills can be, so they don't advertise attacks."

"Twenty-seven *million?*"

"That gold dome, for one thing."

"You're telling me it's gold, Oscar."

"There isn't an ounce of papier mâché in the place, Sam."

"All right," I said. "But the security isn't just because there's valuable metal up there."

"That's right," Oscar said, and sipped at his vodka-mar. "Some religious leader in the Middle East, I don't remember the name, he announced about six months ago that Al-Gazel is a false mosque in a Satanic nation, and whoever destroys it gets Allah's unlisted phone number."

"Sure," I said. "It had to be something like that. And six months ago, plenty of time to set up."

"Not against that place."

"What I think this group around my friend is up to, there's somebody important going to be there next week some time, they plan to break in and kidnap him."

"They'll never get in, and they'll never get out."

"But they're going to try," I said. "The question is, who are they likely to be going after?"

"Beats me." Oscar shook his head. "Next week? The opening ceremonies are this Friday, day after tomorrow, the first holy day's activities, and from then on it's a going concern. I suppose they'll have important people in and out for some time, religious types, some politicos, affirming which side they're on."

"One of them is a target."

"If he's in Al-Gazel, he'll be safe from all alarm."

I remembered the elaborate care and patience with which these people had set up Ross, and how complicated they'd been willing to get to make my own death look accidental. Was this a group who were likely to just climb over a fence and walk onto a guard room's television screen? "I hope you're right, Oscar," I said.

"Well, look at that," he said. "My glass is empty."

38

THE MIND IS A STRANGE OBJECT, sometimes. If the phone rings at Bly's place when we're both there asleep, Bly wakes up and I don't. But if it rings at my place in the same circumstances, I'm the one who comes awake.

We'd spent the evening together, going out to dinner, talking mostly about the possibility that her actor friend had been murdered, and not at all about my quick trip to New York; that would have required some eventual reference to Anita. I did my best to discourage Bly's becoming an amateur detective, a role I could see her leaping into with both feet, but I didn't get very far. She was determined to find some mutual friend who could introduce her to Beau Sheridan's widow, because the woman just might, all unknowing, have some clue as to who had hired her husband for that non-union job last fall.

Well, if I couldn't stop Bly's sleuthing, I could at least change the subject, which I finally managed by getting her to talk about the script she was writing. From there the evening turned pleasant, and we eventually wound up at my place, which is where we were, asleep, when the phone rang at quarter to four in the morning.

I found the receiver in the dark. "Hello?"

"Sam?"

The reason I was whispering was not to wake Bly. The reason the female voice at the other end was whispering I hadn't yet figured out. I whispered, "Yes? Who is it?"

"Doreen," came the faint and guarded voice.

I sat upright. As Bly mumbled and thrashed her legs a bit, I whispered, "Where are you?"

"At the house. I want out, Sam."

"Just a second. Let me get to another phone."

I put her on hold and hurried to the office, where I could switch on a light and talk in a normal voice:

"Hello? You still there?"

"Yes." She, of course, was still whispering.

"What is it, Doreen? Tell me about it."

"I was crazy to come back here." Through the whisper, and through that veneer of hipness she affected, I could hear how tense she was. "I couldn't say anything when you showed up with the police; they were at the windows with guns."

"Terrific."

"Everybody's asleep now. Would you— could you help me get out of here?"

"Sure."

"The way to do it— you know this house, don't you?"

"I've been there; I don't know it that well."

"If I try to get out the front, that's no good. The lawn lights go on at night when you open the gate."

All that excess security Ross had never bothered to remove when he bought the place. I said, "Is there another way?"

"On the side— not the side where the driveway is, the people next door are home there, but on the other side, downhill, you know the one? The big brick house with the pillars?"

"I know it."

"There's a pear tree up near the house, over on their

side of the wall. If you could like come over the wall there, with a ladder or something, I don't know, I could meet you, you could help me climb over. Okay?"

"The side with the brick house with the pillars. It's— let me see, it's ten-to-four. I'll, be there in fifteen minutes, twenty at the most."

"I can get out of the house all right, it's just climbing over that damn wall."

"Wait for me by the tree."

"I will," she promised.

39

THE IDEA BEHIND *PACKARD*, and I guess what made it so successful, was what is called "casting against type." They chose a physical guy—me—to do a cerebràl part, the kind of role that would usually go to somebody like Jack Klugman or E. G. Marshall. Putting me in there meant they could have it both ways: I could ratiocinate away like mad for a while and then go climb a wall. The ratiocinating was actually done by the scriptwriters and directors, but the wall-climbing was done by me.

I climbed the other wall beside Ross's place, opposite where I was to meet Doreen, dropped, and landed on soft sod. Crouching a minute, I looked up toward the garage and the darkened house beyond it. Nothing moved. There was no sound.

Driving over in the Porsche, making better time than I'd expected on the empty streets, it had occurred to me that if I was going to sneak onto Ross's property anyway, I might as well poke around some. But if I was going to do that, I'd want to enter on the uphill side, where the garage would screen me from the house. Then I could make a quick reconnaissance as I crossed the property.

Neither of Ross's next-door neighbors had heavy security, with walls or gates or fences. Having left the Porsche a little farther up the street, I walked back down and went cautiously into the driveway next door on the uphill side.

The house at its top showed one dim amber upstairs rectangle, where a night-light burned. The day's cloud-cover still blanketed the sky, making the night very dark. I went up the blacktop halfway to the house, then pushed my way through the tall ornamental hedge on the right, into the night-cool air between shrubbery and rough fieldstone wall. It was about six feet high, just a bit too tall to see over, but the ragged edges of stone made for easy climbing. I went over and dropped to the soft ground on the other side, and waited a long silent minute before moving up toward the house.

Ross, uncharacteristically, had been letting the grounds get shaggy; too busy with his real-life project, I supposed. *Fire Over Beverly Hills.* The unshaved grass, wet with condensation, swished against my feet as I moved up the slope, keeping the pale rectangle of the garage between me and the house.

I skirted the garage, blundering once into some shrubbery, then coming out to the brighter area in back, where pale stone terraces and the white rear wall of the house, unshielded by trees, reflected and increased whatever light there was. Lawn furniture and plantings were dark mounds along the way, and just to the right, parked on the lawn behind the garage, was the pool-company van.

I went over to look at it, not opening the door for fear of switching the light on inside, but at least touching it, seeing it up close. The windows were open and a faint, unpleasant odor emerged, both clammy and sharp. I went around to the back, and the rear doors stood open, but the interior was pitch black. I leaned in, trying to see anything at all, and my hands touched cardboard cartons.

I patted the cartons and found they were stacked almost to the roof. They were about the right size and shape to carry four gallons of paint, and when I tried to lift one, they were very heavy. The van seemed to be full of them. I started to slide one out, to see what was inside, but my fingers touched a metal band strapped around it; so much for that. Leaning forward, I sniffed at the cartons and smelled mostly cardboard, with the sharp metallic smell faintly within. The clamminess wasn't evident back here at all.

Giving up on the cartons, I hunkered down to try to read the license plate, but it was just too dark. On a *Packard* one time I'd read a license plate in a darkened garage by feeling the raised numbers with my fingertips, but when I tried that now, I couldn't make it work at all. Very disappointing.

Moving away from the van, I looked out past the swimming pool at a kind of muddied darkness that would be trees and shrubbery on the hill climbing up away from Ross's landscaping. Up in there somewhere was Al-Gazel.

There was nothing here, no profit in staring around at emptiness in the dark. Doreen would be waiting, probably getting nervous. I turned away to go between the house and garage, but then paused to look back at the swimming pool.

What was wrong with it? Something out there bothered me, but why? It was merely a full swimming pool in the darkness, like a thousand others in these hills, rectangular, not quite Olympic-size. But something troubled me about it, and I walked slowly toward it, frowning, trying to make sense of my unease.

Unease—that was it. Something about the swimming pool made me uneasy. And yet it was simply there, a black rectangle in the night, surrounded by pale stone walks.

A black rectangle. But doesn't water reflect whatever light there is? Why could I see the stone walks, yet the pool was merely a bottomless black rectangle? It certainly wasn't empty, or I'd see its pale wall on the farther side.

I was reluctant to get too close, and only partly because I would be outlined against the light stone terraces in case anyone was looking out an upstairs window of the house behind me. There was also a faint touch of a kind of atavistic dread as I looked at the wrongness of that enigmatic black. A chilly breeze ruffled the hair at the back of my neck; why didn't it ruffle the surface of the water?

I had no choice, really, atavistic dread or not. I had to walk out over the stone slabs to the pool, I had to go down on one knee and lean forward and reach my fingers down into the cold loose...

What?

Still unbelieving, I lifted my hand, the dark coolness in my palm, some of it trickling out between my fingers, dropping back into the pool. The clammy smell was here again, stronger than it had been in the cab of the truck.

This entire huge swimming pool was filled with dirt.

40

WHY?

I looked out over the pool, and it was all earth. Not mud, but ordinary dirt, so the water must have been drained from the pool before it had been dumped in.

A grave? What was buried down in there?

The dirt I was holding felt unhealthy; I flung it back into the pool, got to my feet, compulsively rubbed my hand on my pants-leg. What was this? Why had it been done? Was it something to do with their religion? Bewildered and crazy ideas crowded through my head, and I backed away from the pool, finding myself thinking, absurdly: How could Ross let them do *this*?

Would Doreen know? She must have seen it, she might have some idea why it had been done. With one last look at that strange casket I turned away and went down between house and garage, then crossed the sloping lawn among the ornamental trees to the wall on the other side.

A pear tree, beyond the wall, that's what she'd said. It was really very dark tonight, I could barely see the wall itself, much less pick out some tree on its far side. I moved leftward along the, wall, staring up into the darkness, and found Doreen at last by stumbling into her where she waited, leaning against the wall. She gave a tiny cry, and I grabbed her arm to keep us both from falling. "Doreen!" I whispered. "It's me, Sam."

"Oh, my God," she said, but not whispering, saying it in a normal tone of voice. "You're inside already."

"That's right. Let's get you—"

"He's here!" she shouted, suddenly flinging her arms around me, draping her weight on me. "He's inside! He's here!"

"What? What are you—?"

Floodlights. The entire house and grounds leaped into existence, and men were running this way across the lawn. I fought loose of Doreen, shoving her away, but half a dozen men crowded around, all with pistols in their hands. I'd never make it over the wall.

I stared at Doreen, who backed away from me, her face bruised-looking in the harsh light. "It was you or me," she cried, defiant. "All right? It was you or me."

Ross was among the half-circle of men, wearing his usual chains and open shirt, his reading glasses nestled on top of his head. Some sort of ghastly smile twitched on his face as he said, "Sam, take it easy. Nobody's going to get hurt. Sam? You're just going to be my houseguest for a while. Sam? Take it easy, Sam."

41

THEY PUT ME IN THE SAFE ROOM, the first one I'd seen since I worked as a security guard out in these neighborhoods nine years ago. Because of the danger of kidnapping, and because there are more Charles Mansons out there in the valleys who haven't exploded yet, a lot of Los Angeles's rich and famous—and some just rich—have installed these safe rooms in their houses. The comic Ross bought this place from used to get hate mail from groups he'd insulted in his act, which was why he'd spent the thousands of dollars such a room costs.

Here's what it is: An interior concrete room, without windows, built either directly on the ground or over a concrete block base extending down through the basement to the ground. Separate electric and water and telephone lines are installed—the utilities around Beverly Hills and Bel Air are old hands at this kind of thing—in underground pipes from outside the property to the base of the safe room, meaning that attackers can't cut off the phone in there and you'll have light to read by while waiting for the police, and a small attached cubicle contains sink and toilet, in case the cops take too long to get there or you have a nervous stomach. Back when I was a guard, I saw the families of famous people practice quite seriously their safe-room drill. Daddy, stopwatch in hand, would shout that the alarm bells had rung, and would then time how long it took Mom and the kids to get into the safe room with the metal door bolted shut.

Not everybody takes their safe rooms that seriously, of course. I remember one place I guarded that belonged to a Las Vegas singer, who had lined her safe room with cedar to make it the storage closet for her costumes. One man used his as a wine cellar. But they always leave enough room for the family to get inside and lock that door, just in case.

Ross used it for his manuscripts and videotapes of his shows and scrapbooks and show posters, but there was still plenty of space for me. The room contained a sofa to sit on, an old sagging one that had been banished from public life, and a coffee table for your feet. The collected works of Ross Ferguson were available, to while away the time. The phone had been unplugged and taken away, but the electricity was on, and the plumbing worked.

They marched me there from the lawn, Doreen fading out of sight almost at once, the exterior lights going off as we entered the house. Four armed men, Ross, and me. Ross led the way to a door that on the outside looked to be an ordinary reproduction of a Colonial style, but when he opened it, the inch-thick steel became visible, and the heavy-duty piano hinges to hold it.

Ross said a word or two before they stowed me away. "I hate this, Sam," he assured me, "I really do, and I know I'm costing myself your friendship. After this is all over and we can all calm down, I just hope you'll be able to understand, to see it from my side just a little bit."

I shook my head, saying nothing. What was the point of talking to him?

He said, "Sam, you wouldn't be here except you'd just never leave it alone. I called you to tell you everything was all right, *you* didn't have to do anything else and *we* wouldn't do anything else—"

"We?"

"For the moment, Sam, yes." Ross looked impatient with my lack of understanding of the artist. "When Capote was writing *In Cold Blood*," he said, "don't you think he thought of Hickok and that other guy and himself as *us*?"

"No."

"Of course he did. Just then, just while it was going on. Not afterward." He sighed, accepting the idea that it was his fate to be misunderstood. "Never mind that," he said. "The point is, you knew I had people listening here, monitoring my phone, I told you that."

"Yes, you did."

"So you made that crack about religious nuts just to let everybody realize you know more than we thought. Jesus, Sam, didn't it occur to you they don't want to be known? And don't you realize they *could* kill you?"

"They almost did."

"They could do it right *now*."

"And bury me in the swimming pool?"

He raised his eyes to heaven. "There you go *again*. Sam, you're going to be here for a few days, and then that's it. I argued like *hell* for you, I really did."

I remember reading once that an insane person is simply a sane person who starts off with one firmly held wrong idea, and then everything else has to flipflop to go along with step number one. If you think Martians are communicating through the fillings in your teeth, for instance, you don't have to have any *more* wrong ideas to be—and act— crazy. It's a kind of colorblindness of the mind: Once you think blue is green, you have to make so many other alterations in your view of the world to accommodate it to your belief that eventually either you or the world must be cuckoo, and it isn't the world.

On that basis, Ross Ferguson was now a certifiable

lunatic, so what would I gain by arguing with him? His one wrong conviction was that he and these Barq people were partners, working together toward a common goal—or at least toward similar goals. He'd negotiate with them, he'd bargain and deal with them, he'd do lots of busywork on his *project*, never knowing that all along they would merely be humoring him, letting him have what he wanted until they didn't need him anymore. At this moment Ross and I were both under sentence of death, but only one of us knew it. And poor frightened Doreen was in it with us, of course, making it all up as she went along, hoping for the best.

Which made me suddenly remember Bly, still asleep at my house. I absolutely didn't want Ross and his business associates to know *she* was there and would miss me. I didn't want them deciding she knew too much. I said, "Ross, how long am I going to be here?"

"Until next week. I can tell you now, since you can't do anything about it. The whole thing will be over next Tuesday, that's when the minister's coming and they'll grab him."

"Minister?" I hadn't thought Islamic religious figures were called "minister."

They aren't. "Oil minister," Ross explained, "from one of the Trucial States. He's the guy they're gonna get."

A Trucial State—would that be Dharak, the oil minister an associate of Hassan Tabari's? But if I asked, it would turn out I was showing too much knowledge again, so I just said, "On Tuesday. So I'm here until then."

"I'm sorry about that, Sam," he said, "but you honest-to-God did bring it on yourself. I'll make you as comfortable as I can, but this is gonna be your home for the next six days."

"Then do me a favor."

"Anything. Something to read? I don't think they'd let me give you a TV."

"Nothing like that. But I'm supposed to see Bly tomorrow afternoon, and she'll worry if I don't show up."

"You want me to call her? Sure."

"No, Ross, I do not want you to call Bly." I was very tensed up and scared with all these guns around, but I made myself sound as sarcastic as possible under the circumstances, to make him do what I wanted without thinking about it too much. "If *you* call her," I said, "what's she going to think? *You're* supposed to be the plot genius around here."

He didn't like that. Face stiffening, he said, "So what do you want?"

"Call my house first thing in the morning. Before eight o'clock, so Robinson won't have gone out anywhere." And Bly won't have started to panic yet, with luck. "Tell Robinson I'm going out on the boat with you for a few days and I asked you to call him while I made my business calls. Tell him I'm supposed to see Bly, and ask him to phone her and make my excuses and say I'll explain next week. All right?"

"Fine," he said. "Consider it done."

"Good."

I was counting on Robinson's having quick reactions here, not blurting out on the phone that Bly was already in the house. But I had to hope for *something* to fall my way. And wouldn't Robinson and Bly then put their heads together and decide it was time to phone Deputy Ken? And wouldn't that be enough to get them onto this property before some of these guns around here started going off?

Six days of this. Good God.

42

DYNAMITE.

No, I don't have six days.

Is Ross lying to me, or are they lying to him? And what difference does it make?

I had fallen into a very uneasy sleep on the sofa, the recessed fluorescent ceiling light still on, and had abruptly awakened with a mind cluttered and confused, but understanding more than when they'd locked me in here.

A truckload of dynamite had been caught on its way to Al-Gazel.

Some Islamic fundamentalist leader had urged the faithful to destroy that mosque.

The pool-company van was filled with metal-banded cardboard cartons of dynamite.

I'd been too distracted by thoughts of Bly when Ross told me the story about the oil minister from the Trucial State, or I would have realized at once that it didn't make any sense. If this small army of people, this Barq group, were really interested only in kidnapping some Middle Eastern country's oil minister, there had to be better places to do it than the Al-Gazel mosque. Of course such a man would have tight security around him all the time, but people who travel a lot—and Middle Eastern oil ministers travel all the time—are constantly vulnerable, particularly to a concerted semi-military action by a large, well-equipped group of men.

An airport, a hotel, a limousine on the freeway; almost anywhere at all would have fewer security problems for the attackers than Al-Gazel.

Did *Ross* believe the story? It was so hard to tell, but his enthusiasm led me to believe the answer was yes. Could he be enthusiastic about a project with real mass murder in it? On the other hand, his working title suggested he knew the truth: *Fire Over Beverly Hills.*

When the van full of dynamite explodes, taking Al-Gazel with it.

On Friday.

That was the other lie, that they weren't going to make their move until next Tuesday. Again, it was impossible to tell if Barq had lied to Ross to keep him controllable or he had lied to me for the same reason, but the lie was still the same. They were not out to kidnap one oil minister next Tuesday; they were out to destroy the entire place. Friday is the Islamic holy day, when the faithful must say noon prayers in the mosque, and this Friday was to be the official opening of Al-Gazel, with major ceremonies. The building would never again be so full. When better for Barq to attack than when Al-Gazel would be packed solid with their political and religious and financial enemies?

I looked at my watch, but of course it was gone. They'd taken that, and my belt, and my shoes, and everything in my pockets, when they'd locked me in here. There were no windows, only the overhead fluorescent as a light source, and so no way to tell what time it was, whether it was day or night.

It had been quarter to four Thursday morning when Doreen had phoned, just a few minutes after four when I'd reached this house, probably no more than quarter past the hour when I was put into this room. Then I'd moped and paced in here for a while, considering flushing all Ross's manuscripts down the toilet in revenge, before groggily passing out on the sofa. I was hungry now, but that didn't mean anything in particular. It seemed to me the time could be anywhere between eight in the morning and noon, but how could I be sure?

In *The Prisoner*, 1955, Alec Guinness played a Cardinal Mindszenty-type priest, brainwashed in a Communist prison, in which one of the techniques was to keep him in a windowless room where he would never know the time, or day from night. There's a strong scene where, in his efforts to invent a clock, he's shown failing to make a pendulum out of a button and a piece of string. His intensity there is so complete, and so apparently natural, and so understated, that I've always used that as my model when I've had a scene to play involving tight attention on a difficult or muddled or futile task. And now I had another use for that scene: It told me not to think about time, not to worry about it. There's nothing to be done. Think about something else.

Like getting out of here.

Like, before that, getting my wits about me.

There was soap in the tiny lavatory, and a small facecloth, but no toothpaste or any way to shave. I stripped, gave myself a rudimentary sponge bath, put my shorts and socks back on, and went out to the other room to exercise. The pale gray industrial carpeting was just soft enough for the purpose. I did my running in place and my arm swings and my knee bends, and was on my back doing my sit-ups when I heard the door being unlocked.

The original purpose of this door, of course, was to keep people out, not in, so it opened inward and was equipped on this side with dead bolts top and bottom. On the other side there was only a simple lock and key, but with this door it was sufficient. The hinge joint showed in here, and with a pair of ordinary hinges I might have been able to remove the pins and get out that way, but this heavy weight was held up and in balance by an entire length of piano hinge, impossible to do anything about.

I was on my feet, trying to take controlled deep breaths, when the door opened. Two men came in, one bearing a tray. Both had revolvers stuck under their belts. One or more other men stayed out in the hall, and with the door open I could hear some sort of twangy plucked music, with a dragging rhythm. Rather loud too.

My visitors glanced at my shorts and socks, but showed no reaction. The one put the tray on the coffee table and stepped back, while the other closed the door (which shut off the music), turned to me, and said, "Eat."

A pretty efficient system. They would both stay until I was finished. Breakfast was finger food—overcooked hamburger on an English muffin, and a pear, so no need for knives and forks. Lukewarm unsweetened black coffee was in a plastic cup.

I forced myself to eat, though it wasn't easy with two armed men standing over me. But at least if they were feeding me, it meant I still had time, they weren't planning to kill me just yet.

I couldn't keep from wondering what the time was right now, but I wouldn't ask. They might have answered—they weren't out to brainwash me, like Alec Guinness's cardinal, merely store me until I could be conveniently killed—but what good would it do to know that right *now* was eight forty-three or ten-seventeen?

I finished eating, and dropped the pear core into the plastic cup. They watched me, standing over by the door, silent and impassive, and when I was done, they picked up the tray and left. The music twanged, then was silent. I heard the key in the lock.

I washed again. For some reason this room made me

feel dusty, a little smudged. I don't like being afraid; the emotion itself can make you feel dirty, abused.

I will break out of here, I promised myself. But there's no point trying anything during the day. Two meals from now, I'll have to be ready. I breathed deep, standing in the middle of the room, commanding my nerves to stop jittering. An actor knows how to deal with nerves, doesn't he? So deal with them.

Where to start? What to do? I looked at the shelves of Ross's old scripts, lined up in their folders, their titles in red magic marker on white Mystic tape on their spines. Would one of those contain some clever way to get out of a locked room?

43

HERE'S WHAT WAS IN THE ROOM:

Two old unpainted wooden bookcases, six feet high by under three feet wide, next to each other, containing scripts in folders, boxed manuscripts, videotapes labeled on tape and box, and one shelf of scrapbooks filled with newspaper clippings about shows or movies Ross had been connected with.

One fireproof metal four-door filing cabinet, not quite six feet tall, with several show posters on top of it, rolled up and secured with rubber bands.

The sagging sofa and the small square Parsons-style wooden coffee table.

Two posters for television series, both about twelve by eighteen, in glass-fronted, metal-sided assemble-it-yourself frames, stored in the space between the side of the filing cabinet and the wall.

Thin wood-veneer paneling nailed to vertical furring strips presumably nailed to the concrete block wall. A. Sheetrock ceiling with a two-by-four-foot rectangle in which the fluorescent light was set, and a foot-square metal grid where air was drawn out. Industrial carpeting glued to the concrete floor, with an air-inlet grid against the wall opposite the door. Sheetrock-and-stud construction of the lavatory cubicle in one corner.

An old-fashioned premodular telephone jack—without

the telephone—close to the floor on the wall behind the door.

The steel door leading out, and the simple flush door leading to the bathroom, the latter with an ordinary brass lockset with a locking mechanism on the inside knob.

The bathroom itself contained a simple toilet, a small corner sink, a small rectangular pale blue plastic waste-basket, a round fluorescent ceiling fixture, and a small wood-framed mirror hung on a hook on one of the Sheetrock walls. The industrial carpeting continued into this room.

And myself, wearing pullover polo shirt, slacks without belt, shorts, and socks. All pockets empty.

That was what I had to work with.

I was mad, and I was scared. Another man's stupidity had gotten me into this mess, his stupidity and my own dumb efforts to be his friend. I did not want to die here in this room. No matter how undeserved my sweet life was, no matter how much it was a result of luck and chance, it was still a sweet life and the only life I had, and I was not ready yet to give it up.

I was mad, and I was scared, and I was mad *because* I was scared. I didn't like it that these people, nothing to me and me nothing to them, could come out of the blue and frighten me. I didn't like it at all.

I have been half-trained in a lot of things: acting, police work, soldiering, basketball, writing. Nobody is actually trained for the kind of position I found myself in now, but still I could have wished I was better at *something* useful. Karate, for instance. I know just enough to make the moves look good for the camera, but not anywhere near enough to deal with two armed men in a small closed room with a lot of their friends waiting outside.

People had tried to kill me twice in the past, before this

crowd here. Both times I was on duty, and the result was that I have killed two men, but none of that trained me for anything. It only showed me I don't have a taste for it, and I don't like the aftertaste. The first time was in Germany when I was on patrol in my MP persona, walking with my partner down a cobbled street in the raunchy part of Kaiserslautern at two in the morning, and a very drunk black GI came reeling out of a bar with a stained bayonet in his hand. Later it turned out he'd just killed his German girl-friend in there. All we knew was that he saw us and, instead of running away, ran at us, flailing with the bayonet.

We tried to subdue him, which was a mistake. My part-ner got cut on the face and the left shoulder, I got nicked along the forearm—I still have the scar, though very faint—and when I tried to whack the fellow with my nightstick, he grabbed it out of my hand, snapping the leather thong around my wrist, astonishing me. Still astonished, I backpedaled, using both hands to unsnap my holster as he pursued me, my partner now on his knees, holding his face. From the bars around, the street was filling up with people who weren't going to be any help. I took the .45 out of its holster, said not a word, and shot him three times. Later, they told me any one of the three would have done, but I'd wanted to be sure. Also, later, I claimed to have yelled, "Stop in the name of the law!" and no one came forward to con-tradict me.

The other time was on the Meadowbrook Parkway in Mineola, when I was a cop there. I'd stopped a speeder at about four in the morning. Afterward, we found out the car contained a shipment of cocaine, from a smugglers' landing place out near the Hamptons, on its way to Manhattan, which was why, as I approached the car, people in it started shooting at me, and all at once the car leaped forward. (I'll never know why they stopped in the first place, since they were going to shoot and run anyway. Belated panic, maybe.) None of the shots hit me. I drew out my own .38 and shot at the tires, but I was shooting in haste, recoil drew the barrel up, and one of my shots hit the front-seat passenger in the back of the head, killing him instantly. The driver went off the road, the car rolled onto its side, and I radioed for help, keeping my distance from those people until a lot of help arrived.

Neither of those experiences could exactly be called *training* in dealing with violence. And both of those times I'd been at least as well armed as the other guy.

Well, I could wish I knew more things by now and had more equipment, but this was it. This man and this room. Knowing I would have only a few seconds' warning before someone came in—the scratch of the key in the lock would tell me—I went to work.

Two screws held the phone jack to the paneling and the furring strip behind it. I had no idea what harm I could do, if any, but it seemed worth the effort, so I worked the jack loose, then turned it over and rewired it so all four wires came together. With any luck I was now causing some sort of short-circuit somewhere in the telephone company's system, and they would have to send a repair crew to fix it.

Next I turned to one of the framed posters. The frame was held together with loosely set screws, which I removed, reducing the thing to its components. The poster I rolled up and slid inside one of the other rolled-up posters on top of the filing cabinet. The glass and mounting board and all but one of the frame pieces I put back in the space between filing cabinet and wall, to be used after lunch, when I'd probably have more time.

There were six rolled-up posters, each held with two red rubber bands. I removed the rubber bands from two of them, and put the posters inside the others. The rubber bands went into my pocket.

I searched under the sofa cushions, and under the sofa itself, but found nothing.

I was slowly and with great difficulty using the metal edge of the poster frame to pry open the filing cabinet, when I heard that scratch sound at the door. By the time the door opened, announced by that twangy music, I was on the sofa, reading an unproduced movie script of Ross's called *Half a League*.

That was lunch: a turkey and cheese and mayonnaise sandwich on rye bread, another pear, another cup of lukewarm black unsweetened coffee. The same two men maintained the same routine, except that one of them looked briefly into the bathroom. I hadn't spoken to them at breakfast, nor did I speak to them at lunch. I acted—I tried to act—as though I were merely resigned and patient.

After lunch I finished breaking into the filing cabinet, which was a disappointment. Notebooks about story ideas. Old checks, year by year, in shoeboxes. Income-tax-supporting documents. More videotapes, these marked only with a woman's name. Nothing sharp, nothing heavy, nothing useful.

The next work had to be done in the bathroom, where I began by removing the mirror from its hook on the wall, tapping the wall with a piece of poster frame until I knew exactly where the vertical stud was—right behind the hook, unfortunately—then beating with my elbow a small hole into the Sheetrock next to the stud. The piece of frame helped me enlarge the hole to about three inches square, and then I moved the hook to a spot just above the hole, so that when I put the mirror back on—it was a bit shakier here without the stud support for the hook, but no matter—the mirror covered both the hole I'd made and the hole from which I'd removed the hook.

My problem was, I was going to make something of a mess in my preparations, and I didn't want trash left around to alert my guards. What couldn't be flushed down the toilet would be pushed into the narrow space inside the wall.

I brought in my equipment and made my preparations. I was very absorbed in my work. Time seemed to fly.

I ALMOST ATE THE DINNER.

I'd planned to go through with part of the meal, behaving exactly as I had the first two times, so they'd be at their most relaxed when I made my move, and I was actually reaching for one of the cups when it occurred to me why I shouldn't.

Hours and hours had gone by according to my stomach, but these were the same two silent waiters who brought me my meal. There was no twangy music to be heard this time when the door was open, but another guard was still visible outside before the door was shut. I hoped he'd turn out to be alone, or at least not with a crowd, when the time came.

The meal this time was in three cups, containing pea soup, and milk, and very weak-looking coffee, plus the usual pear, and I was actually reaching for the pea soup when the word *drug* came into my mind.

Why wouldn't they? If it were up to me to keep somebody quiet and imprisoned for a day or two, I would be very likely to put a lot of sleeping pills or some such into his evening meal, and hold off the evening meal until late, so he'd scarf it down. I'd give him milk, to relax his stomach, and the weakest coffee I could get away with. I'd give him thick liquids in which he'd be unaware of the extra ingredient. Then, knowing that he was safely asleep, I could take some time off as well.

"What is this?" I asked, changing my movement from a reach for the cup to a pointing at it.

"Eat," the talkative one said.

I hadn't known the performance would start this early. You have to psych yourself up to perform, and I'd thought I would have a few minutes to get used to the stage and the other players while I ate, but now the red light was on before I was ready, and my question had been simply a stall, a chance to reorganize my mind, to get ready for my entrance.

"I don't like pea soup," I said, gesturing with my left hand while my right hand went under the sofa cushion. Improvisation; the scariest part of acting.

The talker took a step forward, glowering at me. Good; take another step. "You eat," he said, padding his line.

I picked up the cup of soup with my left hand, as though to smell it, leaning forward over the coffee table, my right hand dragging behind me under the cushion, holding on. Shaking my head, I looked up at the talker and flung the soup and then the cup into his face. At the same time, just as I had been rehearsing it over and over for the last few hours, I pushed up with the back of my closed right hand, shoving the sofa cushion out of the way, so that when I stood, right hand swinging forward, the spear came with it. The spear: two long triangles of broken glass that had been part of the pane mounted in the dismantled poster's frame, their wide ends wrapped in a couple of Ross's old checks and attached by four red rubber bands to the end of one of the long lengths of metal poster frame.

The second guy was still reacting with shock, staring as his friend pawed at the soup on his face. That one was occupied for the next few minutes, so it was the silent one I lunged at, spear out, gashing a great ragged tear along the left side of his neck. There's an advantage to being six foot six, to having the kind of reach I possess.

But I hadn't thought about the blood. It spurted out like somebody finding oil, as though under terrific pressure. I jumped to the side, turning toward the other one, and the spray of blood splashed onto the wall and the sofa as the dying man made a bubbling noise, arms up like a doctor drying his hands, already falling backward.

The talker was reaching for the automatic tucked into his belt. I slashed at him, and he threw his arms up, and the pieces of glass drew a pair of red lines on his right forearm. I drew back the spear and cut at him again, but he was backing quickly away, making a guttural shout.

Would the guard or guards hear that outside? I had not been able to hear the music when the door was shut, not even when I pressed my ear to the crack beside the jamb, so it should be safe. But not too many shouts, please, not too many. I lunged again, this time slicing sharp glass across the backs of his fingers as they closed on his gunbutt.

He tripped over his fallen friend, and as he toppled backward I jumped forward and landed with both socked feet on his chest. His mouth opened, his eyes looked agonized, and before I could tell myself not to, I swung my spear like a golf club across the exposed target of his throat.

God, it's different. On *Packard* I'd done most of my own fights, being pretty good at pulling the punches and doing the falls, and the difference was like the difference on that videotape of Ross's between Delia West "dying" and Delia West dead. Already this small room was filling with terrible cloying smells. The things on the floor were too horrible to look at, and I had done it. I had been angry, and I had been afraid, and that's a dangerous combination; it can make you do atrocious things.

But now both those emotions had suddenly simply vanished from my mind, burned up in the adrenaline surge. My condition was almost as desperate as it had been, my being here in the first place was still just as random and unfair, and yet neither fear nor fury was in me anymore. What I felt now was mostly sick.

I didn't want to look at the people I'd killed, but I needed their weapons. My eyes kept squinting and I swallowed bile as I went down on one knee in the open space of the V their bodies made. First one gun, then the other, and I could concentrate now on the tools rather than the human beings.

These were both standard .45 caliber Colt automatics, not precisely like my issue back in the army, but close enough. Ours had been black, these were a foggy brushed chrome. Nor, now that I looked at them, did the word *Colt* appear anywhere on them; they merely each had a set of numbers and letters stamped into the left side below the safety. Third World ripoffs of the Colt design, probably a little less precise, possibly a much cheaper grade of metal that would stretch and warp from the heat after not much use at all. But enough, I hoped, to get me out of here.

Out of here. The look of them, the smell of them. If I stayed in here much longer, I'd be sick. Worse, I'd lose my strength, my resolve; I'd merely collapse in here until they came to get me.

I put one of the automatics in under my belt, butt to the left for my left hand. The other was in my right hand as I reached out to open the door.

45

THE GUARD OUTSIDE, like the two I'd just killed, was dressed in worn boots, dark trousers, and a dark cotton workshirt. His complexion was olive, his hair black and curly, and he wore a thick moustache as though it were a badge of rank, or a requirement for the job. His gun was tucked in under his belt, so when he glanced in a bored way at the door when it opened, and then saw me with the gun in my hand pointing at him, he at first looked startled, then made as though to reach for his own weapon, then realized that was hopeless and froze.

Were there others, out of my sight? I put my left forefinger to my lips, to shush him, then patted the air downward to tell him to look more relaxed, then crooked my finger at him to say he should come join me in the room.

He didn't want to. He stood there blinking at me, quite naturally afraid of the unknown, so the second time I made the invitation I gestured as well with the automatic, and made myself look very stern, and that had the effect. In he came, walking reluctantly, and he would have put his hands up in the air if I hadn't repeated that down-patting motion.

I didn't want him to see the bodies too early and panic, so the instant he was across the threshold I took his arm and turned him to face the wall just beside the door. Even if he looked to his left now, across the doorway, the open door would block his view. With my own gun in his back I reached around and relieved him of his, then very cautiously leaned my head out through the doorway to look in both directions at what proved to be an empty hall.

All right. I searched my man—I couldn't bring myself to search the dead ones—and came up with Marlboro cigarettes, you-can-complete-high-school-at-home matches, some change, a four-inch switchblade knife, some sort of stringed prayer beads or worry beads, a plastic card all in Arabic, and a thick wallet. I left everything else, took the knife, and relieved him of his belt, to replace my own.

The Yale-type key was in the lock on the outside of the door. Making the shush gesture again, not speaking, I stepped outside and locked him—them—in.

I was in the downstairs hall now, and as I remembered the house from my occasional visits, the dining room and kitchen were down to the right, with the front door beyond. Living room, library, and perhaps other rooms were the opposite way. The door diagonally across the hall from the safe room was the downstairs powder room, and just beyond it, toward the rear, were the main stairs up to the second floor.

I must have looked just then like a close business associate of Pancho Villa's. I had an automatic pistol in my hand, no shoes, and two more guns tucked into a black leather belt going one and a half times around my waist. Still, I doubted I'd impress the Barq crowd by my appearance alone, so the thing to do was get out of there. I moved silently—in socks—down the hall, listening, moving with extreme caution.

There was no more twangy music. In fact, there was no sound at all. The house couldn't possibly be empty, yet that was the way it felt. I checked before crossing the open kitchen and dining room doorways, and both rooms were empty, though well lit. Could it be this easy?

No.

At the front door I saw what my problem was going to be. The exterior lights were on, or at least some of them, not enough to attract a lot of attention from the neighbors, but sufficient to bathe the house itself in illumination. From the front door, looking out through the curtain and the glass, I could see two Barq people, one on the lawn in front and one around to the side on the slate walk between house and garage. Both were seated on folding chairs, facing the house. There would surely be two more of them as well, in the rear and on the other side, so that the whole house was under surveillance, and the fact that they were out there mostly because of Ross and Doreen rather than me didn't help that much.

How much time did I have? The food deliverers would be missed eventually. Before that, someone might stroll down the hallway and wonder why the guard wasn't on duty in front of the safe-room door. But there wasn't any way I was going to get out of this house and across the well-lit grounds and over the wall, not without being seen, and my height and hair color made it unlikely I could disguise myself as just another passing conspirator.

Well, if I couldn't get out, maybe I could bring rein-forcements in. The phone here was monitored, I knew that, but a quick call from one of the extensions—maybe up-stairs—should do the job. With one last look at the patient sentries on their folding chairs, I turned away and hurried back down the hallway, past my former prison, and on up the wide doubling-back stairs.

I'd never been up here before. As with downstairs, a broad carpeted hallway ran the width of the house, but up here there were more doors, a few open, most closed. For no particular reason I chose to turn right—toward the front door, that would be, downstairs—and passed one shut door before coming to an opening on my right which, when I peered cautiously in, turned out to be Ross's office.

Why not? I went in, closing the door behind me. Like the other rooms I'd seen, this one was well-lit, from a fluorescent lamp on the desk and a glass-shaded floor lamp over by the black leather reading chair and a pair of ceiling spots aimed at a giant six-foot-square acrylic painting of tumbled gray boulders.

Crossing the room, I went around behind the desk and, before seating myself, glanced out the window.

There was the rear of the house, the dirt-filled pool very obvious now with the exterior lights on. There was the expected guard, seated at a white wrought-iron chair on the patio, his ugly little machine pistol on the white round table beside him, looking like some obscure tool in the plumbing trade.

The pool-company van was gone.

From this angle I could see the right rear corner of the garage, and the space behind it where the van had been. That area was mostly in shadow now, but out a ways it seemed to me I could see faint indentations of tire tracks in the shaggy lawn, out beyond the pool, angling out away from the house.

I knew, from previous visits here, that the stone wall at the front and sides of this property gave way to a high chain link fence at the back, topped with a spiral of razor wire, the whole thing artfully overgrown with vines and shrubbery. To make a new entrance in a stone wall would be time-consuming and difficult, but to make a new entrance through vines and a chain link fence required only wire cutters. And out there somewhere was Al-Gazel.

I turned to the desk, which was a more elaborate version of Ross's complex miniature habitat out in Malibu. There was the phone. There was the digital clock, reading 11:04, switching to 11:05 as I looked at it. There were the keyboard, the monitor screen, the printer, and there was the drawer of floppy discs. There was more neatness in this office than in Malibu, the vast scumble of research materials having been forced back to the outer suburbs of the desk, leaving only one pale blue manila folder centered in the main work area, just to the left of the word processor's keyboard.

I sat down. The phone, tan in color, was part of a minor switchboard operation, with several incoming lines and an in-house intercom; all in all, a more elaborate setup than mine at home. The push buttons were in the receiver, between the ear and mouthpieces, but when I picked the phone up and put it to my ear—a green light showed on the panel—there was no dial tone.

They've turned it off? Just at night, that would have to be. By day they would need the phone working so Ross could continue to create the appearance of normality here, but at night they could switch it off, protecting themselves, just in case Ross or Doreen had a change of heart or, more remotely, in case I broke out of my prison.

How much longer would they need Ross and, by extension, Doreen and me? They would be setting up tonight, and I had no doubt they'd figured out a way to neutralize those microwave barriers, so after their preparations were complete they would still be undetected. In the morning there would probably be very heavy security throughout this entire area, with the police possibly doing telephone checks and even random checks in person of the houses all around here. Then there would be the explosion.

They'd want to still be here for that, wouldn't they?

Partly to see the results of their labors, but mostly because remote-control gizmos can fail, and they would want to be *sure*, after all their work. So they would be here at the time of the explosion, this army of people—how many? A dozen? Two dozen?—and for some time after all the dynamite blew it would not be possible for them to leave here and try driving away from this part of town. The police presence after the explosion would be intense, and Ross would still have the job of front man, sounding chipper and normal on the phone, being friendly but firmly aware of his householder's rights if any lawmen actually came to his gate.

(Would Deputy Ken be back at Ross's gate, seeing the connection, more insistent than last time? It would be too late for Al-Gazel by then, and all the people in it, even if he did come back, and Ross, the plausible middle-class householder in this affluent neighborhood, would probably still be able to stall and stall and hold off police interference until he'd managed to get us all killed.)

So it would go on until tomorrow night, probably, when under cover of darkness the Barq group could leave, either openly through the front gate or, if the police were showing too much interest outside, surreptitiously through neighboring yards and houses. Just twenty-four hours from now, maybe a little more, and Ross's partnership with Barq would be over, closed out with bullets in three heads. A great relief to those boys, no doubt, not to have to play the game anymore, not to have to go along with Ross's stupid demands, not to have to accommodate his girlfriend and his actor pal. And then, a few hours later, away the whole company would go, free and clear.

I need my own army, I thought. But how? I couldn't get out of the house, and the phone would stay dead until it no longer mattered.

Looking around, I noticed again the blue folder centered on the desk. It was pale blue, and a white label had been pasted to it, with a title:

FIRE OVER BEVERLY HILLS

Ross's file. Ross's file on this. I reached out and opened the folder.

46

IT WAS DEDICATED—I still find this hard to believe—it was dedicated to Doreen and me. This is what was typed on the first sheet of paper I came to inside the folder:

> For Doreen Kaufman and Sam Holt, who put
> up with a lot—
> I hope they think it was worth it.

Insane. The man was completely involved in the fantasy.

But still a professional, I saw, as I turned beyond the dedication page. The material in the folder consisted of three sorts of things: first, variant outlines of the book, with notes for treatment and viewpoint and why thus-and-so should go before this-and-that; second, rough first-draft segments, none more than a few pages long, of specific moments in the story, such as the first time he saw the Delia West tape and the first time he met with the Barq people; third, extensive notes on the conspiracy itself.

Barq, it turned out, was actually who they were. Their organization's precise name was Barq Cyrenica, which Ross translated as "Cyrenician lightning," explaining that Cyrenica—or, more usually, Cyrenaica—was an ancient coastal North African region around the once-important port city of Cyrene, variously a part of the Egyptian and Roman empires, and now, with Tripolitania and Fezzanya, one of the three segments of Libya. Barq Cyrenica was a rogue fundamentalist Islamic sect, at times pledging itself to the Iranian ayatollahs or to Libya's Colonel Qadhafi. It had been held responsible for several murders of Arab emigrés in Europe, but this was apparently its first operation in the United States.

Ross's notes suggested that he'd been trying very hard to pin down the Barq Cyrenica leaders on exactly who supported them, both politically and financially, but had not been successful. It seemed to be true that Qadhafi had never disavowed them or put any obstacles in the way of their basing themselves within his territory, but that might merely have been political discretion on his part. On the other hand, he might be financing them or absolutely controlling them. Ross's frustration in not being able to answer this question was very clear in the notes, and I could see why. If he could name names in his book, fix responsibility on some well-known international figure, it would increase the book's news value and therefore its sales.

Barq Cyrenica's object here was the destruction of the mosque, blowing it up during the first day's prayers and ceremonies, while it was full of dignitaries, as I'd supposed. But what was their method? How did they plan to get through Al-Gazel's security? I was leafing through the pages, looking for the answer, when a voice said, "A writer hates to see that, you know."

I looked up. It was Ross, in the open doorway, a long-barreled target pistol in his hand. He smiled at me almost sadly, playing the scene for all its melodramatic potential, enjoying himself. "Skipping about, you know," he explained. "A writer thinks his every word is golden. Take your time, Sam. You're in no hurry."

47

MY FIRST THOUGHT WAS: Have they found the bodies? I half-turned, looking out the window behind me, and was relieved to see the same sentry still out there, still seated by the dirt-filled pool. So my luck was bad, but not as bad as it might be, because all I would have to contend with now was Ross and his target pistol, not the entire army of Barq Cyrenica.

And the pool was filled with dirt because they're digging a tunnel.

The thought just came to me. I wasn't looking for it, it was probably the only time all day I hadn't been looking for it, the reason to fill a swimming pool with dirt, and in that moment of distraction I'd seen the pool again, and I'd seen the faint tire tracks leading out across the unmown lawn, and there it was.

Why they needed four months to get set up.

How they meant to get past Al-Gazel's security.

How they would manage to put an entire vanload of dynamite *under* the mosque.

When you dig a tunnel, a long and fairly complicated tunnel, one of the major problems you face is what to do with the dirt. A certain amount they could just distribute in the woods back there, but not all of it. The rest had to be stored where it wouldn't look like what it was, particularly from the air. Police helicopters, small private planes, the helicopters of traffic reporters, all would occasionally pass overhead. A brown or tan swimming pool would look odd from the air, but not impossible, and nothing to cause unusual interest or concern. But a big pile of fresh-dug earth in a woody area behind the controversial new mosque would bring *a lot* of attention.

I sighed, preparing to deal with Ross. He had his target pistol in his hand, and I had three pseudo-Colts, two tucked inside the borrowed belt and one in plain view on the desk, between the open folder and the word processor keyboard. So now it was time to do my Clint Eastwood impression. "Ross," I said, keeping my voice very soft, "have you ever killed anybody?"

"I will if I have to." He was grimly determined.

"How do you think I got out of that room?" I asked him, and picked up the automatic from the desk.

His eyes widened. The guy with the gun wasn't supposed to be challenged. "Hey," he said. "Watch that, Sam."

I pointed the automatic at him. "One," I said.

"Don't make me shoot, Sam!"

"Two."

Face agonized, he threw the target pistol away to his right with a sudden convulsive movement. It bounced on the arm of the easy chair and fell into its seat. Embarrassed, resentful, Ross glared at me, saying, "I can't shoot a friend, you knew that."

What I knew—and what he was finding out—was the difference between appearance and reality. "Close the door," I told him.

He turned to do so, but as he did Doreen came snaking in through the opening, her small face tense and determined. Doreen!" he said, astonished.

We were both astonished. Neither of us moved as Doreen headed straight for that chair, grabbed up the target pistol, turned with it in both hands, and shot Ross three times. He was still falling when she lowered the gun, looked in my direction, and said, "He attacked me! It was self-defense. You saw it."

What I saw, when I looked out the window, was the sentry by the pool grabbing his machine pistol and running for the house. Doors down there slammed.

Low and intense, Doreen said, "I hated him. He didn't care what they did. He was supposed to protect me, and he didn't *care*."

Opening the window, I said over my shoulder, "You can explain it to the guys coming up." Then I went over the sill.

48

BLUNDERING AROUND IN THE DARK. The distant glow from Ross's house seen down through the trees behind me was my only guide as I headed out, following the direction the tire tracks were taking when they'd gone beyond the light, just past the new hole in the chain link fence at the back of Ross's property. The tumbled land climbed steeply back here as I moved up in the general direction of Al-Gazel, hoping to find their fence before Barq Cyrenica found me. I'd climb over it and gladly appear on their security's television screen.

Except it didn't work that way. For five minutes I scrambled up into the wooded and eroded hills, taking the easiest route through the tangled underbrush, constantly looking back at those houselights for guidance, and then one time I faced forward to see light *ahead* of me. A house? The light seemed very dim. Cautiously, I moved forward.

The van. Probably it had been the thick shrubbery on both flanks that had kept me on the van's new-beaten path even when I couldn't see it. In any case, there it was, just ahead, facing this way, backed up into a steep gully.

The light came from behind the van, and seemed to flicker and move as I watched, throwing shadows across the scrubby face of the hill. I inched forward, and from two or three car-lengths away I could see through the windshield and through the body of the van that the rear doors were open and men were back there, in the light, moving around.

Unloading the cartons.

I crept forward, and when I'd reached the van, I went down on my stomach to look under it and count feet. Eight of them.

Could I make it away from here, through the thick brush, without getting lost, without these people hearing me, without pursuers from the house finding me? Would I become too turned around to find the Al-Gazel fence?

What was the alternative?

I hate derring-do. Usually you're merely risking the game and your own personal survival for no good reason, which is the lesson I learned both in the army and on the police. Routine and care and thought are almost always the better way. In *Mark of the Vampire*, 1935, Lionel Atwill's police captain summed up the alternatives: "Well? Are we going to sit around and think, or are we going to do something?" I know it isn't the answer he wanted, but I believe that most of the time we're all better off to sit around and think.

However, there do come those exceptions to the rule. Not liking it, I got to my feet, put an automatic in each hand, and walked around to the back of the van.

Here was the scene: Two kerosene lanterns stood on the ground, illuminating the work without sending out a lot of glare to the surrounding countryside. Several feet behind the van, where the rear gully wall turned sharply upward, an oval hole about three feet high and two feet wide had been dug into the ground. The four men were unloading the dynamite from the van, two men toting each heavy carton across the packed-down empty space to the tunnel entrance. Inside, the oval was pitch black, but apparently they had some sort of plastic sheet in there, or something else to make a smooth slide down the slope from the entrance, because each carton was maneuvered into the hole, then given a push, and away it went.

The van had originally been full, and was now about half-emptied. Presumably, more men at the bottom of this first slope were dragging the cartons the rest of the way—a quarter mile, perhaps—to an opening readied for them beneath the mosque. So much effort for such a miserable goal.

The men were too involved in their work to notice me. I had to attract their attention, so I stepped clearly into the light and said, "Stop."

They gaped at me. I'd chosen a moment when they all had their hands full and wouldn't be able to reach for their guns, and in the uncertain light of the kerosene lanterns they looked angry and surprised and chagrined and humiliated. One of the pair over by the tunnel entrance dropped his end of the carton and reached for his pistol anyway, while the other three just stared.

No more killing, not if we can avoid it. With my right-hand gun I fired one shot into the ground at his feet, the sound flat and hard in the night air, like a dog's bark. I knew it would carry, the people at the house would hear it, so I didn't have a lot of time. "Don't die, my friend," I told the fellow with his hand on his gun.

He considered. It was the situation between Ross and me again, except that this time both people knew what the story was. Ross had let me point my gun at him, which had made us physically even and given me the psychological advantage. This fellow knew by looking at me that I wouldn't let him get that pistol all the way out from under his belt; after a few seconds his hand came away empty.

I gestured at the other two guys with my left-hand gun, saying, "Put it down." When they looked at me blankly, I pointed the gun at the carton and made downward movements, repeating, "Put it down."

So they put it down, back in the van from where they'd just picked it up. The fellow who'd decided not to point his gun at me said in heavily accented English, "You should not stop this."

"But I'm going to stop it," I told him.

"Our war," he said. "Our God. Our enemies."

"My neighborhood," I told him, and gestured with the right-hand gun at the tunnel entrance. "Get in there."

His eyes widened, and he pointed at the hole in the side of the hill almost as though he'd never seen it before, had no idea what it was.

"In there? All us?"

"That's right. Quickly."

One of the others said something in some language, and all at once they were all jabbering back and forth.

Before they could decide to fan out and attack me from every side, I fired again, this time shooting one of the kerosene lanterns as a dramatic way to hold their attention. It worked, too; a large amoeba of flame from spattered kerosene on the bare ground flared up, showing their startled faces.

For all I knew, only the one guy spoke English, so I spoke directly to him: "I killed them in the house, to get out here. I'll kill you, too, if you argue. Go in the tunnel."

His eyes flickered away from me, toward the house. I could see him thinking, working it out. Was it possible this one man had killed all the people in the house? But if not, how did he get out here?

"Quickly," I said, and spoke more, generally. "First, all of you, with thumb and one finger, take your gun by its butt and throw it on the ground."

"They have no American," the talker said.

"Then you tell them. Very fast." I found it not at all hard to portray growing hysteria; letting some of it out, I said, "If it's easier to kill you all, I'll kill you!"

The talker spoke to his comrades. It was hard to watch four of them at once in the lesser light of the one remaining lamp, but they did as they were told, littering the ground with sidearms. Then, the talker first, one at a time they climbed into the hole and slid away out of sight.

Close the entrance—but how? Other people inside would have guns, so if I showed myself at the opening, I'd be shot.

The van. I ran to its front, and the keys were inside. So were three shovels, leaning against the passenger seat, no doubt the reason for that clammy smell I'd noticed last night.

It was an old, small van, badly beat-up by life, but it contained a good engine, which caught right away. Looking out through the opening at the back, I put the van in reverse and drove it hard at the entrance to the tunnel.

I don't know what shoring-up arrangements they'd made farther along, but near the surface they'd relied on roots and natural density to keep their tunnel open. I drove the van up, the slope increasing so steeply the rear bumper dug a groove into the ground and the straining wheels threw up mud and twigs and dead brush. Then the bumper was over the entrance and the wheels were on both sides, and I could hear the pop-pop of guns going off, bullets caroming from the undercarriage. That was dumb; if one of those had hit the gas tank, it wouldn't have been good for any of us.

The top edge of the opening stopped the van with a jerk. I shifted into drive and mashed hard on the accelerator, spinning the wheels the other way before they caught and jolted me forward. Reverse again, and back up, the wheels slipping and sliding, the heavy weight of the half-loaded van grinding down into the soft ground. Forward, and I could see the blurred edges of the hole back there, where part of the surrounding earth had already given way.

It was on the fourth hard reverse that the van suddenly side-slipped a foot or two and dropped with a thud, snapping my teeth so hard my jaws ached. I shifted into drive and accelerated, but the van merely slewed and settled.

Was that it? I got out and went back, and the answer was yes. The tunnel sides had fallen in enough for the rear wheels to drop down into the hole, and now the van's undercarriage was pressed firmly to what was left of the opening. If they tried to dig out from underneath, all they'd do would be bring the van more and more into the tunnel with them.

But what about their friends from the house? First, I threw the car keys far off into the woods. Then I shot all four tires. Then I searched the van, and under the front seat I found the wire cutters I'd been hoping they'd still have with them. And finally I took the surviving kerosene lantern with me (the fire from the other had gone out) and plunged on, looking again for the Al-Gazel fence.

I found it about five minutes farther on, an eight-foot-high chain link fence topped with a spiral of razor wire and liberally provided with metal warning signs that talked about private property and tight security measures without ever mentioning exactly whose property or what measures.

I respect razor wire. If you grab it, you'll never own those fingers again. The kerosene lantern made it possible to see what I was doing as I clipped an opening in the fence with my borrowed wire cutters, doing just enough so I could slip through. (Without them I guess I would have used the gun to dig a hole underneath.)

On the other side, before proceeding, I disarmed myself, leaving all three guns on the ground there. I continued to carry the lantern, but now I walked with one hand up in the air, to show I came in peace. I had no idea how soon I'd show up on their monitors, or how long it would take them to come out and collect me, so I just kept walking, on level ground now, away from the fence.

I was walking. And then I was lying flat on my back on the ground, the low boom still reverberating; the wind knocked out of me, the lantern gone somewhere, the hill beneath me quaking like a water bed.

49

THEY WEREN'T GENTLE. I told them I could walk and they paid me no attention, just went on carrying me through the woods, four of them holding my four limbs while one went ahead with a flashlight and the last two trailed, shining their own flashlights left and right into the shadowed trees. "I really can walk," I repeated, and one of the ones behind me said, "Shut up, you."

It had taken them only two minutes to reach me through the woods, where I lay on my back, catching my breath and trying to figure out what had happened and whether or not anything on my body was broken. I was about to sit up, in fact, when I saw the lights coming and decided the safest thing was to make no sudden moves. I was therefore still lying on my back on the ground when they reached me, seven men who looked uncomfortably like the members of Barq Cyrenica, except that they were more neatly and expensively dressed. Flashlights shone on my face, and when I raised a hand to shield my eyes, a tough-sounding voice snapped, "Don't move!"

So I didn't move. They studied me, approached me, patted me down where I lay, and talked me over with one another in a language I didn't understand. I might have tried to explain myself, but what was the point? These were just the low-level troops, who would eventually bring me to someone of authority; that's when the explanations could start.

One of them had a walkie-talkie, which from time to time barked in that same language, and the fellow barked back at it, and after a couple of minutes they picked me up and hauled me away with them through the woods. That's when I told them I could walk, and they let me know they didn't give a damn.

The mosque loomed in the darkness, with a few lit windows on the ground floor and the rest just a massive domed shape in the dark. The man in front opened a door, spilling more light out onto the ground, and I was carried inside and down a long cream-colored corridor with recessed ceiling lights. I tried to look left and right, catching glimpses of doors, some open and some closed, but my captors were all so close to me and hustling me along so quickly that I got very little sense of where I was.

Then they turned left and, with some difficulty, steered me through a doorway, the man in front switching on the same sort of recessed ceiling light as I'd seen in the hall. When they got me inside, there were more quick orders in that language and I was set on my feet, abruptly and rather roughly. Most of the men left. I stood there swaying, my sense of balance lost for the moment, and the man who'd told me to shut up faced me from near the door, his expression cold and hostile. "You will wait," he said, and turned toward the door.

"For what?"

Ignoring me, he went out and shut the door, and I heard the scratch of the key. All over again, locked in. I can't go through it all twice, I thought.

But I shouldn't have to. These were legitimate people, not terrorists; sooner or later they would connect me to the authorities. In the meantime they quite understandably wanted to keep me on ice, and all I should do at this point was, as the man had said, wait.

In a small and nearly empty windowless office. A small metal desk bore a telephone, a blotter, and empty In and Out trays. A wooden swivel chair behind it, a square metal wastebasket beside it, and a leatherette chair with wooden arms in front of it completed the furniture. When I opened the desk drawers, they were all empty. An office not in use at the moment, that's all.

How long would I have to wait? Long enough to think about what had happened outside, certainly. I'd been walking along and all at once the earth had shrugged, knocking me down the way Sugar Ray is knocked down in the back of the station wagon when I make a sharp turn. I hadn't heard anything—or I didn't remember hearing anything—but what could that have been other than an explosion?

The dynamite in the tunnel. The mosque was still here, obviously, so they mustn't have had the dynamite in the right position yet, but surely that was what had gone up, with who knows how many of the men of Barq Cyrenica trapped inside it by the van with which I'd corked the entrance.

Was I responsible? Was something I'd done with the van the cause, several minutes later, of the dynamite blowing up? That was an uncomfortable idea, and I was just settling down to study it, pacing back and forth in the small room, when the sound of the door being unlocked was followed by its opening, and the entrance of Hassan Tabari.

I stared at him. This was the last thing I'd expected. "By golly, you do get around!" I told him.

"So do you," he said coldly. Two more men came in after him and shut the door. These were a very different type, obviously Americans, in slacks and sport coats, white shirts and modest ties. "These men," Tabari said, gesturing to them, "are from your FBI. Perhaps now you will answer the question you wouldn't answer when we talked on the plane."

I didn't get it. "What question? I could never figure out what the hell you were up to. You didn't ask any questions."

"I asked you what your relationship was with Arab groups," he said. "Not in so many words, of course. But that was the question."

Thinking back to our conversation on the plane, I could see that he had in fact been fishing for an answer to that question, but of course at the time I'd had no relationship with Arab groups, at least none I knew about, so his subtlety had got him nowhere. "All right," I said, nodding. "My primary relationship with Arab groups is that one of them, called Barq Cyrenica, tried to kill me and then later on kidnapped me."

One of the FBI men said, "How long have you known about Barq Cyrenica?"

"I learned the name less than an hour ago. Their try at killing me took place on Monday of this week, only I didn't know who they were then. I reported the attempt to the Los—"

"We know about that."

"This makes no sense," Tabari said. He was angry and baffled, and didn't like to be either. None of us had taken either of the room's two chairs, but while the FBI men and I stood facing one another, Tabari paced back and forth beside us, from time to time throwing me discontented looks. Now he stopped and said, "Why were they interested in you in the first place? That was the question, that was why I traveled with you. Here is a group of extremists, operating in this part of the world for the first time, and we have information that they are taking a great interest in one television actor named Sam Holt. Why? Is Sam Holt a sympathizer with these ruffians? Is Sam Holt a person connected to some *other* part of Islam, opposed to the terrorists? We search Sam Holt's background, we come up with nothing, we have no idea if he's someone we should protect or some-one we should guard ourselves against. *Why* is Barq Cyrenica so interested in this person? What do these people have in mind to do in California? I traveled with you and learned nothing, but the next day Barq Cyrenica people were found in your house in New York, and of course you insisted you knew nothing about them."

I said, "So that *was* you in the cab! I saw you going up Sixth Avenue."

Ignoring that, Tabari said, "And now, accompanied by an explosion, you climb the fence and walk into our arms, in the middle of the night."

"I'll tell you the whole story," I promised him. "Some of it I've already given the L.A. County Sheriff's Department, but the rest I didn't know until after I was kid-napped."

"If you have a story to tell," an FBI man said, "now's the time to tell it."

"Wait," Tabari said, moving toward the door. "I wish this to be recorded."

"We both do," the FBI man told him.

While Tabari opened the door and spoke briefly to somebody outside, the FBI man took a mini-cassette recorder from his pocket and placed it on the desk, saying, "Why don't you sit there?"

"Behind the desk?"

"Yes."

So I sat down, and he adjusted the recorder so its built-in mike faced me, a tiny round black ear eager to know all. A somewhat larger recorder had been handed to Tabari, who put it on the desk next to the first one and started it recording. One of the FBI men, clearly for the benefit of the record, said, "You're telling us your story of your own free will, Mr. Holt?"

"Absolutely."

"Good." Then my audience of three stepped back, arms folded, to watch and listen.

I looked at the tapes turning in the machines. "Well," I said. A strange place, this, for an actor to have stage fright. "All right," I said. "The beginning of this story is last winter, in New York, when an old friend of mine named Ross Ferguson phoned..."

50

"**T**HE FIRST THING," Deputy Ken said, looking very earnestly into my eyes, "it didn't blow by accident."

"Meaning they did it on purpose?"

"Meaning it wasn't your fault," he said, and showed a trace of grin. "I had the feeling you were worried about that."

"Okay. I was."

"Also, yes," he went on, and nodded. "They did it on purpose."

"How can you be sure?"

Chuck said, "The technical people can be sure. From the way it blew, and where we found the bodies."

I looked out across my pool. It was a sunny warming day in early March, two weeks since Barq Cyrenica had blown itself apart in its tunnel under Al-Gazel. Bly paddled around in the clear water, decorative in her peach bikini, giving me privacy for my talk with the deputies, who'd arrived unannounced, so that I sat with them in my pale blue terry-cloth robe. We three were around the table near the pool, Sugar Ray watchfully asleep beneath and Max patrolling the far side, on the alert for enemies and disturbances.

But the enemies and disturbances were all gone, most of them dead on that night, the rest captured when the police finally swarmed onto Ross's property after the explosion. Bly and Robinson, after Ross's phoned message from me, had called Deputy Ken and managed to interest the police enough so that they were watching Ross's house by that time, but they'd been maintaining a low profile—to protect *me!*—waiting for something to come out of there, and if they'd stuck to their original script, they wouldn't have intervened until it was too late. The explosion, of course, had made them rewrite.

The explosion. Only about half the dynamite had been moved into the tunnel when I'd come along to interrupt the process, and not all of that had been shifted into final position. The tunnel, nearly a quarter-mile long, was less than four feet tall and three feet wide, shored up where necessary with boards and sheets of thin paneling, illuminated by flashlights, and running very gradually uphill to a widened-out room just beneath the mosque. Perhaps a third of the full store of dynamite was in position there, and fourteen men in the tunnel, when it blew, killing them all.

That explosion had been echoing in my mind for two weeks, and no point denying it. I brooded about it by day and dreamed about it at night, when I was usually one of the men inside, struggling along in the grave-smelling semi-dark, dragging the heavy cartons, sweating but chilled, bent almost double under the low earth roof. In my dream I was following some antlike compulsion to do this work, without understanding why. I would do it, and then I would see the red ball flashing toward me down the tube, I would feel its heat, and I'd wake up sweating, panting for air.

Had it been my fault? In crushing the entrance, packing the van down into it, had I created the circumstances that made the dynamite down there blow fifteen minutes later? I didn't see how it could be a direct result of what I'd done—if it were, wouldn't it have gone off right away?—but I couldn't be sure, and the uncertainty had left an opening for nightmare.

Until now. If Ken was right, if indeed the "technical people" did know what they were talking about...I said, "I have trouble believing it, that they did it to themselves."

"It wouldn't be the first time, the political suicide, with people like that," he said. "You'd trapped them down in there. Sooner or later the law would come along and dig them out."

"Humiliation," suggested Chuck. He was mostly watching Bly swim.

"That's right," Ken said. "Public shame. Failure. And maybe even exposure of whoever finances them."

"And the point from the beginning," Chuck added, "was to blow up the mosque."

I said, "Which they didn't even manage to do."

"Well, they hurt it," Ken said, giving them their due. "There was some structural damage."

"But you're right," Chuck told me. "They didn't bring it down."

"But they *tried*, right?" I wanted to hear that again, to be certain about it. Looking at them both, I said, "That's what they were doing? Turned it into a suicide mission, on purpose."

Ken nodded. "Said their prayers, burned their incriminating documents, gave each other the secret handshake, put their detonators in place—"

"That's one way we know it wasn't an accident," Chuck said.

"Right," Ken agreed, and finished his sentence. "Put their detonators in place and went to talk it over with Allah."

I sighed and smiled. The day was getting warmer and brighter. "Then it's done," I said.

Done. Finished. Nothing left over. I had, of course, backed up Doreen's self-defense story about killing Ross, and her doctor father had provided heavyweight legal help before taking her back to Santa Barbara, so she was out of it. Besides, nobody much cared how Ross had died. His file on *Fire Over Beverly Hills* was enough to make him a co-conspirator in official eyes, whether he'd been coerced into it in the first place or not.

Given the various newsworthy elements in the story— a twenty-seven-million-dollar mosque, an underground mass suicide, a tunnel full of dynamite, a shootout in a Beverly Hills mansion, the presence of a former TV star—the Al-Gazel people and the authorities between them had done an amazing job of smothering the flames of publicity. There had been newspaper stories and television reports about the explosion immediately after it happened, and the phone here had rung off the hook for a couple of days (everybody being referred to my PR outfit for a handout full of vagueness and generalities), but the follow-up was astonishingly meager. The mosque wanted it kept quiet, their enemies had no reason to trumpet this failure, the city always tries to downplay the growing Arab presence here, and the federal authorities feel understandably nervous about public reaction whenever foreign disputes get fought out on our turf, which does sometimes happen, so the story merely faded and died.

Ken made as though to get to his feet. "We just thought you'd like to know," he said.

I said, "Duty calls?"

He grinned. "We're late for our break, actually."

"Then take it here. Dive in the pool."

Ken laughed as though I were kidding, and Chuck said, "Not in uniform."

"I keep spare suits in the poolhouse there," I told them. "Top drawer on the left."

"Thanks for the offer, Sam," Ken said, rising, "but we've really got to get—"

"Why? I'm serious. It's a warm day, you've just brought me peace of mind, I think you ought to have a nice swim."

They looked at one another, considering the idea, surprised at themselves that they were considering it. Beyond them I saw Robinson coming this way from the house, carrying the phone. I said, "An invitation from an ex-cop. How can you turn it down?"

They grinned at one another, and Ken said, "You're right. Top drawer on the left, you say?"

"That's it."

Robinson, arriving, put the phone on the table and politely waited. Ken and Chuck went off toward the pool-house, and Robinson said, "Mr. Novak."

"Ah-hah." Could this be work at last? I took the phone and said, "Zack?"

"Danny Silvermine—"

"No, Zack."

"Just listen," he said.

"No. I told you almost two weeks ago, when Silvermine said no to the idea of me doing an original. I don't want it. His scripts were adequate, but—"

"Sam, darling, *listen*."

When Zack Novak calls me darling, it means he's nearing the end of his rope. "All right," I said. "I'm listening."

"Forget the dinner theater," he told me.

"I already did."

"Good. Our good friend Danny Silvermine has come up with a brand new— Oops!"

"Oops?"

"Hold it! Don't go away!" And here came the unmistakable woolly sound of hold.

"Not again," I told the dead phone, then hung it up and handed it to Robinson. "Take this away," I said.

"Of course," he said.

"When Mr. Novak calls again, tell him I'm not interested in anything Danny Silvermine thinks."

"Yes," he said.

"Tell him I'm not interested in recycling Jack Packard in the theater, in bubble gum cards, in needlepoint pillows, or anywhere else."

"Very well," he said.

"Tell him I want *work*, real, honest-to-God, legitimate acting *work*."

"I shall," he said.

"And tell him I said, 'Don't put me on hold!' Direct quote."

"Quote don't put me on hold unquote," he said.

"Exactly. Oh, and bring my guests a couple of Tabs. Chlorine makes people thirsty."

"Will that be *all*?" Robinson asked, and arched a stern brow at me.

I didn't feel like being browbeaten right now. "For the moment," I said.

Robinson nodded, accepting the inevitable, and departed. I stood, shrugged out of the robe, and went over to the edge of the pool. For just an instant, I saw again that other pool filled with dirt, imagined again the distorted bodies in the black tunnel, blood coming from their ears. But then the images faded for the last time. It was better to be up here, where I could stretch myself and feel the sun getting warmer every day.

Dancing water sparkled shards of sky in my eyes. Bly drifted through it, head raised, grinning up at me. "You're smiling," she said.

"Why not," I said, and dove in.